I0668251

Lee Hunter
Private Detective

Bodies on the 9th.

The second book in the Lee Hunter
Crime Files.

Contact – Olmi Publishing© -
Olmipublishing@yahoo.com

Many thanks to:

Andy Rymer – Technical Content.

A word about the author.

I live in breath-taking southern Italy. The views of the magnificent mountains, rolling countryside and the Adriatic Sea are a great inspiration for my work.

I have been here for several years now, enjoying the atmosphere, the people and the wonderful traditions of this little-known region of Italy.

I would normally write adult fiction, of which the Lee Hunter and Peter Parker series are examples, although I do occasionally write for children.

My latest children's book is "Popysan, the Green Dragon", which is also available on Audible and Apple iBooks. Have a look at that book and the other books in this series on Amazon.

I also have a Facebook page, Russell B. Smith Author. This contains my latest releases and information.

Books by Russell B Smith.

The Peter Parker Series.

<u>The Beyondness of Things.</u>
Published December 2020
ISBN 978-1-8383146-0-6

The Beyondness of Fear.
Published April 202.
ISBN 978-1-8383146-2-0

The Beyondness of War.
Published August 2022.
ISBN 978-1-8383146-4-4

The Beyondness of Peace.
(Expected 2022/23)

Children's books.

<u>Popysan, The Green Dragon.</u>
Published March 2021.
*Also available as an Audio and Book from Amazon,
Audible and Apple*
ISBN 978-1-8383146-1-3

The Lee Hunter Crime Files.

<u>Five Murders and Counting.</u>
Published 2022.
*Also available as an Audio and Book from Amazon,
Audible and Apple*
ISBN 978-1-8383146-3-7

<u>Bodies on the Ninth.</u>
Published May 2023.
Also available as an Audio and Book from Amazon, Audible and Apple
ISBN 978-1-8383146-6-8

Characters in the book.

Lee Hunter.
Private Detective, Ex-Metropolitan Police Force.

Detective Inspector Deborah Smith.
Murder Squad, Merseyside Police.
Detective Sergeant Sharron Shacklady.
Murder Squad, Merseyside Police.
DC Stephen Burton.
On detachment to the Murder Squad, from the Serious Crime Unit.

Kaye Marie.
Senior Scenes of Crime Investigator.

Russ Broadbent.
Radio DJ, Radio Rock n Roll Lancashire.

Adele Wood.
County archaeologist.

Jan Talbot.
Lee Hunters P.A.

Ms Janice Greenwood.
Daughter of the Goldsmith.

Charles Creighton-Ward.
Grandson of the man who commissioned the rings.

Thomas (Tom) Toc.

Grave digger and handy man in the local church.

Detective Sergeant Craig Jackson.
Missing Person Team, Merseyside Police.

Charles Brightling,
The General Manager of the Southport and Lancashire Golf Club.

Toni Bianchi.
Local gangster and friend of Lee Hunter.

Henry Cormack.
Employee of Tony Bianchi.

Three weeks ago.
Southport and Lancashire Golf Course.

The snow was blowing in from the west, straight off the Irish sea. It was swept along on a biting gale force wind that almost knocked Kaye Marie off her feet. Her hands had long since gone numb, as had most of her face and legs in the sub-zero temperatures.

The hastily erected crime scene tent had been ripped by the force of the elements, and portions were now flapping uselessly in the storm. It made sharp slapping sounds as it danced an unrestrained ballet in the fearsome gale.

She pulled her mobile phone from her pocket, looked at it in an attempt to ascertain the time, tapping the screen with numb fingers. Almost dropping it into the snow as her now freezing and useless hands refused to obey her commands. The screen burst into life, shining a clear bright light into her face, it almost felt warm as it illuminated her features.

"Bloody hell, it's half past ten, why the hell did I agree to turn out to this? Surely it could have waited until the morning. I don't care if the crime scene will be two feet deep in snow by then. I could have dug it out, better than standing here in this shit storm"

The Hyundai generator coughed and spluttered, then ran back up to speed. This caused the lights illuminating the scene to darken a little, before returning back to their normal brightness. The snowflakes were caught in the light, dashing about and blowing in horizontally, biting into Kaye's face like a myriad of stinging insects.

Somewhere inside the remains of the tent was Adele Wood, the County Archaeologist. Kaye had summoned her to the scene because of the skeletal remains. One of the golf course greenskeepers had been tasked to construct a new bunker adjacent to the 9th green. It was during this work that the remains had been discovered, and the Police had been called. As the duty CSI, Kaye had received the call and had reluctantly agreed to attend the scene.

She was hoping that Adele would say they were several hundred years old and therefore not to be considered as a crime scene. This would mean she could go home and leave it to Adele and her department, she knew all too well that this was not going to be the outcome, especially on a night like this!

It seemed like and age before Adele exited the remnants of the tent and walked towards Kaye Marie, stumbling occasionally in the deepening snow. She looked just as cold, rubbing her hands together in a vain attempt to warm herself up. She put her head close to Kaye's, taking a deep breath and shouting through the storm.

"Well, they are certainly skeletal, a few strands of hair and maybe the remains of some skin, but I can't be sure until I get them back to the University"

"So, how about age Adele, please tell me early medieval"

"Sorry to disappoint you Kaye but it's not what you want to hear. Judging by the condition of the bones and what I know about the soil around these parts, relative humidity and rainfall, and its effects on the human skeleton, I would say, about eighty

to a hundred years old! Maybe sometime just before the second world war, can't be certain at this time"

"Great, that's just what I need, a bloody murder case in the middle of the worst storm in fifty years, on a golf course in the arse end of nowhere. Why didn't I turn my phone off, let someone else take the call?"

"Because you love what you do Kaye, and you wouldn't just let someone else get into an incident like this, could be very interesting? In any case, it's not necessarily a murder, could be some kind of suicide pact or something!"

"Oh, I somehow doubt it, these things are never that simple. Did you find anything else, a weapon, ligature?"

"Nothing like that but there were a couple of nice-looking rings, they are encrusted in sand so it's difficult to give any precise information. Heavy gold band, three stones, not sure what they are yet, they had one each, on their big finger, right hand"

At that precise moment the generator coughed, blew some white/grey smoke into the night, and gently faded away. The lights now starved of their power quickly followed, plunging the whole scene into darkness.

"Right, that's it, I am off back to the office, no way I am staying out here any longer. I will get the local 'plod' to stand guard over this in the morning. Doubt if anyone will be playing golf in two feet of snow"

Adele laughed, "how about a quick drink on the way back, a brandy might be nice, warm us up a bit"

"Best bit of thinking all night Adele, let's go"

Present Day.
Radio Rock n Roll Lancashire.

"Well good morning everyone, and welcome to the breakfast show. This is your host Russ Broadbent, taking you all the way from 7am to 10am on this crisp February morning. It's been a rough couple of weeks with all of the snow and freezing temperatures', but stay tuned, I am sure we can warm you through and through.

I guess you have all been reading about the bodies found on the 9th hole of the Southport and Lancashire Golf Course. Well, this morning I have on the show Detective Inspector Deborah Smith, she is here to ask for our help in trying to identify the two bodies. But first, Linda is here with the news and latest traffic reports, over to you Linda"

Deborah slid into the seat opposite Russ Broadbent, the studio was warm and well lit. Consoles and equipment made the space seem like something off a science fiction film. A young assistant brought two coffees, some milk and sugar and carefully placed them on a table to Deborah's left. The young girl smiled, turned and quietly left the studio, closing the door behind her.

Linda delivered the local and then national news with her usual cheery tone, almost making the increasing levels of unemployment seem somewhat trivial. Then came the weather, cold and snowy, she even made that sound like fun. Eventually she handed back to Russ Broadbent, signing off, "this is Linda Lofton, see yeah later"

The station producer counted them down with his fingers from the other side of the glass partition. There was an advert running for a local restaurant, it would finish in, two, one, "go Russ"

"Welcome back everyone and I have in the studio our very own Detective Inspector Deborah Smith, Southport Murder Squad. She is here to talk about the two skeletons found on the golf course, and hopefully some of our listeners can help with the case. Ok Deborah, how's the case going, do we know who these two people are yet?"

"Well Russ, I have to be honest and say no we don't. They were found by the greenskeeper when he dug a new bunker on the Southport and Lancashire golf course. We sent a crime scenes specialist out to the grave, who in turn called the County Archaeologist, but they found nothing particularly obvious as to why the remains were there.

There has been no information coming into the office, no reports of missing relatives and nothing in our records. The Coroner has examined the remains and between him and the

Archaeology people, we think they are about one hundred years old, give or take ten years. There is no sign of abuse, no weapons, no bindings or broken bones, nothing at all"

"Did I read something about them being posed in the grave?"

"Well, they were facing each other if that's what you mean, in a lovers embrace, I guess that's why the press is calling them, 'the lovers in the sand'. Anyway, we haven't got anywhere with our enquiries, so anything your listeners can help with, would be very much appreciated"

"We will see what we can do Deborah, what about the rings, I heard something about them?"

"Yes, unique to say the least. A heavy gold band, set with a single emerald and two flanking rubies. Also, on the back is engraved what can be best described as a dragon. Each ring was worn on their big finger, right hand"

"Yes, we have photos of them on the station's website, have a look people, see if you recognise them, if anyone has any information Detective Inspector, what should they do?"

"Well Russ, they can get in touch either through your station or directly with my department. All the email addresses, phone numbers and the crime stoppers telephone line, are all on your station's website along with the photos"

"Well Deborah, thanks very much for popping in this morning, I am sure our listeners will be able to help, have a look everyone, see if there is anything you recognise"

The producer started the next advert off, the green light illuminated on the top of Russ Broadbent's console, indicating that they were now off air.

"Thanks for that Deborah, if there is anything more we can do, just give me a call"

"I will Russ and thanks for your time. I am off back to the office, see if anything comes of this, to be honest, I am not sure anything will!"

Lee Hunter's (new) Office.
Lord Street, Southport.

If I am honest, things have been going rather well since the last case. I guess getting shot by that ex-cop made good headlines in the local newspapers, "local detective saves the life of a CSI and solves a case of five murders"

Not sure that I can take all the credit for that but the increase in business has been very welcome indeed. To be honest, I did enjoy the interviews and the get well soon cards, and the chocolates were very nice indeed. It was my ten minutes of fame, I guess I deserved that.

I have moved office as well, away from the smelly little place above the taxi firm, and into an office a couple of yards further down Lord Street. Here there is room for two people, more about that in a minute. A reception area leads to my office, and a spare workplace, that feels very posh indeed. There are toilets, mixed, I couldn't afford ladies and gents. A small but functional kitchenette, and a video intercom connected to the entrance on the ground floor. The central heating works as does the internet. Oh yes, the windows don't leak and there is no smell of cigarettes either.

So, where does this leave me and the business, well I am busy, money in the account and I have stopped getting threatening letters from the bank. Oh yes, then there is Jan, my new P.A., she has really helped, turned my record keeping and my diary around, what a blessing!

To be honest, she has made such a difference, she does bully me, perhaps I deserve that, but now I turn up to meetings on time and all my accounts are completed when they should be. So, I can't complain, the only worry I have is that she will leave and go and find a better boss, let's wait and see.

It's also nice to have a woman about the place, she has an eye for detail, doesn't give up on paperwork and is great with customers. Does that sound sexist, I didn't mean it to be. She is a little younger than me, five foot nothing, short brown hair, full of energy and loves life, what more can I ask for and before you ask, we are not an item!

Anyway, it was just about home time when the phone rang, Jan picked up the call and wanted to put it through to my office. I thought about telling her no, I was tired. Also, it was 6pm and I was ready for home, a shower and feet up watching the football, my little treat. However, business is business, and I am a sucker for making money, so I picked it up, oh boy, was that a mistake!

"There is a lady on the phone Lee, says she has some information about the people in the sand, I guess she means those two skeletons on the golf course. Do you want me to put her through or get her to call back?"

"Put her through Jan, saves her ringing back tomorrow, what's her name?"

"She won't say, says she has to remain anonymous, might be a bit of a crank"

"Go on, I need to get home for the football, so let's sort this out and get off early for once"

The phone clicked, I am not certain, but I am fairly sure I could hear Jan giggling in the outer office, it wouldn't be the first time she had stitched me up with some crank. There was always some odd ball who wanted something sorting out. "The neighbour stole my cat", "the people above me are Russian spies", "my doctor is an alien". Oh yes and last week someone called saying "an illegal immigrant had cursed them, and now they couldn't turn right". You have to be respectful, I know it's unlikely that any of these tales have any kind of factual substance, but some people can't help being, well just a little strange, can they?

So, I picked up the phone, "Lee Hunter, how can I help?"

"Ah, Mr Hunter, I have been reading about your work, very interesting case with those corrupt Police. How brave you were in apprehending that man in the recycling centre, near to Formby"

The woman on the other end of the phone sounded very cultured indeed, cut glass diction, and a nice calm manner. She sounded older, maybe in her seventies, and thankfully didn't sound too insane.

"Thank you, Ms?"

"I would prefer to remain anonymous Mr Hunter, the reason for that will become clear once I have explained a little further"

"Ok, please continue"

"Have you seen the photographs of the rings found on the skeletons, the poor unfortunate souls found in the sand?"

"I have, the Police are very keen on finding anything out, they seem at a loss to identify them"

"Well Mr Hunter, I don't know who they are, but I certainly know who made those rings and for whom. I can even tell you when they were made"

This information certainly stopped me in my tracks, it seemed very specific, how on earth could she know that kind of detail?

"Go on Ms...."

"It's simple Mr Hunter, my father made them, he was a master goldsmith, as was his father, and they kept records of every single item they ever made. That would include photographs, customers names, dates, even costs. They were meticulous, everything was crossed referenced, every single detail was listed, even down to where the materials had been purchased from and how long it took to complete the work. My middle room is full of their records, all in filing cabinets, each one with dates of the records they contain"

"Gracious, two whole lifetimes work, I bet you are very proud of what they achieved. Have you contacted the Police, they will be very interested in those records, I have the name of the Detective Inspector in the Murder Squad if it helps?"

"No Mr Hunter, I won't be contacting the Police, and I would appreciate it greatly if you didn't either"

"Look Ms…. these graves are a hundred years old at least, nothing is going to come of it if you contact them, whomever did this is long dead. You need to come forward and disclose the information you have, it will help solve this case"

"No Mr Hunter, I will not be doing that, under any circumstances"

"Ok, so why have you contacted me?"

"I want you to look into something, based on the records I hold, try and find out something for me

Mr Hunter. You are welcome to take details, names, dates etc, so long as you promise not to contact the Police. If you give me those assurances, then I will engage your services and pay for your time. I will even add on an amount of money in order to secure your discretion in this matter, your complete discretion Mr Hunter!"

I thought about what she had said, she emphasised 'complete discretion', this meant 'keep your mouth shut', not easy when you are dealing with a live Police case. In fact, it's also very illegal and guaranteed to piss off the local constabulary. I have no intention of doing that, I nearly went to jail last time, I still don't fancy 10 years in Strangeways, not even for Ms….

"You see Ms……, there are laws regarding withholding evidence……."

"Mr Hunter, I am fully aware of such things, but are you prepared to undertake this work for me? I will pay most generously for your time and your discretion"

Now, you must understand that I am for the most part, a law-abiding citizen. However, there is something about money, it casts a strange spell over you. It has a habit of pulling you into all kinds of situations, including a lot of bloody woes. I had to make my mind up, do I say, "sorry Ms….. but no", or do I risk getting into trouble, but earning a lot of money along the way?

"Ok, Ms….. let's set up a meeting, discuss things a little more, no promises though, just an hour of your time"

"Thank you Mr Hunter and you can call me Janice, Ms Janice Greenwood. Do you know where Saint Cuthbert's church is Mr Hunter, in Churchtown?"

"I do Ms Greenwood"

"There is a bench, set just outside of the main entrance, I will meet you there tomorrow, 10am sharp"

With that, the phone went dead. It felt a bit like a cheap spy novel, Mrs Janice Greenwood seemed very keen on protecting her anonymity, no harm in that I thought. Tomorrow was going to be interesting, she had certainly stimulated my interest.

My office door opened, and Jan walked in, with a big smile on her face.

"Another crank Lee?"

"Well actually Jan, it might turn out to be a very interesting case, so you can take that smirk off your face"

She laughed, placed a load of paperwork on my desk and wished me goodnight, turned and left the office.

"See you tomorrow Lee, I am off, enjoy the footie"

I sat there for a few minutes, thinking about what had just happened. I sometimes get this feeling, I guess it's some primeval sense telling me to walk away. That particular 'sense' was screaming at me like some deranged banshee.

Why the hell was I thinking like this? It was just a meeting with some old lady, she had some information. It would probably turn out to be useless and I would just hand her my bill and walk away…..done…..well probably.

Outside Saint Cuthbert's church.
Sunday morning.

She could have picked a better day to meet and most certainly a better place. I got out of the car and immediately felt the sub-zero blast rip through my clothing, turning every part of me icy cold. It was coming straight from the north, that's not what I had been told last night on the TV. To be honest, the weather forecasters had said the cold artic winds would be replaced by a warmer westerly flow, but that was two weeks ago! I don't know why I bother watching the weather on the TV, I should just wet my finger and stick it in the air, perhaps that's what they do in the weather centre.

Anyway, I am here now, so I turned up my collar and leant forward into the freezing wind. My eyes immediately filled with tears and my right knee began to ache, a horrible throbbing pain, roll on the summer! I was hoping my mobile would start to ring, "it's Mrs Janice Greenwood here, sorry Mr Hunter but I can't make todays meeting". No such luck I'm afraid, so I continued towards the ornate wooden gates at the entrance to the churchyard.

Surely the old lady won't be sitting on that bench, not in this frigid nightmare of a bloody morning. It's cold enough to freeze a polar bears nether region, let alone a doddery septuagenarian. I stared through the fog of my watery eyes and thankfully she wasn't sitting on the bench, but someone was standing in the open church doors. From twenty feet or so, I could just make out the outline of a diminutive lady, wrapped up in an ankle length fur coat, topped with a matching dark brown fur hat. She had white gloves on and stood bolt upright, rather like my old school mistress. I must admit to feeling some dormant fear and dread. My old headmistress, Miss Bentley-Hayes, was not a woman to be messed with. She would wheel her cane with consummate ease, whooshing through the air and impacting on unsuspecting children with surprising alacrity. I remember the fearsome pain of those blows, the red marks on my legs, the anxiety caused by those early school days are as clear as the football match last night.

Putting my mental mutilation to one side, I marched confidently up to the entrance of the church. The lady standing there was no more than five feet and a bit tall, very refined features, perfectly dressed, a young and spritely looking seventy. As she looked at me, I detected a confident air, someone with an ease about themselves but always in control of those around them.

"Good morning, Mr Hunter I presume?"

"Good morning Ms Greenwood, pleased to meet you"

I extended my hand, but she just looked down at it with an amount of disgust on her face. She turned and without speaking, walked into the church, I followed like a naughty boy. She walked halfway down the aisle before turning to face me once again.

"Mr Hunter, shall we take a seat, there is no one in the church, perhaps if we sit here, we can speak discreetly without the fear of being overheard"

She moved into the line of pews and sat down, never looking at me but staring forward towards the alter.

"Ms Greenwood, may I ask why the level of secrecy, it seems a little extreme....."

"Mr Hunter, when I have explained to you the nature of the work you will undertake, I think you will come to understand why"

"Then please make a start Ms Greenwood, I am freezing cold, hungry and I am not keen on churches"

"Right Mr Hunter, please listen to what I have to say and treat it with complete confidentiality. The rings found on those two bodies in the sand were made by my father in 1933. They have dragons engraved on the back, as described by the Inspector on the radio. I have spent a lifetime researching and admiring my fathers and grandfathers work, so as soon as I heard about the rings, I knew who had made them, and when"

"Ok, so we know who made them, but how does this help the case?"

"As well as knowing who made them and when, I also know who the rings were made for Mr Hunter. I have their full name and address, so perhaps that's a good place to start. You need to find out why they were made Mr Hunter, why the rings were commissioned in the first place"

"Ms Greenwood, your father made those rings 89 years ago, whomever he made them for will surely be long dead!"

"Most probably Mr Hunter but the family most certainly still exists, they are a well-known local family of some distinction. Might I suggest you start with them. I will give you the name of the person who commissioned the rings, perhaps they might be able to advance your enquiries from there"

"That's very good of you Ms Greenwood but I must say I am more than a little puzzled by all this. Why not just give the Police their name and address? Also, why am I doing this work for you? As soon as you give me the details, I will no doubt establish that the person in question is long deceased and that will be it, job done!"

"It won't be 'job done' as you put it Mr Hunter, there will be further work to undertake in this case. This is just the beginning, I can assure you, but that will have to wait until later, after you have first contacted the family"

This all seemed bloody strange, what the hell was this lady up to? She could just give me the name and address and I will go and ask them if they know anything. They would say no and that would be the end of the job. In all probability they will know nothing and slam the door in my face. Or better still, she could just tell the local Police and they can get the door slammed in their face, saves me the trouble.

Also, what did she mean by 'further work', I wanted to ask her, but I knew that would get me nowhere at all. Oh well Lee, just stick with it, so long as she was paying the bills then I shouldn't complain, it's a nice easy job and a guaranteed fee.

"Ok Ms Greenwood, if you give me the details I will go and ask the family, see what they have got to say. I need to mention Ms Greenwood that they will probably know very little if anything. This all happened many years ago, I wouldn't be surprised if no one knows anything at all"

"Thank you Mr Hunter. Here in this envelope is everything you need at this time. There are some details from my father's records, photographs of the rings, also my telephone number. I will await your call after you have contacted the family, please remember Mr Hunter, complete confidentiality please"

With that she got up and without so much as a goodbye, left the church. I sat there for some considerable time, brown A4 envelope in hand, wondering what the hell had just happened. I made my mind up just to go along with the whole performance, after all she was paying the bill so why should I care? Also, it will make a pleasant distraction from the day-to-day work of a private detective.

I was just thinking about popping into the Bold for a coffee and a piece of cake when my phone started to buzz in my pocket. I reached in and tapped the screen, it was Jan in the office.

"Hi Jan, what's up?"

"You will never believe what I have just heard on the radio"

"After the meeting I have just had, I will believe anything. Go on, see if you can surprise me"

"Well Lee, it seems that those two skeletons in the sand were not alone, not by any stretch of the imagination!"

The Southport and Lancashire Golf Course.
9th hole, the previous day.

Kaye Marie and Detective Inspector Deborah Smith stood outside the new scenes of crimes tent. The biting wind had abated somewhat, but the chill remained, seeping deep into their bodies, causing shivers to race through them. Each word uttered was accompanied by clouds of steam that were immediately taken away by the breeze.

They were joined by Detective Sergeant Sharron Shacklady, all wrapped up in a long duffle coat, hand knitted scarf and bobble hat. Deborah laughed as she approached, all she could see were Sharron's eyes and the tip of her nose.

"Listen boss, you can stop that laughing, it's bloody freezing out here and I am not going to get cold. Now please tell me I can go back home to my lunch, I don't like golf and I don't like working on my day off"

"Sorry Sharron but things have just taken a turn for the worse. The greenskeeper has been at it again, this time on the other side of the 9th green, and guess what?"

"Let me have a go boss, he has found another body?"

"Nope Sharron, he has found another four, two pairs, both posed like the first couple, 'lovers in the sand', the press are going to love this. Adele Wood from the County Archaeology Team is in there, I know that she is going to say they are modern, but we had to get her to check things out first"

"That's just what we need boss, three staff off sick with covid, one detective short, and now this lot!"

"Well Sharron, it's what we have, so let's get ready, here comes Adele"

The Head of the County Archelogy Department came out of the white and blue tent, ducking under the ridge as she did so. She had worked with the Murder squad several times in the past, but this was turning into a major and very interesting case.

She smiled at the three women waiting, then laughed a little as she drew closer. She scanned across the waiting three, trying to judge who would best take the news.

"Well spill the beans Adele, if I don't get out of this freezer soon, I will die of hyperthermia I am sure"

"Sorry Debs, it's not what you want to hear, I am sure. One couple must have been placed here about the same time as the ones found the other week. The third couple I guess somewhat later, maybe deposited in the sixties, ish?"

"So, Adele, we have two couples pre second world war, maybe 1930's and the third couple 1960's. Any signs of foul play, weapons, ligatures?"

"Not that I can see, but they are posed all the same, like the papers say, 'the lovers in the sand'. Oh yes, they all seem to be wearing the same style of ring. Hard to tell, they need to be cleaned up, but my guess is they are the same rings as the first couple"

Kaye started to laugh, "this is just what we bloody need Debs, a sextuple murder! I don't suppose that dam detective, what's his name, Lee Hunter has got anything to do with it"

"I don't think so Kaye, the last time he got involved the killing stopped at five!"

The four women laughed, more out of frustration than humour. This was turning into a potentially huge murder enquiry, and the truth was, they didn't have the faintest clue where to start.

"Right Kaye, let's get the coroner over, get these skeletons out of the ground. Adele, can your people do some scanning of the area, see if there are any more out here? Sharron, we need to seal the area off, no golf until I give written permission, do I make myself clear?"

"Yeah boss, on it"

"I will get the geophysics people over this afternoon. They will determine what, if anything is out here, I will report directly back to you Debs"

"Thanks Adele, let's get moving, the press are going to have a field day with this. We need to play it close to our chests, but that will probably be a waste of time, the greenskeeper and just about everyone else has seen what's going on. So, no mention of the rings, even if the press ask, let's just keep quiet on that one"

Back in the office.

This was getting messy, another four bodies, or should I say skeletons' on the golf course. It felt a little like my last adventure, dead people popping up everywhere and no bloody answers!

I ripped open the A4 envelope Ms Greenwood had given to me, I couldn't help thinking that I should have just given it back to her. After all, why the hell did I want to get caught up in this lot, and this might have been just the beginning. Trouble was, my curiosity had been pricked, so as much as I wanted to throw it into the shredder, well…..let's just see hey.

I sat back and started to read through the documents, she was right, they were very detailed indeed. Names, dates, costs even the supplier of the stones and gold. The problem was, they were dated back to the 1930's, so there was no way any of this was still relevant, anyone mentioned here would more than likely be long gone. The only thing that might be of use was the name of the customer, a Mr Edward Creighton-Ward. Sounded posh, as did his address, 'The Old Manor House, Hillside, Lancashire'. I do know that location, I used to go walking out there, not far from Southport, very exclusive, huge houses, plenty of expensive cars and well-dressed women. You don't buy anywhere in that area for less than a million, and that's just the garage!

I dropped the contents of the envelope on my desk, this was going to be a wild goose chase, that address probably doesn't exist anymore and even if it does, the Creighton-Wards almost certainly don't live there. Just ring Ms Greenwood and say that I am busy, plenty more Private Detectives about, any of them would be happy to take on the work. I was just reaching for the phone when my office door opened. Jan was standing there, a cup of coffee in her right hand and a look of shock on her face.

"Lee, you will never guess what I have just heard"

"Go on, surprise me"

"I had the radio on, and those latest skeletons' are all wearing the same rings as the first two found. How odd is that, and apparently, they are searching for more, what the hell is going on Lee, it's a mass grave or something!"

That was a surprise, it kind of hit me like an express train, a mass grave she said, not sure about that but six skeletons' out on a golf course, all wearing the same rings? Now if that doesn't get you thinking then nothing would. I picked up the documents again, this time I wouldn't be putting them down!

"Ok Jan, I need to get in touch with DI Smith, see what she can tell me, nothing I expect but it's worth a try. I am also going to have a drive out to Hillside, see if a family is still at an old address. Keep in touch, especially if there are any more developments in relation to this case"

"Will do. Just be careful Lee, I know these bodies have been there for a long time, but you never know if anything is still going on. You don't want to be the next skeleton on the 9th, do you?"

"No chance Jan, I am way too clever for that"

You know when you say something and instantly regret your bravado, I must admit to having that feeling as soon as those words came out of my mouth! Anyway, I brushed those regrets away and reached for my phone, I hit DI Smith's stored number and waited for an answer, the case was on.

"DI Smith's phone, Detective Sergeant Shacklady"

"Hi Sharron, Lee Hunter here, where is your glorious leader then?"

"Hi Lee, she is in with her boss trying to beg for some more staff, some hope there. We are one detective short, now three office guys off with covid and two uniforms away on a course. If things stay the way they are, we will be lucky to man the local school crossing this dinner time.

Anyway, enough of our woes, what can I do for you?"

"It's about those skeletons Sharron, I have been contacted by the daughter of the man who made the rings. I am sure it won't come to anything, but I am going to follow it up"

"Hang on Lee, you know the score, that's an ongoing case, if you know something then you need to tell us"

"Well, that's what I am doing Sharron and, in any case, are you in any kind of position to actually do anything about it?"

"That's not the point and you know it Lee, you have to divulge what you know, so what do you have?"

"I will do you a swap Sharron, and I will keep you informed every step of the way, and that's a promise"

"Swap what Lee?"

"What I have for what you have"

"Go on, amaze me"

"Ah, wait a minute, you go first. I need to know if those remains discovered the other day have the exact same rings as the first two, that's all"

"Lee, you know I can't tell you things like that, it's part of a live case"

"Ok, well if they did, I might be able to ascertain the dates of those rings, that's going to help you date the deposition of the bodies"

"And how might you be able to do that?"

"Like I said, I know the daughter of the man who made them. Now, do we have a deal or not. It's going to save you quite a bit of time if I can find out that information for you, and given your staffing issues, that's going to be a big help"

"Lee, I can't tell you anything, you know that, but I can confirm that there were some similarities to the remains, if you get my drift?"

"Thanks Sharron, that's a big help, I will keep you in the loop"

"Lee, if that information gets out, I will personally lock you up for the next thirty years on some trumped up charge, and that's an absolute promise, do I make myself clear?"

"Crystal Sharron, Crystal"

I said my goodbyes and immediately dialled Ms Greenwood's number, we needed to have a chat! The phone rang several times before it was answered, I had to play this very carefully indeed.

"Good morning Mr Hunter, what can I do for you?"

"Ms Greenwood, good morning, can I ask you a question please, about these rings?"

"Most certainly Mr Hunter"

"How many were made by your father and grandfather, to the same design found on the bodies on the golf course?"

"That's a good question Mr Hunter. If my memory serves, I think there were around fifty"

"Just to be clear Ms Greenwood, around fifty rings were made, solid gold band, with a central emerald and two flanking rubies, each with a dragon engraving on the back?"

"Why do you ask Mr Hunter?"

I felt a hot sensation well up inside of me, fifty, my goodness. If these rings were given to each one of these poor souls before they were killed, how many more bodies are we likely to find?

The thoughts running through my mind became chaotic, I wondered where the hell this was going to end. I thought about telling DI Smith, if she thinks that she has problems now, that's nothing in comparison to what might be coming down the line! I would leave that particular issue until later, much later. Let's concentrate on what's in front of me right now and find out who these rings were given to.

"Oh no particular reason Ms Greenwood, no particular reason at all. Would it be possible to take a look at your records, I wonder who these other rings were made for?"

"Well, if you call to my house tomorrow morning, I will let you see any of my records you wish Mr Hunter, shall we say 10am? My address is 29 Akers Close, not far from Birkdale station, do you know it?"

"I don't Ms Greenwood, but I am sure my sat nav will find you. I will be there at 10"

"Excellent, see you at 10am sharp"

The phone went dead, dam this case is getting bigger and bigger, where the hell is it going to end? I had that feeling, you know, I wish I had not started this, I should have turned my back and gone the other way. Well, it's too late now, so let's make a start, the first thing to do is go and see Mr Edward Creighton-Ward's decedents at the old manor house. That's if they or the old place still exist.

The morning was bright and clear, this made a change to be honest, this winter had been a bastard, it was time the sun made an appearance. Living in London for most of my life, the winters were mostly bland and somewhat mild. This winter however had taught me a lesson and that was, 'never take any dam notice of the weather forecast, it's never right'

Anyway, spring was about to make an appearance, so things were looking up, probably. I entered the manor house postcode into my sat nav, Jan had been good enough to find that online, at least the place still existed. I wasn't so confident about the Creighton-Wards though, 1938 was the date of the sales invoice, that was a long time ago. Also, was this date when the job had been completed, or sometime after?

The chances of the same family still being there were, well very low indeed but at least the drive out to Hillside had been pleasant enough. The early morning commuters were now gone and the roads nice and quiet. Eventually my sat nav informed me, "you have reached your destination"

The building was out beyond the town itself, around 5 minutes from its nearest neighbour. I found the sign at the edge of a leafy country lane,

The Old Manor House – Private Road – KEEP OUT.

Well, that was plain enough, especially the block capitals telling me to keep out! Still, I was on an official investigation, and besides which, I didn't really give a dam. So, I turned right and proceeded up the gravel track. About 100 yards in, I came to an entrance, a large five bar gate cutting across the whole track. I quickly nipped out of the car, opened it and drove on. I didn't bother closing the gate, I would do that on the way out.

Eventually, the track made a turn to the right and swept into a large wooded area. This was turning into one of those 'Hammer House of Horror' films that I used to watch on a Saturday night. I used to pretend I was scared, but to be honest, the Brides of Dracula was never the most terrifying film ever made.

As soon as I entered the woods, the light almost disappeared completely, the darkness was pervasive, it made me feel uneasy, uncomfortable. The whole place had a damp muggy feeling, it felt different from the winter sunlit day. I expected to see a ghostly figure running across the track, it had that sad air, as if something had happened here, something evil perhaps.

Eventually the woods opened up and to my right was what looked like a large stable block. It was a couple of stories high in the middle, made of Cotswold stone, and with a huge set of green wooden doors at this end. Numerous windows opened up from the front and sides, to be honest it was so large that it could easily have made five or even six family homes. There was no doubt that whoever lived here was not on the poverty line, not even close!

That stable block was really impressive, so much so that I almost missed the little wooden bridge that led over a small stream. At the last second, I pulled my self together and managed to steer the car over the bridge and continued on the track towards the looming grand house. It was huge, a central façade, four stories high with two identical wings sweeping in an arc forward, like two huge embracing arms. There were huge windows, spires, balconies and a central turret. This wasn't a house, it was more like a small palace, a stately home for curious visitors on a weekend coach tour.

I steered my car around the circular drive and stopped outside the front doors. Several stone steps led up to a pair of oak doors with a highly polished brass knocker. I must admit to feeling somewhat intimidated by all this grandeur, this wasn't anything I had any experience of. I took a deep breath and got out of my Ford Mondeo, I do like my car but for the first time it did feel a little cheap! Right Hunter, pull yourself together and go and knock, what's the worst that could happen?

I felt like a naughty schoolboy getting ready to knock on the headmaster's office door, something I had done on several occasions. Goodness only knows why, it was just a house, ok, a very posh one and it probably didn't even house the family I was looking for. I raised my right hand, lifted the very heavy knocker and started what I had come here to do.

Eventually, after what seemed like and age, the door opened, there stood a stunning woman, perhaps late fifties, dressed casually in a sweater and jeans but looking a million dollars. She was tall, blond hair, flawless skin and perfect teeth. Not the kind of woman that would even glance in my direction, let alone start up a conversation with me.

She stared out at me, a look of perplexed annoyance on her face, eventually she drew an audible breath and spoke. Her accent was perfect, public school educated with a clear and measured pace.

"Yes, can I help, I assume you know this is private property, did you not read the sign?"

"Sorry madam I didn't mean to intrude. My name is Lee Hunter, I am investigating the case of the remains found on the golf course"

"So, you are the Police, why didn't you call ahead, please don't just turn up it may be inconvenient"

I was about to tell her that I wasn't actually the police, but we had started the conversation so I thought I would take advantage of that.

"Sorry madam, but this is rather urgent, I wonder if Mr Creighton-Ward is at home?"

I knew this was a long shot, but I might as well give it a try. Why ask if that family still lived here, just to give her an opportunity to slam the door in my face.

"Charles is very busy, you need to make an appointment. He has just returned from a long business trip, he is trying to catch up on things"

"I understand Mrs Creighton-Ward, but this is very important indeed"

Just another punt on my part assuming this was the wife, but it was worth a try. It's surprising what you can find out without actually asking anything!

"Oh, very well, this is extremely inconvenient, I will go and ask but I am certain that he will require an appointment"

She slammed the door in my face and left. I expected to be standing there for some considerable amount of time and then be told to go away, but it didn't take long for the door to open once more. This time it was opened by a tall slightly greying man, in his late sixties, very upright, athletic, reminded me of an army colonel.

"Can I help officer, I am Charles Creighton-Ward?"

"Certainly, and thank you for your time. I wonder sir, was your grandfather, Edward Creighton-Ward?"

"What is this about officer, I don't understand?"

"I wonder if I might come in sir, it's a rather complicated story?"

"Very well, but I have a call booked with New York in fifteen minutes, so you better be quick, do I make myself clear?"

He showed me into the hall, closing the oak doors with a dull thud behind us. There was a central staircase, marble everywhere and paintings that wouldn't have looked out of place in the royal collection. Chandeliers hung from the ceiling that glittered and shone and were probably worth more than everything I owned. We turned right into a drawing room, you can guess what that looked like, more paintings, leather sofas, carpet an inch deep and the smell of beeswax, it was stunning.

"Now Mr…….."

"Sorry sir, Lee Hunter, this won't take a minute, just tying up a few loose ends. You may be aware of some remains being found on the Southport and Lancashire Golf Course. Those remains included gold rings and our enquires suggest that they were commissioned by a Mr Edward Creighton-Ward in the late1930's. Can I assume that this gentleman was your grandfather, or family member?"

"You can assume some of that Mr Hunter, he was in fact my grandfather, as for commissioning rings in the late 1930's however, that would be impossible"

"Oh, why is that?"

"He died in a flying accident in 1930, he was in the RAF you know, dam fine pilot, that is until his Gloucester Gauntlet fighter collided with a flock of seagulls. Sent the dam thing into a spin and boom, that was the end of grandpapa"

"Was there any other Edwards in the family, perhaps living in another part of the country?"

"Impossible Mr Hunter, this is the family seat, this place was the home of the entire family back then, I can absolutely assure you of that"

"That's strange, I am certain that the records are correct"

"Well Mr Hunter, I can absolutely assure you that your records are in fact wrong. Edward Creighton-Ward died on the 1st of June 1930, just outside RAF Andover in Hampshire"

"Where is he buried sir?"

"In the family crypt, as are most of the Creighton-Wards. Now, if there is anything else I can help you with Mr Hunter, I am really busy?"

I stood there for a few moments, this was very disappointing. I had assumed Ms Greenwood's records were correct, they clearly were not. This threw the whole thing into disarray. I decided to go to the local churchyard where I would most likely find the Creighton-Ward crypt, just to confirm the death of Edward and the dates. Then off to Ms Greenwood's house to break the bad news and present her with my bill.

The journey to the old church didn't take more than a few minutes but I felt flat, the news about Edward was very disappointing. The truth was, we didn't really have a clue as to who made the rings or when, as the records could no longer be trusted. Oh well, I would just have to hand the records over to DI Deborah Smith and let her and the team sort it out. I had enough work to be getting on with, four acrimonious divorce cases and a man defrauding the Department for Work and Pensions.

I pulled up at the front of the churchyards, the clouds had begun to gather, bringing a chill in the air. I looked up, please no more snow, I am dam sick of digging my car out every morning. No sooner did I say that than the rain started to fall, a fine penetrating drizzle, soaking everything it touched. I grabbed my coat from the boot of the car and made my way into the graveyard, not knowing for a minute where the Creighton-Ward crypt actually was.

It didn't however take long to find what I was looking for, thank goodness. A huge sandstone monument, adorned with statuettes and gargoyles on each corner. It was very impressive indeed, and must have cost a fortune to build, and all for what, a house for the dead! It glistened in the rain, a strange almost ghostly sheen, I shivered and not just because of the wet and the cold.

Anyway, on the northern face was a list of all those interred within, complete with dates and any honours bestowed. There were four Knights of the Realm, one Dame, two doctors and several military honours, and a governor of a colony in Africa that I had no idea even existed. The trouble was, as much as I checked and re checked I could find no mention of an Edward Creighton-Ward. I thought perhaps he might have been known by another name, perhaps just Teddy, but there was no entry for 1930, not even within 5 years of that date!

This is dam odd, maybe his name was omitted for some reason, maybe he joined the RAF but was supposed to enlist in the Guards. These things did happen, members of a family completely obliterated from the records, I had come across this on several occasions during my time in the Met. I needed to check the official records, there was no way they could have been glossed over just because Edward was some kind of outcast.

I turned and looked around, maybe the vicarage was still here, perhaps the local Priest could help. He would hold the local records, all I needed to do……

"Hello sir, I hope this rain doesn't turn to snow, I am sick of digging my car out in the morning"

Did I just imagined that, did I think the exact same thing a couple of minutes ago? I turned to see a ruddy faced, rather round chap, no more that five feet six tall, thinning grey hair, maybe fifty or even more. I tried to look relaxed, opened my mouth and listened to what came out.

"Oh, good day, erm, no, it's supposed to clear up later, I think"

"Let's hope so, the name is Thomas Toc, most people call me Tom"

He had a rather annoying jolly nature, not really what I wanted standing in a graveyard getting piss wet through. He had a stocky build, a thick neck and workman's hands and I couldn't help noticing an inward turned right foot.

"Hi Tom, my name is Lee Hunter, do you know anything about this crypt and the Creighton-Ward's?"

I guess it was a little abrupt, but I thought is prudent to come to the point before we both died of hyperthermia.

"I certainly do sir, my grandfather was the batman to Colonel Cyril Creighton-Ward, they both bought it on the Somme, November 1916. My uncle worked all his life over at the manor house, head gardener and chauffer, and my old mother was the head housekeeper"

"That's interesting, did you work for them?"

"No sir, didn't fancy all that bowing and grovelling, so I ended up as the grave digger and handyman to the church and the Vicarage, it's been a good life to be honest"

"I am looking for the grave of Edward Creighton-Ward. I am told he is in the family crypt but there is no mention of his name on here"

"Come with me, the records are in the office at the back of the church. Everything and everyone who has gone into the ground here will be recorded in that book"

I couldn't believe my luck, I almost pushed him forward towards the church, this would confirm the accuracy, or not, of Ms Greenwood's records or perhaps the memory of Charles Creighton-Ward!

It was a relief to finally get under cover, it wasn't any warmer in the church but at least the rain wasn't drenching me, and the cold northerly wind wasn't freezing my nuts off. He pulled a large bunch of keys from his overcoat pocket and started to open doors that lead to corridors and then more doors. This place was like a bloody TARDIS, I am sure it wasn't this big from the outside!

Eventually we found the office, if you could call it that, more like a tiny little storeroom with a desk and chair shoehorned in between the filing cabinets and boxes of records. He opened one of the grey and very dusty cabinets and then turned to me.

"Right, when did you say this Edward chap was buried?"

"I don't think I did but I was told 1930"

"Hang on"

He pulled some large leather-bound record books from the top drawer, inspected them for dates and then pushed them back. Then the second and then the third drawer before he found the year we were looking for.

"Right, 1st of January 1930 until 31st October 1930, what was the date?"

"1st of June, he was killed in a plane crash, somewhere in Hampshire but I was told he was interred here"

He placed the volume on the desk and started to flick through the yellowing pages. Every turn got us closer to the date before he eventually stopped.

"Here we go, 18th of May, Doctor Claude A Durand, 24th May, Mrs Susan Sutton, oh look at this, 26th May, the local Vicar, Simon Boulter. That was a busy month, next one.......that's strange, 20th June, hang on let me check"

I gazed over his shoulder, he was right, there hadn't been anything recorded between the 26th of May and 20th of June.

"Could it be he isn't recorded in here, maybe in a private Creighton-Ward book?"

"Nope, certainly not, these are legal records, they are not subject to money or privilege sir, never! If you get buried here, you are in these books, guaranteed"

"Maybe he wasn't buried here until later, if he was killed in Hampshire, it might have taken some time to get his body here……"

"Let me stop you there sir, according to this book, there is no record, at all, of an Edward Creighton-Ward, anywhere up until this book finishes at the end of October 1930. I would suggest sir, he isn't in that crypt at all, you need to check back with whoever gave you that information"

This was looking dam strange, Edward Creighton-Ward was supposed to have died in 1930, but Ms Greenwood's records stated that he commissioned some rings to be made years later. His grandson told me he had been buried here, but the official records give no mention of that at all. Someone was wrong or was lying, or both!

I needed to get to the bottom of this, there had been six bodies found on the golf course and around fifty of these rings have been made. I was hoping that we wouldn't find those rings attached to another 44 skeletons!

A Dark Place.

She shivered uncontrollably, the pain was unbearable, the nausea overwhelming. It was dark, completely void of light, the floor felt wet and slimy beneath her bare feet. The cable ties had bitten tightly into her wrists, even though they had now been removed, the pain that remained was more than she could stand. Searing hurt flashed around her body, utter torment and agony filled every sense.

She had lost any perception of time and how long she had been down here. She had woken, crumpled and naked on the stone floor, two, three or even four days ago, with her hands tied behind her back. It had started with a Saturday night out with friends, a few drinks in her local pub and then on to a club in the city centre. She remembered getting out of the cab and going into the club, chatting with friends, being approached by a good-looking young guy around her age.

That was about the last memory she had before waking in this dark and cold place. There had been a couple of visits, the wooden door being thrown open, some old clothes, a track suit top and pants handed to her. An older man coming in, bringing her food and water. He had pulled her up to her feet, turned her around, examined her body before leaving, slamming the door behind him.

It was during these visits that she caught site of her surroundings. It was a long stone cell, maybe six feet wide and ten long. There was a bed with no mattress and a child's wooden chair all standing on a very cold and wet grey stone floor.

She had stopped crying, the fear and utter helplessness of her situation had overtaken her. All that remained was terror, panic and a certain inner acceptance of her impending death. She wrapped her arms around herself in a futile attempt to bring some level of comfort. It didn't work, only serving to reinforce the utter futility of her position.

As she lay shivering on the floor, she heard approaching voices, feet on hard stone, echoing noises. Their conversations were distorted, reverberating, unintelligible, but as they came closer, some words and even sentences started to become clear. There were two men, one with a refined accent, softly spoken, in control. The other was deeper, more excited, louder, it was this man who she came to understand first.

"So, when do we start, I thought it was supposed to be last Saturday?"

"It was, but he wasn't able to be here, so we had to postpone"

"That's tough, he knew when the ceremony was planned, he should have been here. What happens if she dies, that's going to fuck things up, the boss isn't going to like that"

"I know, but he is as you put it, the boss. If you want to tell him he had better be here, then be my guest. I can assure you it'll be the last thing you do"

"You lot are all fucking terrified of him and I don't understand why. He is just a jumped-up prick who thinks he is better than the rest of us, and he's not"

"OK, let's just calm down, she is here and still alive. The doctor tells me she will be fine for the next few days, and he should know. In any case, it's not as if she is going back home afterwards, is it"

The two men laughed as they continued passed the cell door and down the corridor.

"Listen, I just want to get this thing on, see her up on that alter, screaming for her life, but we are late, we should have done this last week. There are rules, timescales, we are pledged to follow the scrolls, they are not optional, they are the fucking law, let's not forget that"

Her head pounded not just with the cold and hunger, but the realisation of her predicament. They had said, 'up on the alter', the 'ceremony', 'she's not going home', what did that all mean?

Of course she knew, deep inside, the truth was by now obvious and going home to her family wasn't part of the plan.

Ms Greenwood's residence.

I knocked on the door, the puzzlement of the morning's activities were still whirling around my mind. Ms Greenwood had seemed so confident in her father's records. Hey, we all make mistakes, and this was just one example. So, what was I going to tell her, "sorry your families records are rubbish, not worth the paper they are written on". Of course, I wouldn't say it like that, she had a lot of pride in her father and grandfather. Those records were clearly important to her. But in essence this was the news she was going to get. Ok, just tell her Lee, not my fault that she has some duff information, if she gets upset then, well……tough!

I could see her outline approaching through the opaque glass in the middle of the old front door. I looked up at the house, a classic Victorian mansion, circa 1850ish, very impressive. What was just as remarkable was it was still a family home, most of these houses had been turned into flats and bed sits years ago.

The door opened, "ah Mr Hunter, please come in. We can take tea in the drawing room, please follow me"

I followed her into a very old-fashioned room, an open marble fireplace, heavy oak furniture, rugs rather than carpets laid on a waxed wooden floor. It felt like something out of a museum. The whole place was spotless, this again was at odds with a bad record keeper, she was more akin to an obsessive! It was no more than a couple of minutes before she returned with a silver tray, holding a teapot, two fine Bone China cups and saucers, and milk and sugar bowls. She sat down, placing the tray on a small table between the two of us, in front of the ornate fireplace.

"How do you take your tea Mr Hunter"

"Black one sugar"

She gently poured the tea, with a loving passion for this English pastime. "How can I help you Mr Hunter?"

"It's a little awkward Ms Greenwood but it's your fathers' records. I went to see the Creighton-Wards and they tell me that Edward died in 1930 and therefore couldn't have commission the rings in 1938. Odd thing was though, I couldn't find any record of him dying in 30 or 38, in fact no records of Edward Creighton-Ward at all"

"Well, I showed you the records Mr Hunter, I am certain they are correct"

"Could it be that your father has mistaken the name of the person who commissioned the rings. Perhaps it wasn't anyone in the Creighton-Ward family at all, someone with a similar name"

"It was Edward Creighton-Ward Mr Hunter. In another file I have the bank document confirming to my father that the money had been paid and by whom. Banks don't make mistakes like that, it was Edward, there is no doubt about that Mr Hunter, no doubt at all"

I sat back in my chair, she was one of those people who just knew her facts were right. In all this paperwork, something would have been obviously wrong, an entry in a logbook, notes from the bank, photos, names. It would have been clear to a person like Ms Greenwood that a piece of information had been incorrectly recorded, either mistakenly or on purpose.

As I sipped my tea, I decided to accept her explanation that Edward had commissioned the rings in the 1930's. I had to at least agree to that, there was too much information supporting it. Assuming of course that those records were accurate, and I had no concrete evidence suggesting that they weren't.

The trouble was, what the hell was James Creighton-Ward talking about, and why were there no records of his supposed Grandfather, Edward. Your grandfather simply doesn't vanish, even if he joined the RAF instead of the Guards or ran off with the milk maid. Also, why did he tell me he was buried in the family crypt, that was odd. He could have told me some other tale, even his body was never found after the crash.

It was all very odd, nothing made any sense. It felt like a was investigating two completely different cases, one involving the Creighton-Ward's and the other Ms Greenwood.

A Dark Place.

He awoke with a start, he was facing the wall, the cold grey stone was not more than an inch from his face. Something had crawled over him in the dark, perhaps a rat or some insects, it wasn't the first time and he guessed it wouldn't be the last. Sleep was the last thing he had thought about, but even the hard surface of the bed had been enough, exhaustion had simply overwhelmed him.

He couldn't understand what the man had said to him yesterday. He had put the tray of food down on the floor and simply announced that he would be getting married in a few days. Getting married, what the hell was he talking about? Why the hell had they drugged him and imprisoned him down here so he could get married? He had asked for an explanation, but the man had just laughed and slammed the door behind him, his last words were, "the fitting for the rings would be tomorrow"

It was a joke obviously, the man was just torturing him mentally, trying to suck away the last remnants of his sanity. Hunger, thirst and sensory deprivation had taken its toll, eating away at his ability to resist, cope and fight back. Part of him hoped this would end soon, no matter the outcome, perhaps every person thought like this, maybe it was part of giving in, dying!

He couldn't get what the man had said out of his head though, that smile as he turned and walked out of the door. Married, what the hell did that mean, married to who, what and why?

It wasn't long before those questions would be answered, he could hear footsteps, that familiar methodical pace, just one set of feet coming in his direction. He dreaded the door opening, he did every time it happened. It was only the arrival of food, a plastic bottle of water but the dread was real. This time the fear was heightened, the ring, the man had said, the fitting would be today.

The key made that familiar slightly rusty sound as it turned the lock, then the door swung inward. The same man stood there, a sickly grin on his face, something in his right hand.

"Stand up now and hold out your right hand"

He stood up, more from reflex than obedience, his knees shaking as he drew himself upright.

"What are you going to do?"

His voice was horse, dry and cracked, it hurt to even speak gently.

"Never mind, you are nothing, just scum, a worthless life meant for our purpose. Don't ask questions, all will be revealed in time and trust me, it won't be pleasant, well at least not for you"

The man stood in the open door, a strongly built individual, thick arms, a powerful neck. He strode confidently into the cell.

"Put out your right arm before I hit you, don't test me you shit, just do it"

There was something inside him, some streak of resistance, a need to fight back. There was no way he was going to do as he was told. Up until now it had just been a delivery of food and water, he had sat in the cell and whiled away the time in the darkness. This time he was being ordered, told, he wasn't about to comply.

"I told you, hold out your right hand"

He stood there, shaking from head to toe, terror raging through his body, he wanted to comply, but his inner self would not let him. He was determined, whatever the outcome, he was not going to give in.

"Last chance shit, hold out your right hand"

The man's face changed, his eyes flared with rage, he seemed to grow, his neck turned purple. He marched into the cell, gritting his teeth, both arms bent, fists clenched. He closed the distance between them in an instance, it was no more than a second before he was on him. When the blow came, it was completely unseen, unexpected.

His world turned white, flashes erupted, a metallic taste filled his mouth. He felt himself falling, his hands impacting on the cold and wet stone. Then a blaze of pain in his right side, a kick and then another. He was pushed onto his back, another blow, this time causing intense burning pain in his mouth, strong fingers around his throat caused him to choke, he began to panic, he couldn't breathe.

"Right, you little shit, now do as you are told and put your right hand out, or do I have to beat you some more?"

More as a reflex than an acquiescence he held out his hand, he caught a glimpse of it as he pushed it into the darkness. His right eye was unable to open, his left filled with a sticky warm substance, which could only be blood. The man grabbed his hand, pulling the second finger straight, he felt it crack, the pain was intense. Something was pushed down his finger, it was tight, constricting.

"Right, it fits, now that wasn't too difficult was it, all you need to do is what I tell you, next time save yourself a beating and do as you are told"

He felt the man rip something off his finger before smashing a couple of blows down onto his face. His head bashed down onto the stone floor, the world started to spin, a tunnel of light flashed in front of him as he fell into unconsciousness.

Murder Squad Offices.
Southport Police Station.

Kaye Marie had been up since five thirty this morning, it seemed Southport had become the murder capital of the UK. The bodies on the golf course were of course part of the problem, six in total, the first two from the late 1930's, the next two from around 1950 and the last couple from the early 60's. The whole thing seemed very strange, especially with such a regular time span. If the murders did in fact begin in the late 30's, and finished in the 60's, that was at least twenty plus years of killing. She knew from experience that such a time span was rare and if it was the case, then in all probability there would be more bodies to find.

In addition, the circumstances were very odd. She had consulted the data base and made several phone calls, but nothing had ever been seen like this before. Male and female couples, buried in the sand, in a lovers embrace. Also, the rings, they were all wearing the same rings, what did this indicate? She had even spoken to several local jewellers, not one of them had seen anything like it, nor could they begin to offer an explanation as to their meaning, if indeed there was one!

She sat back in her office chair, her full English breakfast and the broken office heating were beginning to take effect, gently lulling her into a light sleep. She wanted to open her eyes, lean forward and carry on with the reports for DI Smith, but her tired mind resisted.

"What the hell does all this mean", she thought as she drifted off, "some lunatic, an occult gang, some crazy worship?"

She was shaken back into life by her phone vibrating in her pocket. Stung by the sudden intrusion she lurched upright in her chair, wiped away the dribble from the corner of her mouth and grabbed for her right-hand pocket. Her shaking hands touched the screen back into life, as she tried to focus on the caller's name.

ADELE WOOD
COUNTY ARCHAEOLOGIST

Kaye cleared her throat and tried to sound awake, she wondered how affective that would be.

"Hi Adele, what's occurring?"

"Kaye, well we have finished the scanning of the whole area, the Geophysics guys are looking further afield but they don't think there has been any additional disturbance"

"So, that looks like the lot then"

"Ah sorry to screw your morning up Kaye, but there has been another find"

Kaye Marie sat bolt upright in her chair, those words blew away any remaining feelings of tiredness.

"Another find Adele, what the hell do you mean?"

"Another couple Kaye, yep, just the same as the first two couples. Judging by some of the remains, including a pair of very expensive handmade boots on the male and a locket found under the woman's body, I can be reasonably certain of the date of entombment"

"Bloody great, that's just what I need, another couple of skeletons, I will be making a whole career out of this before I retire. Ok go on, when do you think they were put in the ground?"

"I am reasonably certain in saying, 1940 at the latest. There was a coin in the grave dated 1939, so they couldn't have been buried before that date. The man's boots are a classic design from the late 30's but no later than 1942, the manufacture has already confirmed that to me. The woman's gold locket was hallmarked 1938, put that lot together and you come up with 1940, put my mortgage on it Kaye!"

"Hang on, so these four couples seem to have been murdered1940, about 1950, 1960 and then around 1970. Ten years apart?"

"Yeah, I can't argue with you there Kaye, we can't be absolutely certain without carbon dating them, but that seems a very reasonable assumption"

"Bloody hell, if that's the case, where are the other five couples?"

"Five couples Kaye?"

"Yeah, five would bring us bang up to date, 1980 through to 2020, one couple every ten years. We are missing another ten bodies! Ok, thanks for that Adele, I will go and see DI Smith and break the good news. Email your report as soon as you can please, I will call you once I have read it"

"What do you mean Kaye, another ten bodies, you are having a bloody laugh right?"

"Sorry Debs but that's what it looks like, one couple every ten years, we are missing another five couples if we take 2020 into account"

"If you are right, and it's a big 'if' Kaye, that means eighteen bodies in total, this is beginning to look like Jack the bloody Ripper part two. When the press gets hold of this it's going to be bedlam around here. Look Kaye, get hold of Adele and tell her to keep this under her hat for now. We haven't got the resources to control this or even answer the questions. No one gets to know about this, not anyone, do I make myself clear?"

"Crystal boss, leave it to me"

"Right, we need to get on, if you are right and there are potentially another ten bodies to find, we need a plan. Trouble is, I haven't got a bloody clue where to start, we don't even know if there are any more than we already have. It's entirely possible that we have the lot, all eight!"

"Want to put money on it Debs?"

"I don't want to think about it Kaye. We are in the shit with this case and if the press gets hold of it, well I don't even want to contemplate that. The top brass will be all over it, the mayor of the town will want it sorted quickly, no bad publicity and all of that. There will be conspiracy theorists around every corner, what a bloody nightmare. Worst of all, when someone asks me the question, who did this, I will have to say, I haven't got a clue"

"Let's just take it one step at a time Debs, see what Adele digs up, so to speak. We should also wait until forensics gets done, I am sure we will have a better idea then"

"A better idea Kaye, you mean any idea at all don't you!"

A Dark Place.

Richard looked across at the man sitting in the old leather chair, in the corner of the dimly lit office. It was a neglected place, something that had certainly seen better days. Three broken wooden filing cabinets from the 50's, two cracked and sad looking leather armchairs, a desk and office chair. The single light bulb hung limply from the electric cable above them, casting a very gloomy yellow light across the whole place. The discoloured paintwork was fractured and blistered, the whole scene smelled of damp and corruption.

"You shouldn't have given him such a kicking, I wouldn't be surprised if we find him dead in the morning."

"Couldn't give a fuck Richard, should have done as he was told. All I wanted was his hand, try the ring on, that's all"

"I know but you should have given me a call, we could have restrained him together"

"This is not some pussy Police station, should have done as he was told"

"Listen, we can't afford any screw ups, they should have done the ceremony two years ago but bloody covid got in the way. They are two years late, should have happened in 2020, so let's not make them mad or we might be next on the list, understand?"

"Yeah, yeah, stop bleating on Richard, he will be ok"

"Well, if he's not, you will be taking his place, ever fancied getting married?"

"Fuck off Richard, they will have to catch me first"

"Well, they won't have a problem catching you, not with that turned in right foot!"

The two men laughed, it was an awkward exchange but one that was certainly meaningful. It was true that the ceremony should have been completed two years ago, but due to the pandemic and other business, things had been delayed. It had been made clear to both men there would be no more delays, there was no room for mistakes, no further postponements, in a few days' time the ceremony would begin.

The silence in the dank room was broken by the telephone ringing. It wasn't a modern ring, but an old-fashioned bell, Richard looked at the cream handset hanging on the wall next to the door.

"I'll get that then"

He stood up and walked briskly, picking the receiver off its cradle.

"Richard here, what's up?"

A whispering voice spoke, the man didn't introduce himself, but Richard was fully aware of his identity.

"Richard, it has been decided. There will be an extra ceremony, it will take place a week after the first"

"Oh really, what the hell for?"

"It's an installation, a new master of our congregation, and it's about time. Might have been done after the 2020 meeting but that didn't happen either. I am looking forward to it, should be fun"

"They are catching up I guess. A new master you say, it's been a few years since that was last done"

"Well it's been decided, so you need to act and act very quickly, you have got just over a week to prepare. Just do what you need to, make the necessary preparations, get everything ready"

The phone went dead, Richard replaced the receiver and turned to face back into the office. He could feel the dismay rising and no doubt it showed on his face.

"What the hell just happened Richard, looks like you just found a penny and lost a pound?"

"Bloody hell, there is going to be an extra ceremony, in a couple of weeks"

"You're joking, don't tell me that they want more?"

"Looks like it, we need to find a couple of extra's and be quick about it. We better get started, get everything ready, we will start looking tonight"

"It's not going to be easy Richard, people are really careful nowadays, it's not easy getting them"

"Look, we need another man and woman, by the end of this week. Get the drugs and the cuffs ready, we start tonight"

Returning Back to the Office.

As I walked through the door, I heard the gentle click of the kettle. Jan was an absolute godsend, not only keeping my diary up to date but managing most everything else in my life. I must admit to being attracted to her, she was good-looking by anyone's standards but after Ruth I was in no mood for relationships. I still had nightmares about the phone call from DI Smith telling me that Ruth had been found murdered at the side of the road. I promised myself that I would never enter into any kind of relationship ever again. Putting someone else's life on the line because of my work was simply not acceptable.

I kicked the door shut with my heel, the warmth of the central heating washed over me with a comforting touch. I could see Jan standing by the kitchen worktop, diminutive but radiating a positive aura. Shoulder length brown hair, soft pale skin, she turned and smiled, a gentle friendly smile, very easy on the senses.

"Hiya, fancy a cuppa?"

I smiled back, she was disarming I must admit, but I needed to be careful. Firstly, after the Ruth incident and secondly, I didn't want to make a complete fool out of myself.

"Yeah please, anything important happening?"

"No not really, Mr Hanson paid his bill, finally! Oh yes, Russ Broadbent from Radio Rock n Roll Lancashire called, he needs to speak to you, he wouldn't say why. I left his number on your desk, give him a call, it sounded urgent"

I collected my black coffee with one sugar, thanked her, she responded with a smile and returned to her work. So, what did Russ want? I knew him quite well, he seemed to have his fingers into many different pies. I never asked were exactly he got his information, but it always seemed to be genuine.

I slumped down in my office chair, placed the coffee on the desk and reached for the yellow post-it note with Russ Broadbent's number. To be honest I couldn't be bothered ringing him, I had more work than I could handle, and this skeleton thing was just about the straw that broke my camel's back. I watched the hot steam whirl off the top of my white cup. Jan had it made, it had the words, 'worlds greatest detective' on one side and 'detectives do it under cover' on the other. Jan did make me smile, perhaps I should ask her out for a drink, but on second thoughts, we worked very well together, let's not spoil that. With some reluctance, I reached for the phone and dialled the number.

"Hello Russ Broadbent"

"Hi Russ, it's Lee, Jan said you wanted to speak to me"

"Yeah mate, got some rather interesting info' for you"

"Go on, enlighten me"

"A little birdie tells me that they have found some more buried lovers on that golf course. Another two in fact, brings the total to eight, apparently, they are still looking for more"

"Who the hell told you that Russ"

"Lee, my old friend, do you really expect me to tell you that?"

"I guess not"

"That's not all, it turns out that they were buried ten years apart, starting from 1940 and finishing in 1970, how cool is that?"

"That certainly sounds like some deranged serial killer, or perhaps a cult. Any ideas of where they all came from, was there ever rumours of a cult around here?"

"Not that I can make out Lee, there has never been anything like that in these parts and I have lived here all my life. This is really odd, mind you if it ended in 1970, that's before my time and a long way back, perhaps people who might have been involved are all gone"

"I wouldn't jump to any conclusions about when it ended Russ. You know those rings they were wearing, well I have reliable information that there were at least fifty made. There might be many, many more bodies yet to find"

The line seemed to go dead, all I could hear was a slight humming in the background.

"Fifty Lee, you have got to be joking right? Where the hell are you going to hide fifty bloody bodies?"

"Listen, we are going to let the Police handle this Russ, this isn't some granny who has lost her cat, or a schoolboy who found an odd piece of military memorabilia from World War two. This is serious and to be honest, I don't want to get involved. Please take my advice Russ, neither do you"

"It'll be ok Lee, what could possibly go wrong?"

"A bloody lot Russ, trust me"

"Well, I can't help myself Lee, it's in my blood this kind of stuff, I am a journalist, I love to get to the bottom of things. Anyway, I think the local papers will be reporting the additional bodies in tomorrow's editions, so no secrets after that"

We agreed to disagree before saying goodbye. Russ worried me, I was a cop for a long time, these kinds of cases can be way more complexed than first meets the eye. There are often shadowy people in the background, unanswered question, unpaid bills. Getting mixed up in them can lead to very bad things happening, mostly out of your control. People end up dead and sometimes it can be you!

The Ceremony.

She had been stripped naked, blindfolded and with her hands handcuffed behind her back. She could feel another person standing very close, that person's skin occasionally touched hers. The place where she was standing had an odd smell, incense burning, and something else woody, maybe cannabis but she wasn't sure.

She was no longer standing on the hard rough stone floor, this was smooth, cold and more like the old marble top in her grandmother's pantry. Her knees were trembling, mouth dry, she found it difficult to swallow. There was no noise, but she could feel the presence of others, she was certain of that.

Two men had come to her cell, removed her clothes and taken her along the narrow corridor and pushed her into a cold shower. From there she had been dried, blindfolded, cuffed and lead to wherever she was now. Nothing had been said, no conversation, nothing at all. Now all she had was terror, utter and complete dread as to what was going to happen next.

A door opened somewhere in front of her, it was some distance away, there was shuffling, perhaps people standing, chairs being pushed about. She wanted to run but someone was behind her holding the handcuffs. The cold steel bit into her wrists, she felt her knees buckle, but those hands held tightly onto her, holding her upright.

He felt extraordinarily defenceless, helpless, he had always been in control of things in his normal life, but now everything was different. He was naked, blindfolded and cuffed, he had no idea where he was or what was going to happen next. Someone was standing right next to him, their bear skin occasionally touched, sending nerves into overdrive. The cuffs around his wrists were being held tightly, this only added to the terror and feelings of claustrophobia.

A door opened, chairs shuffled, the room fell once more into silence. He couldn't see anything at all but his senses and perhaps imagination warned him of impending doom. The smells of incense and fear filled his mind, his consciousness screaming at him, the sound of his heart pounding in his ears. Feelings of nausea rose inside, acid reflux burned his throat, sweat ran down his back. He wanted to pee, but he knew nothing would come out, fear would restrict everything. All he wanted to do was run but that was impossible, he senced only one thing, death.

A strong and well-educated voice began to speak. It was controlling, persuasive and emanated directly in front of him, maybe just a few yards away.

"Brothers, we are here today to enact the ceremony sadly postponed from 2020. Our master upon high was no doubt disappointed at the lack of reverence shown to him by this postponement. Tonight, we will once again demonstrate our utter and complete obedience to him.

Standing before us are two pathetic and unworthy beings, one woman and one man. They will be joined in marriage before progressing to the ultimate stage, and gladly giving themselves for the greater good.

Are there any amongst us brethren who object to this ceremony or to the marriage of these two pitiful wretches. Is anyone here tonight who would bring forth any reason not to complete tonight's celebration and acts of obedience?"

The gathering once more fell into silence before a booming deep voice came from the back of the room.

"There are no objections Principal, the brothers they are in agreement"

"I thank you for your observations master of rituals, have the couple seated"

He felt rough hands pushing him forwards, into the darkness before stopping him. Next, they pushed him backwards and down. He wanted to resist, he could feel himself falling but the hands were strong, he had no choice but to obey. In no more than a second, he hit hard onto a wooden seat, he was pushed forward, and the cuffs removed. Both his wrists were strapped tightly to the thick wooden arms of the chair and both ankles were fastened roughly to the legs. There was then a thick strap put around his chest and tightened.

She felt completely immobile, unable to breath properly let lone move. The straps around her ankles, wrists and chest bit tightly into her flesh. Her whole body shook uncontrollably, she began to cry, someone whispered in her ear, "shut up bitch or you will regret it"

"Master of rituals, bring the rings for the couple, let the marriage begin"

"Your wish is my command Principal Brother. Novices, bring forth the rings as commanded by the Principal Brother. Holy Minister, are you ready to carry out the wedding ceremony?"

"I am master of rituals, as commanded by our most gracious Principal Brother and for the benefit of our master upon high"

"Then master of rituals, remove the blindfolds and let the wretches observe their ceremony"

"I will gladly Principal Brother"

The hood was pulled slowly off her head, at first the blinding wall of light prevented anything from being seen. A few outlines, some figures perhaps, but nothing certain. She squinted, the pain from her eyes as they reeled at the sudden blast of white was overwhelming. She looked down and waited for her vision to return to some semblance of normality. She blinked, closed then opened her eyes, she looked up, fear surging through her every nerve. The man in control of the ceremony was standing in front of her. His magnificent robes flowing from his broad shoulders. He had an ornate and heavy gold chain around his neck and at its center was a bright star with a huge green emerald at its centre. She stared at this adornment, its magnificence was obvious, the green of the emerald was perfect and clear.

He stared at the person standing to his left. He was dressed in a long black robe that reached to the floor. He had black gloves and a pointed black hood on, with small slits cut in for his eyes. He was standing to attention, holding in front of him a small silver tray. On the tray was a gold ring, a thick band with a single green emerald flanked by two bright red rubies.

He turned to his right, sat next to him was a woman, bound as he was and naked. She was looking at the ground, sobbing and to her right was another black robed person holding another small silver tray with and identical ring. Looking to his front he could see a long table, about twenty feet away. In between was someone this time dressed in a gold robe and hood. This person was flanked on each side by four people dressed in bright red robes and hoods.

He looked nervously around the room, all around where people dressed in various coloured robes and hoods from blue, green and yellow. He couldn't get an exact idea of how many people were in the room, but he guessed at least fifty. The booming deep voice from the back of the room started again.

"Holy Minister, advance to the couple and begin the ceremony"

"By your command master of rituals"

A hefty round person in white robes and hood, edged in bright gold cord with a large maroon x in the middle, appeared in front of the couple. He stood there for a second before drawing a deep breath. He was holding in his hand a large book bound in crimson leather with gold accents.

"By the letter of the law bound in this book I command you to obey. For the pleasure of our master upon high and to show our utter obedience, I now begin the ceremony of joining.

You will be married in accordance with our law before giving yourself to our master upon high for his pleasure. Your sacrifice will make our master stronger, enable his power to reach out and dominate, bring control and order to this world.

Novices, place the rings on this book for my blessing"

They turned and put the rings on the now outstretched crimson leather book.

"I bless these rings in accordance with our law, they will act as a symbol of your joining and accompany you in your journey. When you meet our lord, as you surely will, he will see your true nature and thank you for your gift of life"

The Holy Minister then commanded the two novices to take the rings and place them on the two naked victims second finger of their right hands. They pushed them on roughly, before turning and walking away. He then opened the book and began to read aloud, sometimes softly, sometimes with great passion, it seemed to go on for some considerable time, but eventually he stopped and addressed to two victims directly.

"You two people, sitting naked in front of our great and magnificent Principal Brother are now wed. You will lay together in a lovers embrace for all time, enjoying the privileges endowed by our master upon high. I now call on the two slayers to advance and take their positions behind you and prepare for the conclusion of this ceremony"

She looked up, the man in the white robes moved to one side, the people sitting at the long table in front of her slowly got to their feet. The whole place fell into a deep silence, she sensed a movement from behind and caught sight of something pass over her, a flash of steel, glistening in the lights. That thing was a long-curved blade, cold and soulless, it was brought to her throat, nicking her, causing a trickle of blood to run down onto her collar bone.

She tried to shout but nothing came forth, the man next to her screamed and thrashed about but his bonds held him tightly. She tried to get up, run away but she couldn't move, an overwhelming explosion of panic crashed into her but there was nothing she could do about it. The leather straps cut into her wrists, scorching her flesh, the pain was overwhelming, but she had to get away.

He screamed again, "let me go you bastards, what the fuck do you think you are doing. My name is Jake Fullerton, you have no right to do this"

The man dressed in gold robes and hood began to chuckle, he held his arms out, his whole body shook as he laughed out loud.

"It is time for you to die, remember to tell our master upon high of our good deeds and our love for him. Slayers, do your work, but slowly, we want to enjoy tonight, it has been far too long since the last ceremony"

A roar went through the gathering, filled with expectation and excitement. She could sense the rising tide of illation filling the room and at the same time, the cold steel strengthening its grip around her throat. She struggled, perhaps for the last time as an acute burning sensation overwhelmed her. There was a sharp searing pain as the steel sliced into her throat.

There was a feeling of hot liquid gushing from her, pouring down her chest, a strong metallic taste and then choking as her red oozing blood spurted and ran down her throat. She panicked, choked violently and tried to free herself but to no avail. The crowd roared, chanted and sang, she felt humiliated as well as terrified, but there was no escape now, her fate was sealed.

He looked over, the woman sitting next to him was covered in thick red blood, it ran like a fountain, her head fell forward, next it was his turn. The knife tore into him, he coughed then choked. The pain was acute, unbearable as was the panic, this was the end for him, but it brought no piece.

Late lunch in the Bold Arms.

I decided Jan and I would go for a late lunch in the Bold, we had to get away from that work environment, email's, phone calls etc. I had to think, the case of the 'lovers in the sand' was beginning to get to me. I had told Russ Broadbent to leave it alone, pity I couldn't seem to follow my own advice. I just knew this was going to end badly, I had spent too long as a cop to think otherwise.

Besides which, this was a serial killer case now, so DI Smith and her crew would be right on top of it! So why the hell was I still even thinking about the case? Well, Ms Janice Greenwood, the daughter of the Goldsmith had got me hooked. What the hell did all these rings mean, what had they been made for? She seemed to think around fifty had been completed. Some of them were found on the remains adjacent to the 9th hole of the Southport and Lancashire Golf Course. It would therefore seem likely that many more victims were yet to be found, possibly!

What of the Creighton-Wards, had Edward Creighton-Ward been a mistake in Ms Greenwood's records, or was his grandson Charles just spinning me a line? There was no doubt Edward had existed, well according to his grandson at any rate. So why the hell was he not buried in the family crypt or recorded in the parish registers?

It didn't seem to make sense, why lie about a family member, was he the black sheep of the family? Maybe he had sold the silver to fund his gambling habit, and so was expunged from the records? Who the hell knows, but I had that familiar little itch on the tip of my nose, this didn't add up, someone was lying to me, and I don't like that!

"Lee, just drink your pint and stop gazing out of the window, and why do you keep scratching the end of your nose?"

I turned to look at Jan, she made me smile, she had that exceptional ability to put someone in their place without resorting to threats. Goodness knows where the business would be without her, she was truly one in a million. I must admit to becoming rather fond of her, her smile, her calm manner and ability to make me feel ok, even if I had a crap day, which was more often than not.

"Sorry Jan, I was just thinking about this case, I don't know what to do next, everything seems to lead to nothing"

"I think you need to go and see the Creighton-Wards again. Edward doesn't seem to have existed, but according to Ms Greenwood he certainly did, there must be an answer to that.

Go and find that Tom Toc, or whatever his name was, he might know a few more things"

"Yeah, good plan Jan but I don't think the Creighton-Wards will allow me anywhere near their place again, let alone speak to me. I could try Tom, see if there is anything else he knows"

"That Creighton-Ward estate is huge, several hundred hectares, maybe you could go poking around, see if anything crops up. It's so large that the chances of coming across anyone are very slim and if you do, just say you got lost. Are there any buildings that might be of interest, maybe hiding a secret or two? If there are a load of undiscovered bodies, maybe they are buried on the estate"

"Oh, hang on a minute Jan, this is not John Christie, the Creighton-Wards don't live at 10 Rillington place you know, they wouldn't bury the bodies in their back yard"

"Just a thought Lee, Edward commissioned fifty rings, eight of which have been found on the skeletons on the golf course. He has now disappeared from the records, and his grandson has been telling you a load of lies, or so it seems. I might be putting two and two together and coming up with six, but I smell the proverbial rat! Not just that but you admit yourself, Ms Greenwoods records are impeachable, so you tell me what's been going on?"

I gazed about the place, people talking, some trying to impress their date, others just passing the time. All these people just leading ordinary lives, so where or indeed who the hell was Edward Creighton-Ward? Had he just been an ordinary guy leading a normal life? Had he in fact existed at all, if so, why was there no record of him? I had to remember that Ms Greenwood was paying me for this work, she would want results, but results of what? She had said to me, it would lead on to 'further work', whatever the hell that meant?

Jan was right, if I was going to persist with this case, then I had to get closer, by legal means or otherwise, and I knew just the right person to help.

The coffee van at the back of the bus station, Southport.

I waited patiently, to be honest when dealing with smelly Ken, patients was certainly a virtue. There was little point in making any real plans, he could and would turn up when the mood, or his need for drugs took him. Mind you, the promise of free money and a bottle of vodka always guaranteed an appearance, at some point or another.

Smelly Ken had few virtues, and even fewer skills but one thing he was very good at though was getting into somewhere and out again without being noticed. I have absolutely no idea how he managed it. I sometimes wondered if he had some kind of invisibility cloak, but however he did it, it was amazing. My idea was to launch him at the Creighton-Ward estate and see what he could come up with.

I wasn't worried about him coming to any harm, in all probability, if he was found wandering about the estate, they would feed him, give him some money and then escort him off the premises. That was another ability he had, making people feel sorry for him, how the hell does he do that? Anyway, I had three bottles of vodka in the boot, a hundred fags and fifty quid, that was certain to secure his services.

It wasn't long before the errant Ken made an appearance, popping out of a dark and narrow walkway like the cork from a cheap bottle of Champaign. He was resplendent in his dirty grey tracksuit and green parker, old Nike trainers, no socks, and fingerless gloves. I am sure a cloud of flies circled around his head like a kettle of Vultures flying in formation, or was I just imagining that?

Anyway, I took several deep breaths and jumped out of the car, dulled my senses and walked over to him. He turned to face me, stubble and greasy hair made up the picture of this underprivileged young man who had a shit start in life. Largely due to drug addicted alcoholic parents who didn't give a dam about him.

That mostly toothless smile always moved me, despite what he was and what he had gone through, he always had time to smile. I wonder what he would have been like if only he had an honest start in life.

"All right boss, what's cookin?"

"Hi Ken, bit of a job on if you are interested?"

"Yeah man, what's the score"

"We are going to pay a call on a family, I am going to talk to the man in the big house, I want you to scout around a bloody great big stable bloc, tell me what you find. Not sure if you will see anything but it's worth a try. Just make sure you don't get caught, no unnecessary risks, understand?"

"Don't take risks boss, just leave it to me, what we looking for anyway?"

"Probably nothing Ken, but this family are mixed up in something. I am not sure exactly what yet. Also, the head of the family is telling me a load of lies and I don't like that. It's a bit of an odd story, have you heard of the bodies on the golf course?"

"Yeah man, eight fuckin skeletons' all tangled up together, like a mass grave. My mate recons it's something to do with aliens, taking humans for food"

"Well, it's not aliens, I can assure you of that Ken and they aren't all tangled up either. Could be some kind of cult, and I think this family have got something to do with it"

"Wow fuckin weird boss, you saying they are sacrificing people and dumping them on the golf course?"

"To be honest, I don't really know. There certainly is a connection to the family and the bodies, they were all wearing a ring commissioned by an ancestor, Edward Creighton-Ward. Trouble is, this Edward seems to have been erased from history, or the boss of the family is telling me a load of bollocks.

Whatever is going on, I am being paid to get to the bottom of it, by an old lady by the name of Ms Greenwood"

"Sounds like an old battle-axe boss, better do as she says"

"She's ok Ken, not sure what her angle is yet though. Why is she paying me, her father and grandfather made the rings for someone, just a normal commercial contract, paid in full, job done. I can understand that it freaks her our somewhat, after all they have been found on eight bodies. There is however nothing implicating her to any of this, or any member of her family for that matter, it was just work, happens every day of the week. All this happened years ago, it's in the distant past, anyone who was part of it is almost certainly dead and buried. She doesn't want me to talk to the Police either, wants it all to be kept under wraps, why?

"Sounds a bit of a mystery man, we need to get started"

"Right, I guess you are in then"

"Yea boss, no probs, what's in it for me?"

"A couple of bottles of vodka, 100 quid and some fags"

"Done deal boss, when we doin it?"

I will pick you up, tomorrow night at five, just after dark"

"Sorted, be here, don't be late"

That made me laugh, Ken hadn't been on time ever in his whole life before, now he's telling me not to be late. I gave him the goodies in the boot and reiterated the plan, with a bit of luck he would remember at least some of it, possibly!

I made my way back to the office, it had been a long day, at least tomorrow might provide some answers, not just for me but for my client, Ms Greenwood. By the time I got there Jan had gone home, I looked at my watch, it was seven thirty, where the hell had the time gone?

Not so Bright and early in the Office.

It was a tale of the night before I am afraid. My friend Lennart had brought over a bottle of his fantastic Norwegian gin. Anyway, we poured a few too many and before you know it, well things kind of disappeared in a haze. I guess it was a relief from the case and all those dead bodies, and the inherent dangers of getting mixed up in things like this. Don't get me wrong, I can handle myself and years in the Met had taught me when to back away, but this was turning into some kind of mass murder mystery and the hackles on the back of my neck were well and truly standing on edge.

"Well look who the cat dragged in, you look like crap Lee"

"To be honest Jan, I feel like it, any chance of a coffee?"

"On its way, extra strong I think"

She walked into my office holding a large mug of steaming coffee, with a great big 'it serves you right' look on her face. She gently placed the mug in front of me and stood back.

"So, what was the party about, looks like you had a good night"

"It wasn't, we just ended up drinking too much I guess"

"Who was the lucky girl then?"

I looked up at her, that smile had disappeared, was she jealous? I wanted to reply quickly, quell any thoughts that I might be seeing anyone. Why would I think that I mused? Had she actually managed to get under my skin, was I falling for her very obvious charms. No Lee, this is work, don't get mixed up with anyone, remember what happened to Ruth, I certainly didn't want to go there ever again.

This is not social, Jan works for me, we are a team, nothing more than that, right! In any case, I was probably reading way too much into this, she was curious, nothing more than that.

"No, just Lennart, we ended up getting waisted on his gin, it's wonderful stuff but bloody potent"

She laughed, "well tell Lennart to keep that stuff to himself, especially in the middle of the week. Now, what's the plan for today, that's if you have one"

It was my time to laugh, that awkward situation seemed to have resolved itself.

"I am meeting Ken this evening, at about five, I am going to pay a surprise visit to the Creighton-Wards, unannounced of course. I will knock on the big house, ask to speak to James, I will drop Ken near to the estate buildings and that huge stable. He can poke around, see what he finds. You never know, might even find the grave of Edward Creighton bloody Ward!"

103

She laughed, "I bet he doesn't, my guess is, he never even existed, all those records Ms Greenwood keeps so well are wrong. It will probably turn out to be a different family altogether, Edward Kempton-Draw or something like that. The Creighton-Wards are a historic and very influential family, why the hell would they simply forget where someone is buried. Why make up some tale about him dying in an air crash in 1930, or denying he lived years later? That simply doesn't make any kind of sense at all. Also, they have staff at the manor house, their own family solicitors, accountants, drivers and maintenance guys, someone would remember Edward, it would be relatively easy to find someone who did"

"Ok Jan, but James did confirm to me that his grandfather Edward actually existed, and that he died in 1930 and was buried in the family crypt. The trouble is there is no record of him actually being there. Why would he say, 'he is buried in the family crypt', when he isn't, and he is not, I have checked.

As you say Jan, that calls Ms Greenwoods records into doubt. It could be an incorrect date by her father, but they clearly say when the rings were commissioned and by Edward, there are even bank statements backing this up"

"Lee, you are the detective, go and figure. My guess is either Edward never existed at all or a general screw up with Ms Greenwood's records, or the records at the church and possibly even the dates James is recalling, or any combination therein. This will turn out to be something very simple, trust me, more than likely Ms Greenwoods father enjoying way too much brandy whilst completing his accounts"

She had a point of course, I was reading too much into this, I wondered if I should call tonight off, go for a pint in the Bold, watch the football on Sky. Something was troubling me though, surely James should know where his grandfather was buried, simple question really, I know where my grandparents are. Maybe there are two family crypts, yeah that's it, I will ask him tonight, clear this up completely. But then there are Ms Greenwoods records and of course the bodies on the golf course, and the 50 rings, only eight of which have been found. This case was beginning to take on a life of its own, rolling like an out-of-control vehicle down a very steep hill and guess who was in the way. Nothing made any sense at all, and it was beginning to drive me insane.

The evening had turned misty and very cold indeed. It reminded me of one of those B list movies I used to watch. Not at all scary even when Christopher Lee went to bite the unsuspecting virgin on the neck. Nevertheless, I had to be ready, I had to settle this once and for all, James was going to tell me the truth whether he wanted to or not.

Anyway, this shouldn't take long, by end of play this evening we would know where Edward was really buried. Ms Greenwoods records would be proved to be accurate or very incorrect. DI Smith and her team could then sort out the rest, solve the bodies on the golf course mystery and any issues regarding the rings, job done!

I was shaken out of my thoughts by the emergence of a horror all of his own, smelly Ken. He broke forth from the mist like a dread creature from another universe, clad in grey and green, with a fur lined hood. He tapped on the window, with some reluctance I wound it down and tried not to breathe in.

"What's occurring boss, ready for tonight's mission. Reminds me of that surveillance job on that tall bird from Birmingham. She was seeing three men, all at the same time, what a woman, love to have met her!"

"Actually, it was four men, yes I do remember that job, not sure she was the right woman for you though, I think she would have worn you out Ken"

"Fuckin good way to die boss, don't have her address, do you?"

"Ken, get in the car, we need to get going"

I tried to drive as fast as I could, it was clearly impossible not to breathe, but with the air con turned up to full, the atmosphere in the car was, well, tolerable. It wasn't long before we reached our destination, the old manor house, and the family home of the Creighton-Wards. I had chosen the same entrance as last time, it was more discrete than what turned out to be the main way in, which was closer to the centre of the village. It was by now completely dark and quite foggy, the headlights of the car illuminated the large gate and the sign, Private Road – KEEP OUT.

"Right Ken, we are here, you jump out and open that gate. Once in, we will drive slowly through the woods, on the other side we should see the estate buildings and the large stable complex. I will drop you off there and go and talk to the head of the family. I shouldn't be long, so I will meet you at the same place where I dropped you off, maybe thirty minutes tops, any questions?"

"No boss, what do you want me to look for?"

"Nothing specific Ken, anything that looks a bit out of place, anything suspicious, including a graveyard"

"Graveyard boss, what the fuck?"

"It's a long story Ken but we are missing a member of the family, and I am beginning to wonder if there are two family burial plots, maybe one of them on the estate. Just see what you find eh"

"Sorted, leave it to Ken"

We quietly wended our way through the woods and eventually arrived at the estate buildings to my right. There didn't seem to be any lights on, in fact no sign of life at all. Ken got out of the car and disappeared into the mist and darkness, I did feel bad about using him, but Ken was a survivor, he would be fine.

I opened all of the windows in the vein attempt to clear the air and perhaps even my clothes of 'perfume di Ken'. Anyway, I was going to be positive, go straight up to the front door and demand to speak to James. Get him to tell me the truth and straighten this mess out, once and for all.

I could see the big house looming large right in front of me, several rooms were fully lit so no excuses as to nobody being in. It was at this precise moment that I noticed something or someone to my right. My first thought was Ken, but this person was way too big, and he was carrying something, a walking stick perhaps.

Rather strange, walking around in the dark, in the fog, in the freezing cold?

I naturally slowed to a stop, he walked in front of the car, it was then I realised the stick was in fact a double barrel shot gun, and it was pointing right at me! He stood there in the headlights, the barrels pointing directly at my head. It made my blood run icy cold. I had trained as a firearms officer in the met but all that was in a controlled environment, there was nothing controlled about this. He could pull those triggers, drag me off into a far corner of the estate and no one would even know what had happened.

"Wind the window down and put your hands on the steering wheel"

I of course obeyed without question. My heart was pounding, the palms of my hands drenched in sweat, I truly thought this was the end.

He sauntered over to the driver's window, keeping the gun pointed at me at all times.

"We know who you are Hunter", he said in a low and very menacing voice, "and we know what you are after. Take this opportunity to turn around and leave, take that tramp with you, he is waiting at the stables. If anyone sees you on this estate again, I will personally put both barrels into you. That's not a threat by the way, that's a solemn promise"

I tried to get my thoughts into some sort of order, I don't like being threatened but he clearly had the upper hand. I decided to play the innocent, maybe it would de-escalate the situation, maybe!

"Liston, all I want to do is have a talk to James Creighton-Ward, I don't know what you think I am up to, but I just wanted a quick chat, that's all"

"Listen Hunter, I know exactly what you want, turn the car around and leave, I won't ask you again"

I looked into his eyes, this man meant business, maybe he would shoot, maybe not but I wasn't prepared to risk it. One thing this incident did confirm to me, the family in that big house had a lot to hide.

"Ok, point taken, I am off but when you see James, please tell him I just want to talk to him"

"Hunter, turn your car around and leave, before I start getting bored with this conversation"

I did as I was told, I pushed down on the clutch, engaged first gear and swung the car around on the gravel track. I looked in the rear-view mirror, the man hadn't moved, he stood there until I turned a bend in the track, before he disappeared into the gloom.

My mouth was bone dry, my shirt was sticking to my back, I had got away with my life. If I came here again, I was certain I wouldn't get away with it a second time. My thoughts turned towards smelly Ken, the man had said he was waiting for me, I guess he had gone through the same experience. I just hoped he would have been sensible enough to do as he was told. I drove as fast as I dared, I needed to get back to the estate buildings quickly before Ken decided to take matters into his own hands.

Thoughts raced through my mind, what the hell did that all mean, apart from the obvious, 'get off my land'. They knew my name, said they also knew what I was after. Ok, my name is Lee Hunter, perhaps that was be easy enough to find. Maybe I had been caught on CCTV on the estate somewhere, take the photo, pass it around the local Police, businesses, someone would ID me quickly enough. What made them think they knew what I was after, come to think of it, what exactly was I after?

I had asked James about his grandfather but that wasn't enough to send an armed guard out after me and threaten my life. Ok, his grandfather wasn't in the family crypt, so what the hell was going on? Did the Creighton-Wards really have a connection to the bodies on the golf course? Had Edward belonged to some sick cult and commissioned the rings for a human sacrifice ceremony? It was beginning to look more likely, there was certainly something going on. Had I got a little too close, had I hit that nerve, exposed the Creighton-Wards? Maybe, it would seem they wanted me out of their lives as well as off their property!

As I turned the last bend, I caught site of a familiar shape standing at the side of the track. He was briefly illuminated by his lighter as he lit up what looked like a very large joint. I stopped the car and wound down the window, through the grey cloud of cannabis smoke, he appeared, coughing but very much alive.

"Hey boss, you will never guess what just happened to me"

"Let me guess, a man with a shotgun told you to leave?"

"No boss, two men with shotguns told me to leave. Fuck, it was like the wild west, they meant it too. They said they knew why I was here and if I came back, they would kill me"

"Same thing happened to me Ken, strange goings on I must say. Put that joint out and get in the car, I think we should move off hey"

He rubbed his cannabis joint out and jumped in, nothing really got to Ken, he was bomb proof and this situation was no exception.

"You must have pissed them off boss. Not even the local drug dealers send an army of men out with shotguns just for being somewhere you shouldn't. What do they think we were up to?"

"It's a long story Ken but suffice to say, I think this lot are up to no good. I am beginning to think they are murdering people for some sadistic ritual. There could be a lot more bodies out there and if we are not careful, we could become the next two"

"Not sure I want to be one of them Lee, bloody strange set up though"

"What did you see in there"

"Much as you would expect Boss, stuff lying about, three huge tractors and farm machinery, bags of fertilizer, a hey barn, that kind of stuff. One odd thing though, upstairs in the stable block was a huge room, lots of marble, chairs around the outside. I was going to have a poke around but that's when those goons found me. They were pissed off I can tell you, I thought they were going to shoot me on the fucking spot!"

"Odd thing to have above a stable"

"Yeah right, guess we won't get to the bottom of that one now"

"You might be right Ken, on the other hand, perhaps we might just have one more try"

Radio Rock n Roll Lancashire.

"Well good morning everyone and welcome to the breakfast show, this is your host Russ Broadbent, taking you all the way from 7am to 10am on this bright early morning.

Don't know if you caught the early news but that young woman, Susan Forbes has now been missing for three days, I bet her parents are beside themselves. If you know anything at all, call Crimestoppers on 0800 555 111.

Someone must know something, she was out with her mates on Saturday night having fun, a few drinks downtown and she simply disappeared. I have Detective Sergeant Craig Jackson from Merseyside missing person team on the phone to bring us up to date. Craig, what do we know about the disappearance of Susan Forbes?"

"Hi Russ and thanks for having me on this morning. To be honest we know very little, her friends first noticed her missing about midnight or shortly before. They contacted the club's security guys but after a search, they realised she was no longer on the premisses. They checked the clubs CCTV and oddly enough, it had stopped recording during that evening, so there was no footage of her leaving the club"

"The CCTV had just stopped? Never Craig, these things are uber reliable, someone must have turned it off"

"We did think about that Russ, but why would someone go to the trouble of turning it off?"

"Well Craig, to get Susan out of the club unnoticed?"

"Well, it's possible I guess but that doesn't answer the question, where is she now? We have posters in the town centre, on our and on your station's websites. I understand her friends are very active on social media. It's imperative that we find her soon Russ, it's now Wednesday, she has been missing since Saturday night"

"Right Craig, so people can contact your team directly, or Radio Rock n Roll Lancashire, or ring Crimestoppers. All the numbers you will need are on our website or Merseyside Police.com."

"That's right Russ, and let's not forget other missing persons, firstly the Italian back packer Vittorio Bruno. He went missing a week ago whilst on his way to a camping site near to Formby point. He was last seen walking on the coast road not far from the pier"

"Is it possible that Vittorio has simply gone home to Italy?"

"No, we don't think so Russ. He left friends in Churchtown and was on his way to an open-air gig. He had been expected by a couple of fellow backpackers from Italy but never arrived.

We checked with the UK Border Agency, and he didn't leave the UK, and the Polizia di Stato in Italy, but they have no record of him arriving back in Italy. It's another sad story Russ and one we want to sort out, very soon"

"Remind us about the others Craig?"

"Right, eight weeks ago, Jake Fullerton went missing from a late-night party. It is believed he was walking home, sometime in the early hours towards his home on Southbank Road. Similarly, Christine Brown went missing from an illegal rave the following night, neither have been seen since. There are full details and photos on our website Russ, please if anyone has any information about these four young people, please get in touch. All calls will be treated in the strictest confidence"

"Is it possible that the four disappearances are connected Craig?"

"Not likely Russ, it's very unusual in these parts for people to simply go missing. Also,

why would someone go to the trouble of abducting the two males and two females, especially given their ages? Youngsters of that age can fight back or run. There would be easier targets, especially given busy weekend nights in town.

"Well, thanks very much Craig, I wish you every success in finding these youngsters as soon as possible and in the meantime, if anyone has got any info' you know how to contact us"

Driving to work.

I had been listening with some dread, at the interview Russ Broadbent had been conducting with Detective Sergeant Craig Jackson from Merseyside missing person team. Another young person had gone missing, followed by another and just to add grist to the mill, they were male and female.

It probably meant nothing at all, people go missing all the time, just because I am in the middle of a case regarding some kind of cult, doesn't mean they are all taken for some sick ritual. I was just getting a little jumpy that's all, putting two and two together and coming up with six. In any case, I had no proof of anything, to be honest I couldn't even prove that Edward Creighton-Ward had ever lived. The whole thing could be a case of fiction, something and nothing, an act of imagination.

I guess if you looked at it from the outside, it would look like the ramblings of a gin-soaked old man. The problem was, I was certain there was more to it that that. Ken and I had been threatened at gunpoint last night, there were the eight bodies on the golf course and now two more missing persons. I debated if I should continue up Lord Street and go and see DI Smith, tell her everything I knew. Maybe she could add it to what she had, together we could put something positive together. Perhaps not, sure I could tell her about the other night, maybe she could send a couple of uniformed officers over there to tell the gamekeepers to back off, but what would that achieve?

No, before I did anything like that, I had to give that grave digger, Tom Toc another go, see if there was anything else he knew. I swung the car around and headed to the village church, hoping I would find him there.

It didn't take long before I arrived at the front gate of the beautiful old church. The sun was out, perhaps spring was finally making an entrance. As I got out of the car the cold air soon changed my mind about spring. I immediately realised that any warmth had been coming from the cars air-con units, and not from any temperateness in the wind.

There was a white transit van parked on a small track behind the church, its rear doors were open, and the engine running. There was someone or perhaps two milling around, in and out of the back. "Maybe it's Tom", I thought, I decided to at least check it out, if it wasn't him I had absolutely no idea where he might be.

I walked purposefully across the graveyard and towards the slightly sunken track at the back of the church. The cold easterly wind bit into my cheeks, stabbing my skin like rusty old razor blades. As I crested the rise, I could see down towards the van parked on the track. Someone jumped awkwardly out of the back, it was Tom, carrying some bags, a spade and what looked like scaffolding poles.

I watched him as he walked down the track towards a concrete building about the size of a large double garage. It had a double green up and over door to the front, and a dirty grey wavy asbestos roof that was half covered in moss and algae. You wouldn't be able to see the building from the road, it was half hidden by the church and its location at the end of the sunken track. There were a collection of bushes and scrubby growth all around it, a perfect little hide-out perhaps! Maybe it was the old cop in me, but I stopped myself for a moment, stood quietly in the cover of a huge Yew tree, its overarching branches produced a dark and effective concealment. I felt comfortable there just watching, absorbing what was going on. Tom went back and forth a couple of times, unloading some wood shuttering like that used when shoring up a grave, as well as a pickaxe and some sacking. Then the second man appeared, tall, long dark hair, muscular build, about thirty-five or maybe a little older. He lit up a cigarette and stood watching Tom unload the van. Tom stopped and said something I couldn't make out, then carried on into the building.

It looked like they had just carried out a burial, nothing strange in that, Tom himself told me that's what he did. Maybe it was easier with two, and why he had an accomplice. That would explain the equipment for sure and why there were two men. It wasn't long before they finished, Tom slammed the doors to the back of the van and jumped in. As I was watching him in the cab, I became aware of someone watching me. I looked slightly to my left and standing down on the track, cigarette in hand was the other man.

"Oy, what are you doing there, this is church property you know, you can't just please yourself what you do here"

"Oh sorry, my name is Lee Hunter, I just popped over to see Tom, we spoke the other day. I wanted to talk to him again about Edward Creighton-Ward, he will know what I mean"

The man dropped is cigarette onto the muddy track and stubbed it out. He looked at the van and then back at me.

"Listen mate, not sure who that is, don't know anything about no Edward here. Suggest you fuck off quick like, we don't like people poking about, know what I mean?"

I could feel a wave of annoyance welling up inside. I had given a perfectly civil answer to his question, and I certainly don't like being told to 'F' off.

"Listen, I just want to ask Tom a couple of questions, that's all"

"Well, I am telling you to fuck off"

That was it, I started to walk down the shallow bank and towards the man. I hadn't got more than five yards when the door to the white van slammed shut. I looked over and Tom Toc was standing at the side of the vehicle, staring right at me.

"Oh, Mr Hunter, isn't it? What do you want over here then, another look at the records? Sorry but we are really busy, me and Richard have just done a double burial, we need to get back and sort the paperwork out"

That was odd, get back where I thought, this is where he worked, get back to what? The other man walked over to Tom, said something softly, I couldn't make out what he had said.

"I just wanted to chat to you about Edward and the fact that he is missing from the records and from the family crypt. I wondered if there was anything else you remembered?"

"Told you the lot Mr Hunter, nothing more to say on the matter"

The other man then piped up, "right, we are off, suggest you do the same if you know what's good for you"

I didn't get the chance to reply, they jumped into the van, revved the engine, and sped off up the track. Within seconds they had disappeared, leaving the smell of diesel fumes and burning oil behind them. That felt strange I must admit, most folk would at least stop for a chat, even pass the time of day for half an hour. This was very different, the other man was agitated right from the start, he sounded and indeed looked like he had been caught with his hand in the proverbial cooky jar! What had they been up to I wonder, why so aggressive, evasive, it didn't seem to make a lot of sense? Maybe they had been doing a cash job for someone, a quiet little number, out of sight of the taxman. I couldn't shake it out of my mind though, another side effect of being a cop I guess. Maybe a little poke about around that building, I wonder if that might shed a light on what they had been up to? Yes, let's have a look Lee, won't do any harm, they have gone, if they haven't got anything to hide, then what's the problem?

I scrambled down the grassy bank and onto the lane and started walking towards the grey concrete building. It didn't take long before I reached the dark green door. I tried to open it but with no luck, however, there was a dirty window on the rear wall. I peered inside, it was like trying to see through an opaque bathroom window, but the cloudy effect on this glass was more to do with years of dust and dirt.

Inside was a general tool shed, lots of wooden shuttering, some scaffolding poles, spades, shovels and a couple of large wheelbarrows. Ropes hung from the roof and on one side was an old desk and a wooden chair. There were a couple of box files on the desk, but it was difficult to make out what was written on them, it could have been 'location of burials', but I wasn't sure. One thing I did become aware of though was the approach of a vehicle down that track. It sounded suspiciously like the Ford transit van that Tom and his mate had driven away only moments ago.

Shit, it too late to run, I crouched down at the back of the shed, with a bit of luck they had forgotten something and would leave quickly. I heard two doors slam and the sound of walking on the gravel trackway.

"I told you Tom, that twat Hunter is poking around, that car parked at the front of the church, no one else is here, it must be him"

"He is nothing Rich, just a two-bit detective, thinks he is on some case, he knows nothing"

"If he knows nothing Tom, why is he here?"

"Because he is looking for Edward Creighton-Ward"

"Why is he looking for him?"

"I haven't got a clue Rich, he just turned up one day asking a load of questions. He couldn't find Edwards name on the crypt, so we had a look in the records. I hoped that would be the end of it"

"Yeah, but Edwards name wouldn't be in the records"

"I know that Rich, but I hoped it would put him off and he wouldn't come back"

I heard someone trying the door on the front of the building, I hoped this would be the extent of their search.

"Well at least this place is secure, we don't want anyone poking around in there. We better go and report what's happened, this could really fuck things up"

"Listen Richard, nothing is going to happen, what's he going to find anyway, nothing of any use and certainly no information from me and you"

"Yeah, but we need to tell them, let them sort it out"

"Ok, if it makes you feel any better, we can go for a pint on the way back, it's been a bloody busy day"

They turned and walked away, one thing stuck in my mind though, one of them had said, "we don't want anyone poking around in there". The only things I could see were some gardening tools, bits of timber and some scaffolding tubes. Not something that might be incriminating or be of interest to the Police! Seemed an odd statement, I wondered if there was in fact something in there that I should have a look at?

I looked out down the side of the building, I couldn't see anyone, they had clearly left, so I decided to try and get inside and see what was so important to them. I pushed my way through the brambles and over a couple of rusting petrol cans, cautiously making my way back to the front and the only means of entry, the up and over sliding door.

I gripped the slightly rusty handle and tried to open it, it was securely locked. Don't know why I actually did that as the two men had found the same only minutes before! Anyway, I looked around for something that might help me force the lock, but apart from a couple of old railway sleepers and a load of broken glass, there was nothing. Dam, if smelly Ken was here, I bet he could get inside, I pondered for a moment, would it be worth traveling back into town and picking him up? Perhaps not, by the time I found him it would be evening and poking around here in the dark, torches lit, might well attract some unwanted attention.

I couldn't stop thinking about those box files on that old desk, what was written on them, 'location of burials' or something like that? Was that what they were worried about, did those files contain information that they wanted to keep hush-hush? Also, why have the records at all, I had seen the official files in the church, what would be the point in another archive in an old grave digger's shed?

I would come back with Ken, I would keep look-out whilst he broke in. We could see what the files contained and move on from there, good thinking Lee. Right, lunchtime was approaching, and I needed something to eat, back to the car, sandwich from the bakery and into the office.

I was about halfway back when my phone started to ring. I looked at the display on the dash, 'number withheld'. Ok, some scammer I guess but it might be a client, so I pressed 'answer' on the steering wheel.

"Lee Hunter, can I help?"

There was a pause, before someone started to speak, a man with a muffled voice, deep, menacing and very precise.

"Hunter, we know what you are up to. We know why you are looking around but stop or we will stop you. You won't find anything and even if you do, it won't be of any use to you when you are laying dead at the bottom of the Irish Sea. You are dealing with forces beyond your control, people and things that you don't understand. For your sake and those whom you love, move on and forget everything you think you know. This is your only warning, take heed and move on Hunter"

The line went dead, I pulled up at the side of the road, had that just happened or had I fallen asleep driving back to the office? Someone had just put the frighteners on me, told me to back of or die. Don't get me wrong, I had been handed many such ultimatums, but that was when I was a cop, not a one-man band with no back-up!

"Laying dead at the bottom of the Irish Sea" he had said, that was explicit enough. Question was, would I do as they had told me, or should I carry on? Thing is, I don't like being threatened, it doesn't sit well with my turgid little mind. If you want me to do something, all you need to do was ask.

In any case, this just confirmed to me they were trying to hide something, something connected to the bodies on the golf course and Ms Greenwoods rings. It went without saying that it must also include the Creighton-Wards and the mysterious Edward. What was it that connected the three elements together? Was it ritual killings, some sort of suicide cult, or some psychopathic maniac who just enjoyed killing people? I guess that's what the phone call was about, someone or some people thought I was getting too close to the truth, little did they know that I hadn't got a bloody clue!

Right Hunter, pull yourself together, either drop this case or carry on, simple choice. One decision might include dying, the other a nice simple and quiet life as a private detective, so decide. Thing is, I hate giving up, even more than being threatened, I wondered if that goon or his boss knew that?

A Dark Place.

"What do you mean she is dying, dying of what?"

"I don't know, it's possibly something to do with diabetes, but I can't be sure. Richard looked in on her this morning and she was unconscious, and he called me over. Her pulse is rapid, her breathing is shallow, and she looks like shit"

"She can't die Doctor, you need to do something, we can't go looking for a replacement, not at this late stage"

"Sorry but there is not much more I can do. In any other circumstance I would call an ambulance and she would be taken to A&E for further tests. Given the situation, I don't think that would be a good idea, do you?"

"So, what are you going to do?"

"I have given her a couple of injections, let's see what if any effect they have. To be honest, I think she is on her way out. It could be any one of a thousand different reasons, a whole myriad of medical issues and diseases. It could be something as obvious as a blow to the head when she was taken, failing kidneys, heart problems', some medical condition we don't know about. Without the facilities of a proper hospital, I just can't tell"

"They are not going to be happy with this Doc', you know what they are like, and the next ceremony is a very special one indeed"

"Sorry, can't be of any more help I am afraid. You need to report this and then get looking for another girl, I am reasonably sure she will be dead by tomorrow"

The Doctor turned and walked out of the grubby little office. As he exited the heavy wooden door at the end of the corridor slammed shut behind him with an echoing shudder, causing little particles of dust to fall from the degraded plaster on the ceiling.

"This is just great, they are going to have my balls in a bag for this"

He slowly got up from the desk and walked over to the phone hanging on the wall. Pressing the saved number 1, he leant back against the wall and waited for someone to answer.

"Yeah, what's wrong?"

"It's the girl, what's her name.......Susan Forbes, that's it. The Doctor has been to see her, he thinks she is dying, and he doesn't know why"

"Dying, that's impossible, what the hell have you been doing to her?"

"Nothing sir, she was found this morning, unconscious on the floor of her cell. The Doctor thinks it's her kidneys or heart or something like that"

There was a long pause, he wondered if the line had been disconnected but eventually the voice returned.

"Ok, these things happen I guess, you need to find a replacement and soon. The next ceremony is a very special one indeed. It's the first installation of a new Master in this century and most likely, the only one we will live long enough to attend. You need to get out and get another girl and soon, do I make myself clear?"

"Yes sir, we will get onto it immediately"

"Hang on a minute, I have an idea"

The phone on the other end clunked as it was roughly placed on a hard surface. He could hear a muffled conversation, two or maybe three male voices. It went on for a couple of minutes but eventually he picked up the handset once again.

"Right, listen to me, this is what you are going to do. That twat Hunter is poking his nose in, we have warned him, but we need to take it a step further. He has a PA, Jan Talbot is her name, nice looking woman. Go grab her, I will get one of the members to take some photos of her, then email them to you. I will send the office address over and her private address.

That will teach the nosy bastard, once we have her, I bet we won't hear from him ever again. I will have the photos over in the next couple of days, so get yourself ready, this needs to be done properly, understand?"

He could hear raucous laughter in the background, and shouts of hear, hear!

"Right boss, leave it to me, I will get it done. One question though, is this Jan woman going to be used in the sacrifice, or do we just hold her here to frighten Hunter?"

"Not sure yet, maybe use her, maybe just hold her. There are plenty of pissed-up women to choose from on a Saturday night, so let's not rush into anything, that other girl we have isn't deceased yet"

The phone went dead, he placed the receiver back on to the cradle and went back to the desk. This job would need some planning and it had to be done properly. The door opened at the end of the corridor, a familiar voice rang out.

"Hi mate, fancy a coffee, I have some chocolate digestives with me"

"Richard, forget the coffee, get down here, I have something to tell you and you are not going to believe it"

The Bold Arms for lunch.

I had decided that a sandwich from the local bakery wasn't going to cut it, so I passed the shop and drove directly to the Bold. I needed a pint or two to settle my nerves after the threats from, well goodness knows who? By the time I got there it had started to rain, it was cold, grey and totally miserable, kind of reflected my state of mind, I guess.

My assumption was the threats had come from the Creighton-Wards at the old manor house, who the hell else would it be? The question therefore was why? What had I discovered, or more likely stumbled upon, why did they want me to back off? It had to be something to do with the bodies on the ninth, I guess. It had to be more than just finding me and Ken wandering around their estate. A quick warning would have done the trick there.

They had something to hide, and they were thinking I knew what it was, or was pretty close to finding out. How wrong were they, but that guy with the shotgun and the goon on the phone just now were in no mood to listen. So, what was it, what did they think I was close to finding?

I sat down at my usual seat and looked around, it was quiet for a lunchtime, a couple of the regulars and a group of middle-class hikers in their expensive walking boots and bright red jackets.

I took a long slow drink of my beer and gazed across the top of the glass. I noticed a coat of arms on the opposite wall, odd how you notice things only months or even years after first coming to a place. Something about it really caught my attention though, not the design itself but it set a thought off in my mind. The coat of arms was of two unicorns on either side of a portcullis. Why was I thinking of a coat of arms, what little spark had been set off in my mind?

I sat there for some time, the waitress brought my lunch, I didn't touch it, I just sat there wondering what idea had been set off. Unicorns, where had I seen something like that, no it wasn't unicorns, it was another mythical animal. Giants, no it wasn't that, knights in shining armour, no, what the hell was it? Then it struck me, dragons, on the back of those rings there was a dragon, why? Was it part of a coat of arms, was a dragon part of a family crest? There must have been a reason why Ms Greenwoods father went to the trouble of carving a dragon on those rings, he must have been instructed to do so.

I needed to find out why, and what the family crest of the Creighton-Ward's is, maybe that would cast some light on the matter, might even give me a few answers. If I could tie them and that dragon together, that would certainly add credence to the documents of Ms Greenwoods father.

Right, have a look on Google, I opened my phone and asked the question, "family crest or emblem of the Creighton-Ward family"

"The Creighton-Ward family crest is a lion and two eagle atop of a crown of thorns"

Ok, well that blew that theory out of the water, I guess the dragon would have to wait until later, it must have some significance though, I wonder if Ms Greenwood might know.

I pulled up her number and pressed call, it didn't take a moment for her to answer.

"Greenwood residence, how may I help?"

"Hello Ms Greenwood, it's Lee Hunter here. I wonder if you might be able to answer a question for me?"

"Hello Mr Hunter, I will certainly try my best"

"On the back of the rings your father made there is a dragon, do you happen to know why he did this?"

"I will check the records Mr Hunter and ring you back. He must have been instructed to do it. I can't imagine why he would have gone to all that trouble just on a whim. He certainly wouldn't have engraved anything on a commission without being told to do so"

"That's my hope Ms Greenwood, if we can understand why, then it will undoubtedly shed more light on the case"

"Right Mr Hunter, I will start checking, perhaps I could ring you back in a short while?"

"I will have this phone ready for your call Ms Greenwood, I look forward to speaking soon"

Good, I bet she comes up with something, if it's another families crest or even one man's emblem or badge, then we are on to a winner. I made a start on the double sausage sandwich with brown sauce, it had cooled down since the waiter brought it, but it tasted so good. Perhaps I was making some progress on this case at last and that made me very happy indeed.

The Greenwood Residence.

Ms Greenwood carefully replaced the handset and stood thinking in the hall for a moment or two. Lee Hunter wanted to know why there were dragons on the rings her father had made, and she wasn't quite sure where to start looking.

The old clock ticked away, a familiar and comforting sound, one that had been part of her life for as long as she could remember. She looked around, photos of her family, and a couple of old oil paintings adorned the walls. She had lived here all her life, her mother had given birth to her in the large front bedroom. Everything she had ever known, all her memories and dreams were in this house, and now she was the only one left. She sighed and then smiled, it didn't seem that long ago since her father was here, laughing and telling funny stories of when he was a child.

"Right Mr Hunter, the dragons, now let's see what the records tell us"

She made her way into the middle room, it was crammed with files, cabinets, ledgers of all sizes and colours. Standing in the middle of the room she made herself stop and think.

"Now, where would father record that kind of information? It's certainly not on the sales receipts, it's not on the commissioning documents, where would it be, if it's anywhere at all? I am sure you would have recorded that father, but where, what would you have listed it under?"

She thumbed over the ledgers, looked at the numerous box files one at a time. She was careful, diligent, she didn't want to miss anything, perhaps a habit inherited from her father and grandfather. Eventually she came across a ledger that caught her attention, it was named, 'additional requirements by customers'.

She opened the book, there were all kinds of entries, mostly mundane things, 'secret wedding gift, only talk to the customer', 'export to the Isle of Man before Christmas', 'don't use Ceylon sapphires'. The entries were not in date order but had been listed alphabetically, she kept flipping the pages, and eventually.

Creighton-Ward. Edward.
Customer requested his 'personal' crest on back (inside) of rings,
Dragon surmounting serpents.
Whole crest impossible to engrave, too large.
Agreed to Dragon only, customer happy, will proceed as requested. Additional cost, 5 shillings per ring.

She read the entry several times, this is what Lee Hunter had been looking for. Standing up, Ms Greenwood cleared her throat, and made her way out of the room and back into the hall. Her fathers' records had come up trumps yet again, she couldn't wait to tell Lee Hunter, this would certainly open up that case.

She was just about to pick up the phone when there was a knock at the door. "That's odd" she murmured, looking through the stained glass insert in the old oak door, "I wasn't expecting anyone, perhaps it was those religious people again"

They had been told several times not to come back! Janice Greenwood went to open the door but thought better of it, something didn't feel right, the look of the man outside, the time of day, the unexpected visit.

"Can I help?", she shouted through the glass.

"I am from the electric company, I need to read your meter"

"My meter is in the cupboard on the front of the house, you don't need to come in to read that"

"Yeah, but I need to see the connection madam, you need to let me in"

She backed away from the front door, she was scared, 'need to see the connection' he had said, what on earth did that mean?

"In that case, you will need to make an appointment, I don't allow anyone I don't know into the house"

The man seemed to disappear for a moment but then, like a charging bull, crashed into the front door. The noise of the impact and the sheer terror of what was happening made her fall backwards onto the tiled floor of the hallway. He hit the door again, this time the stained glass cracked, one or two pieces fell onto her.

She pushed backwards with her feet in a vain attempt to get away, but she just slipped on the polished floor. She turned over onto all fours, started to crawl away as the door took another huge hit, splintering wood, sending coloured glass flying in all directions. She instinctively knew that one more blow would be it, the door would crash inwards, and the man would be in.

Scrambling to her feet she looked around, where to run to, upstairs, lock the bathroom door and scream from the window? Perhaps run out of the back of the house and into the garden, maybe the neighbours would hear her shouts. No, the main bedroom, it had a good lock and an old-fashioned heavy wooden door. There was a phone in there, she could phone the Police.

Ms Greenwood ran for the stairs and as she began to climb the third and final blow smashed into the front door. There was the most terrible sounds of splintering wood and breaking glass before the unmistakable deafening crash as the door hit the hallway floor. She didn't wait to see what happened next, with nerves jangling and terror raging through her every fibre, she ran as fast as she could. She desperately wanted to turn around, see where her tormentor was, any second now she would feel his grip as he caught her on the stairs.

By now her lungs were running short of strength, her whole body was gasping for oxygen, breathless she turned to start the second flight of stairs, every breath vital. Light-headedness was closing in, nauseous, any second now he would have her for certain. Daring not to glance down, stumbling for a second on the next flight of stairs, only seconds from the bedroom now and safety. Running into the bedroom she glanced down the corridor and slammed and then locked the door, but much to her surprise, he was not there!

"Right Janice Greenwood, pull yourself together, pick up the phone and ring the Police"

With trembling hands, she picked up the phone at the same time sitting herself down on the large double bed. Putting the receiver to her ear she began to dial but there was something wrong, dial tone, there was no dial tone. She pushed the buttons on the top of the phone down two or three times but there was no response, the phone was dead.

"He must have cut the phone line, now what am I to do?"

Fear raged through her mind, shaking uncontrollably, she looked around the room, perhaps she could open the window and shout to anyone passing on the street below. The problem was, the gardens at the front were large and this was a quiet neighbourhood, it might be some time before anyone passed by, there must be another alternative. As she was thinking, she could hear a commotion on the ground floor. Filing cabinets being opened and closed, box files being thrown about, he was in her father's records room, searching, ransacking.

"What was he searching for, what did he need to find out, all he needed to do was ask! There is nothing in those records that was secret, why all the fuss over that?"

At least she knew where he was, and thankfully it was nowhere near her. She looked out of the window, but no one passed by, she started to realise, even hope that he wasn't after her but her father's records. She shook her head in disbelief, "why didn't he just ask?"

After some time, the commotion stopped, Ms Greenwood remained seated on the bed for at least another hour before deciding to go downstairs to see what had happened.

Quietly she unlocked the door, "what happens if he is on the other side, he might grab me. No, if he was, he would have tried to break this door down as well, in any case, I can't stay here for ever"

Slowly and with great dread she opened the bedroom door but there was no one on the other side. Gradually she made her way down both flights of stairs and quietly began to explore the ground floor rooms. Her head was pounding, her throat dry but she pushed on, the house seemed to be deserted, the man was nowhere to be seen, he had gone.

The only room which bore any indication of the man being present was her father's records room. It was in a state of total disarray, papers, records, and ledgers strewn all over the floor. She began to cry, what a state, her fathers life thrown all around the place and for what?

She was shaken out of her melancholy by a voice coming from the front of the house.

"Ms Greenwood, what the hells happened to your door, are you alright?"

It was a man's voice, someone familiar but in her state of distress she couldn't quite remember who.

"Come in, please can you phone the police, there has been a break-in"

She turned to see Lee Hunter standing in the doorway, a look of total shock on his face.

"What the hells happened here?"

"A man smashed down the door and he………"

She couldn't finish the sentence, she crumpled to the floor and held her head in her hands. Sobbing uncontrollably, she fell onto her side, "why, why did you do this?"

The ambulance drove away from the front of the house, en-route to Southport Hospital. Hunter was very relieved to see it go, Ms Greenwood was in a terrible state and hospital was the best place for her, at least in the short term. The Police squad car remained, blue lights flashing, it stood empty at the front of the house. Another unmarked Police car was parked behind.

Two uniformed officers took notes at the scene, and a plain clothed detective wandered about the house checking for any additional clues. Eventually he came into the front room where Lee Hunter was sitting patiently. He looked very young to be a detective, tall, light-coloured hair, a strong muscular build. He approached Hunter, sat in the chair opposite and took out his notebook.

"Ok, it's Mr Lee Hunter, is that right?"

"Yes…… erm detective?"

"Sorry sir, detective constable Stephen Burton, serious crime unit. Can I ask you what you were doing here and what Ms greenwood said to you?"

"Serious crime unit, well that's a turn up for the book's detective, glad to know Merseyside Police are treating this as a serious crime. To be honest, I just decided to come and see Ms Greenwood, she is a client of mine. She was examining some records for me, but I thought it would be easier to come and see her in person rather than talking over the phone"

"What work are you doing for her Mr Hunter?"

"Look detective, this is really complicated, and you wouldn't believe me even if I spelled it out for you. Can I make a suggestion, let's go back to the station, grab DI Deborah Smith and possibly DS Shacklady and all sit down with a coffee and discuss what's happened?"

He looked a little puzzled, that was the first time anyone had actually wanted to go back to the station, let alone ask to speak to two members of the murder squad.

"Detective, they both know me, and this can be sorted very quickly, might I suggest you make the call and save us all a hell of a load of time. This case is really complicated and involved those bodies on the golf course. I am not sure DS Smith will really want to chat to us, but it's her case so I think we need to at least try, don't you?"

Southport Police Station, interview room 8.

The tape recorder clicked into life as Detective Inspector Deborah Smith pressed the buttons. It made a high-pitched whine for a few seconds before settling down, indicating it was ready to record.

"The time is 16.45, interview room 8 Southport Police Station. Present are myself DI Smith, DC Stephen Burton and Lee Hunter. The purpose of this interview is to ascertain the reason behind the attack on MS Greenwood's property, and any connection to the remains found on Southport and Lancashire golf course.

Mr Hunter, you stated that Ms Greenwood was searching her files for a crest engraved on the rings, is that right?"

"Yes DI Smith, I think the dragon engraved on the back of the rings is in fact part of a family crest. If this is the case, then we can narrow down who the person was that commissioned the rings. I assumed it might be the crest of the Creighton-Ward family, but this turned out to be incorrect"

"Why the Creighton-Wards Mr Hunter?"

"It's a long story DI Smith but in summation, MS Greenwood's father and perhaps even grandfather were commissioned to make 50 such rings for an Edward Creighton-Ward.

Having checked with the family, it seems that Edward died before the rings were even commissioned, that was confirmed by his grandson James"

"So, it's an error by Ms Greenwoods father"

"That's what I first thought DC Burton. The thing is, having seen these records and having spoken to Ms Greenwood at length, I think they are correct in every detail. Also, I can't find any record of Edward either alive or dead. His grandson told me he was buried in the family crypt, but he isn't, and the church records have no entry on Edwards death, on any date"

"Well," DI Smith spoke slowly, "something or someone is wrong. James is wrong about his grandfather's death and place of burial or Ms Greenwood's records are a load of crap! They can't both be right, that's impossible"

"Maybe Edward didn't commission the rings, maybe someone was using a false name"

"Good point DC Burton, but I have also seen detailed bank records connected to the rings, they confirm on several separate occasions the identity and payments of Edward. It was Edward Creighton-Ward who commissioned these rings and later paid for them, that's certain"

"So, getting back to our original question Mr Hunter, why do you think Ms Greenwoods house was broken into?"

"I think someone, or some people were after parts of those records DI Smith. There was something that potentially incriminated them. Some details of names and places that they had to take and destroy. Why else would someone break into her house, ignore her money and jewels, the expensive paintings on the walls, the gold clock in the front room? No, they were after information, records and I bet when Ms Greenwood returns to her house, she will discover what was taken"

"Hang on, just take us back a minute Lee, did you say 50 rings?"

"I did Deborah, 50 and you have how many, eight?"

I felt the whole room gasp a collective intake of breath, just how many bodies were still out there?

"Wait a minute Lee, I thought there was only going to be another five couples?"

"Five couples Deborah, what do you mean?"

Well, the first four couples were murdered ten years apart, 1940, 1950, 1960 and lastly 1970. It had been assumed that there would be another five couples, 1980, 90, 2000, 2010 and 2020. You are now telling me there are potentially 50 rings, that means we could be missing thirty-two dead bodies. This is turning into a bloody nightmare, who the hell is this lunatic?"

"That's about it Deborah, those ten couples are potentially only the tip of this iceberg"

"Hang on, if DI Smith is right and these people are being murdered ten years apart, maybe the killer has not used all the rings, maybe they are to be used years into the future"

"You better hope so DC Burton or Deborah is going to be very busy over the coming months"

"So, we have eight bodies, there might possibly be another ten, and the rings could be used for decades to come. This is not just a murder case but a crime prevention exercise on a monumental scale"

I stared across the table at Deborah, the look of shock and horror was clear to see. She ran her fingers through her hair, then tapped them on the table.

"Right, Lee, I want you to get lost and not interfere with this case. I know you won't take a blind bit of notice, but I needed to say that. You can't interfere in a live investigation and if I catch you doing so, I will arrest you, do I make myself clear?"

"Yes Deborah, scouts honour, I will be a good boy"

"DC Burton, you are with me. We are going to see your boss, I have no staff and a multiple murder case, you are working for me from now on, ok?"

Deborah reached out and switched off the recorder, then looked up at DC Burton.

"Go and wait in my office, I will be up in a minute, mine is a white tea, no sugar, now go"

DC Burton hurriedly left the room, leaving just me and Deborah behind.

"Lee, I am serious about you interfering, but I also know you won't take a blind bit of notice. This is bloody grim stuff, bodies everywhere, I have no staff and absolutely no clue where to start.

You say it's the Creighton-Ward's. Well, I can tell you taking them on won't get me anywhere. They are well connected and able to bring favours in, but I will do what I can. There are eight dead people, please don't become the ninth, this could turn out to be one twat of a case. Whomever is responsible is well organised and highly motivated. Stay out of the way Lee, you managed to escape death on the last case, your luck will run out eventually"

"Thanks for the warning Deborah, I will be careful and very discreet. For what it's worth, I am certain it's the Creighton-Ward's and James in the big house is the man at the centre of all this. Also, it's not my life I am worried about, it's the people around me, they are the ones who tend to die, and all because of me"

Apart from the gentle hum of the air conditioning unit, the room went quiet. I finished by telling Deborah about the incident on the estate but left out the part of being held up at gun point! I thought about reporting the death threats to her, but I was certain that it would absolutely end any concession she would give me, and result in some kind of court order to stay away. We agreed to stay in touch, I decided to go back to the office and catch up on the day's proceedings.

It was late, past 6pm by the time I got back to the office, I could have gone to visit Ms Greenwood, but I decided to leave that until the morning. The Paramedic had suggested given her age, the level of shock and the possibility of physical injuries, she would be kept in at least overnight and more likely much longer. I had contacted a joiner friend who said he would go and secure the property immediately, the uniformed police confirmed that they would wait until he turned up.

So, there wasn't much else to do I guess, I had hit a brick wall. The only lead I had was the dragon engravings and the name of Edward Creighton-Ward, who seemingly hadn't existed, or at least not in the time that the rings were commissioned. I needed to think carefully about my next move, going to the big house to see

James was likely to get me shot. I had death threats hanging over me, nothing new there then, and goodness knows what had gone missing from Ms Greenwood's records! I couldn't involve DI Smith and her team, that would get me arrested, smelly Ken was an option, but he would probably end up getting killed, so what to do?

I needed a break, one of those, 'out of left field' moments, something completely out of the blue. Trouble was, I didn't see anything like that ever appearing, let alone it being of any use! I had to shake things up a bit, that was one thing I had learnt over the years, if you make enough fuss, often something just turns up. You need to create sufficient pressure on people, then things start to go wrong, they create indecisive actions, ill thought-out plans, just a little panic starts to set in.

That 'out of left field moment' thankfully occurred, just as I pushed the radio button on the dashboard, "this is Radio Rock n Roll Lancashire, tune in to Russ Broadbent on tomorrow's breakfast show, 7am right the way through to 10am, the best sounds, latest news, and just a little gossip on your number one radio station"

That's it, Russ Broadbent, now there is a man who could stir things up a little and everyone would know about it, after all, "it's your number one radio station!"

A Dark Place.

He pushed his way towards the half open cell door. The man who had brought his food and water had turned his back on him once too often. The years of martial arts training, self-discipline and sacrifice had now paid off. Vittorio Bruno had launched himself at the man, kicked him squarely between the shoulder blades which sent him crashing into the heavy wooden door. He had bounced off it like a rubber ball and as he fell backwards, Vittorio brought a fearsome blow down on the man's neck, causing him to crumple like a rag doll onto the floor.

He wasn't finished yet, there was no way the man would be putting up any kind of resistance or prove an obstruction to Vittorio's escape. He knelt down by his side and reigned several more blows down on the man, blood flew in all directions, if he wasn't dead already, he would be very soon.

The young Italian stood up, opened the door slowly and looked down the corridor. To his left was a dead end, to his right a dimly lit passageway, flaking whitewashed walls and a stone floor. There were four or five cells, each with a different coloured door. Near to the end of the passageway was an open doorway, perhaps that of an office.

He prepared himself, anyone who ventured out would be attacked straight away, there would be no mercy or humanity, just force and violence. Taking care not to tread on anything fragile, and with his senses turned up to maximum, he made his way towards the door at the end of the corridor.

His first obstacle would be the office, was anyone in there, were they armed? He decided to act and bring the fight to them. The surprise and shock would buy him valuable time, enough to overcome anyone who even tried to resist. He positioned himself by the door frame, took several deep breaths and moved in, ready for the fight.

Within a split second his adrenalin calmed as no one was inside, just the usual things you would expect in a grubby little office. He spun and moved back into the corridor, the next barrier was the heavy oak door at the end of the passageway, just a few feet away. Vittorio hesitated, what if this door lead into a place where he couldn't escape from, maybe where several people sat? There was no point in hesitating now, the next person might come through that door at any second and he might not be such an easy target as the man in the cell.

"Right, open the door and burst in, there is no other way Vittorio Bruno. If I just walk in there, they might overcome me in seconds. Take the fight to them, bring violence, it might be enough to get me out of here, wherever here is?"

He took some more deep breaths, checked his shoes to make sure the laces were tight, looked up and opened the door. He ran into another corridor, almost crashing into the wall opposite. He looked to his left but immediately sensed something or someone to his right. He spun to see a man running towards him, he had a look of anger and perhaps a little fear on his face.

"What the fuck are you doing, get back in your cell twat"

Vittorio balanced himself, allowed the man to close the distance between them and then struck, with a clear and decisive kick right into the mans face. It knocked the man backwards, but also sent Vittorio tumbling to one side. It was clear his assailant was much the worse from the encounter though, he sat on the floor, blood pouring from his nose and mouth. The young Italian regained his composer and kicked the man in the face two or perhaps three more times.

He slumped backwards, chocking on his own blood, Vittorio stepped over him and proceeded down the corridor. There was now a need to act expeditiously, there was one man, perhaps dead in the cell. One man laying covered in blood in this corridor, his escape would be discovered at any moment. He could feel his heart pounding in his chest, he was a very fit man, but the adrenalin rush and the events of the last few minutes were now slowing him down.

Next, he burst into a large room, a white marble floor, seats all around the walls, and on a raised platform at one end several large gold-coloured chairs. He looked around, it was a strange room with a foreboding atmosphere. Fear and pain overwhelmed him, this place was evil, he needed to get out as soon as he could.

He looked about for another exit but there was none, so he turned to go back the way he came. As he approached the door, much to his horror it opened, and in walked a tall man, shoulder length hair, he was holding a shot gun with his right finger on the trigger.

"Ah Vittorio, there you are, did you really think you could escape? You should have looked up when you left your cell, there are CCTV cameras all down that corridor. I am surprised you got this far to be honest, guess the guys in the estate security office weren't doing their job, I will have a chat to them later.

My name is Richard by the way, and your attempt to escape has now come to an end. In case you are wondering, yes I will blow your fucking head off if you don't do as you are told"

He looked left and right, surely there was a way out of this place, there was no way he was going back into that cell.

"Listen Vittorio, you aren't getting out of this room alive, some of those estate security men are on their way here, they should arrive in a few seconds. If you do as you are told you will live, if you don't you will die. That's not a threat by the way, that's a solemn promise, so think on"

"Then I die, I am not going back into that cell, no way. I don't know why you have me here but it's too late now to try and stop me"

With that, he launched himself at Richard, sprinting the few feet towards certain doom. Richard lifted the gun and pulled the trigger, Vittorio felt the hammer blow as the first load of lead shot hit him, just below his right shoulder. The pain was immense, almost paralysing but he pressed on. Richard pulled the trigger on the second barrel, Vittorio felt the blow, it spun him around like a rag doll, the fire in his chest and arm tore into his nervous system, shocking every part of his conscious mind.

It took a second before his brain re orientated itself, re engaged, he was kneeling on the ground, clasping an open wound with his left arm. He looked up, Richard was looking down at him, holding the shotgun, ready to use it like a club. Vittorio tried to get up, but he couldn't move, loss of blood and pain prevented anything other than the smallest of movements.

"You prick Vittorio, what the hell did you think you were going to achieve, I had a loaded shotgun you idiot, there was only going to be one winner, and that was me"

He caught site of the two security men as they entered the room, dressed in black boiler suits, boots and baseball caps.

"Right, you two, get on the phone and make the call, we need this lot clearing up and this dick head burying. Tell them to get here as soon as, I don't want this place stinking of dead men, understand?"

The two men didn't wait around, they knew what to do and who to call, Vittorio heard them running down the corridor.

"So, I guess you heard that, sorry boy but I can't have you bleeding to death in here and you are certainly no good to me dead. If you had just done as you were told, you would be alive tonight but no, now you will be saying hello to your god, if you have one"

Vittorio never felt the blow Richard swung at his head, his last thoughts were for his mother in Abruzzo and the family he left behind.

Dawn, My Flat.

I absolutely hated getting up early, I never did get used to it, no matter how many times I was required to haul my sorry arse out of bed in the morning. Anyway, I reached over to my digital alarm clock and pushed the snooze button, it would only give me ten minutes of peace and quiet, but it was worth it.

It seemed like only an instant had passed before the alarm went off for the second time. Ok, I had to make the effort, the only way I was going to talk to Russ Broadbent was to call him, or at least leave him a message whilst he was still on the air. I knew from experience that once he signed off at 10am he could be anywhere, probably in bed having a nap, if he had any sense.

I reached out for the mobile, unlocked the screen, opened WhatsApp and scrolled down to Russ's number, blinking my eyes in a vain attempt to get them to focus. Right, I better make this interesting, but I don't want to tell him too much, just enough to get his attention. I carefully typed out my message, reading it back several times before I pressed send.

Hi Russ.

Listen, re the lovers in the sand thing, you know the skeletons found on the golf course? I have a couple of leads, trouble is, the cops have told me not to get involved, nothing stopping you broadcasting something though, is there!

If you give me a call, I can fill you in on what I have, see what turns up eh?

I pressed send in the sure and certain knowledge that he would ring me back. I knew Russ, he was a journalist at heart, and he couldn't resist a juicy tip like that! It wasn't more than five minutes before my phone bleeped, I opened it up.

WhatsApp message from Russ Broadbent.

Hi Lee, sounds interesting, bit busy this AM, loads of callers waiting on the line, how about breakfast, no wait a minute, pub lunch in the Bold, say 12ish?

Hi Russ.

I will be there, lunch is on me.

Well, that didn't take long, all I had to do now was to convince him to join in, that might prove a little more difficult than it seemed. I was banking on Russ and his insatiable thirst for a story, the latest headlines, I was sure this would get him on board with the plan.

I walked into the Bold at precisely 12, the place was quite for a weekday, maybe it was an hour or two before the main lunch crowd turned up. I looked around but I couldn't see Russ anywhere, so I got myself a pint and grabbed a seat by the door and waited until he made an appearance. The beer went down very nicely but knowing my past and the evil drink I had to take it easy, this stuff can really take hold of your life.

"Well, as I live and breathe, it's Lee Hunter private detective"

I turned round to see Russ standing there, pint of beer in his hand. He had that usual relaxed style about him, nice shirt, leather jacket and jeans. He must be in his sixties but to be honest he didn't look a day over 50!

"Hello mate, glad you could come, grab a seat, I have a menu here, burger and chips for me, nice low-fat option hey?"

We both laughed, he sat down in the seat opposite and picked up the menu.

"Right Lee, what's this 'thing' you have in mind. Knowing you it will be bloody complicated"

A smartly dressed waitress came over, note pad in hand. "What can I get for you gentlemen?"

We both looked up and said the same thing at precisely the same time, "burger and chips"

We smiled, she wrote something on her pad, turned and disappeared.

"Well Lee, let's have it, I don't want to be talking when my lunch turns up"

I spent the next ten minutes going over what I knew, Charles and Edward Creighton-Ward, the crypt, church records and even the death threats. I went over Ms Greenwood's father's records and the connection to the family. I still had to visit her in hospital, so if anything was missing from her house, that issue would have to wait for a later date.

"To be honest Russ, I think we will find the records pertaining to the rings are what's been taken, but we will need to do a stock check with Ms Greenwood once she is discharged. I am going to see her this afternoon, so I will have a better idea when that might be"

"Right Lee, so what's my part in all of this? I am not going poking around in the big house and risk having a shotgun stuffed up my nose"

"No, that's not it, all I want you to do is broadcast something on your breakfast show. We can then just sit back and see what falls out of that, simple really"

"Right Lee, so for the third time, what the hell is it you want me to do?"

Southport Hospital.

By the time I got to the hospital Ms Greenwood was sitting in reception seemingly ready to go home. I must admit to being taken aback, I know she was a strong woman but what had happened to her would have destroyed most other people. She had called me as I was leaving the Bold, wondering if I could offer her a lift home, I of course was more than happy to do so.

Once we had the go ahead from the doctor she virtually sprinted out of the place, across the carpark and into my car. There was no doubt as to where she would rather be, or at least where she didn't want to be!

"So, Ms Greenwood, where are you staying tonight, surely not at your place?"

"I am staying at my friend Gloria's house for a while, she lives a short drive from my house, but I need to find out what that man took from me"

She tried to sound strong, but I could sense an underlaying emotion in her voice. She had led a completely honest and open life up until now, but that had all changed with the arrival of that man a couple of days ago.

It must have been a terrible shock on so many fronts. She had been thrust from a moral law-abiding existence into an immoral pit of treachery and deceit. Her whole outlook must have been shattered and from my time as a cop, I knew that life for victims like her would never be the same again.

At least she appeared to be fine, oddly calm and assured, strange really. Maybe it was just denial, most people would be rambling wrecks but not Ms Greenwood. It was if nothing had really happened, perhaps it was just her way of dealing with it.

"Your place is secure Ms Greenwood, there is no need to go back there for a while yet"

"I want to go back, I need to find out what was taken"

She cleared her throat as she finished speaking, I could tell what that meant, an overwhelming wave of emotion had just broken over her.

"Ok, but we are not staying long, just until you find out what's missing. Afterwards, I will take you to your friends and go and see the police with the list"

"Thank you Mr Hunter.......sorry Lee"

The rest of the journey was conducted in complete silence. Eventually we arrived at her house, it looked as if nothing had happened. The joiner friend of mine had done a great job repairing the front door, apart from a few cracks in the paint, nothing seemed to be amiss.

She pushed her brass Yale key into the lock and turned it, I had to give it a bit of a shove but once inside, it was if nothing had ever happened. That was until we entered her middle room. A once perfect and well-organized area, records and documents in their assigned place, sorted by date, type or customer. Not anymore, files, logs and paperwork lay strewn all over the floor, chaos had replaced order, anarchy ruled over control.

Much to my surprise, Ms Greenwood stood up to the shock amazingly well, and within a second or two was rummaging around in the documents and taking complete control.

"Lee, put this file on that left hand shelf, take these papers and put them on the desk, these go in the red file, sort these out into date order"

The quick job lasted most of the night, we ordered in pizza and Ms Greenwood or Janice as I was now calling her, found a couple of bottles of rather nice red in the back of a cupboard.

By the early hours the room looked to be back in some kind of order, in fact to my eyes, it looked remarkably neat and tidy. I could tell that it wasn't up to Janice's standards, but at least it was close enough, and it made the job of identifying what was missing much easier.

"So, Janice, what do we think, can you tell what was taken or was it just an attempt to wreck the place and send a message?"

"No, there are records missing Lee and I know exactly what they are. The files containing payment details for the rings, for example, who paid for them and when. That's critical because we would know the actual name of my father's customer. Also, the bank details to back that payment up"

"Right, so in essence, we can't accuse anyone because there is no evidence that any kind of transaction took place. Therefore, there is nothing that the police could use in a prosecution against anyone"

"Correct, the rest are just names on various forms, dates, specifications but with no actual proof that anything was bought and paid for!"

"Surely your father kept a record of addresses, if I order something off Amazon or from the local supermarket, they will want to know my address"

"Yes Lee but that's because they need to deliver it. As I discussed earlier, you need to understand that my father was regularly asked for complete secrecy or at least a high level of confidentiality. Some of his orders were secret love tokens to a mistress, a bribe to facilitate an order or new contract. It could have been a secret wedding present, a gift to a friend on their birthday, he operated in a very discreet world.

That's why we needed that payment ledger with the bank details. That was the only way we could get to know who made an order or more appropriately, who paid for it. The bank payment details would certainly contain the person's real name, not some pseudonym. Banks in those days dealt in facts, not deceptions or secrets, that ledger would prove who actually paid for an order.

I understand that it wouldn't have contained anyone's address, but it would tie a name in the order book, for example Edward Creighton-Ward, with the name of the person who actually paid for that order. Now all we have is the ledger with a name of someone who placed an order for 50 rings. Was that person who they actually claimed to be? Were they using an alias or someone else's identity? That payment ledger would have confirmed all of that, and now it's gone"

There was now a question about someone perhaps using Edwards name? I hadn't thought about that one before, I had just gone with the records and assumed Edward was the man who ordered and paid for the rings. Could it be possible it was just an alias used by someone else. Had this in fact been confirmed by Edwards grandson, James, when he told me Edward had died several years before the rings were commissioned.

Dam it, how could I have been so bloody stupid, just picking up the first story and running with it, instead of taking a step backwards and analysing the whole picture. My first boss in the Met would have run me out of the department for such a schoolboy error. Dam it Lee, you are slipping, you need to get your edge back before someone else pays the price.

So, what did I know to be fact? Well, there were still eight unidentified bodies, all found in a lovers pose and wearing identical rings, 50 of which had been commissioned. They had been buried in ten-year intervals and there were no signs of foul play. They had all been buried in the same place, near to the ninth hole of Southport and Lancashire Golf Course.

The Edward Creighton-Ward in Janice's records clearly wasn't the one who had been killed in an aviation accident years before. Having said that, where was that Edward, certainly not in the family crypt or church records? Come to think of it, why would James feed me a line about his grandfather, what could he possibly gain from telling me about a tale like that? Was he covering up for Edward, was he actually the man in Janice's records?

I was beginning to get a headache, I had been on this case for a while, and I knew less now than I did when I started. I had death threats hanging over me, DI Smith had warned me off and the payments ledger was missing, bloody hell, what a mess! If only I could find something, a little chink in this sordid tale that would allow me to gain some traction.

I curled up in a very comfortable double bed in one of Janice's spare rooms, I quickly found myself dozing off, encouraged by the late hour, red wine and way too much pizza. The light was still on, I couldn't be bothered to get out of bed and turn it off. As my eyes closed, I noticed a small trophy on the dressing table, it was the last thing I saw before I fell asleep, but it jolted me awake again with a rush of adrenalin.

I opened my eyes, any thought or feelings of sleep had been stripped away. I focused on that little shiny object, it was a man holding a golf club. I swung my legs out of bed, I wasn't sure why it had set off a firework display in my brain, but it had. I picked up the little object, just a few inches tall, made of metal with a shiny finish set on an alabaster base. There was a small inscription, I strained my eyes to see what it said.

Awarded to-Jonathon Greenwood

Best young golfer 1929.

Perhaps it was Janice's father, but why had it woken me, what was its significance? It was then that it hit me. It was the bodies, they went back to the 1930's but how old was that golf course, surely the course was older than that? If they were still burying them on that spot in the 60's and 70's, why didn't anyone notice the disturbance, digging graves is a messy business.

Don't get me wrong, I am no golfer, but these places are manicured to death, they aren't some suburban back garden. They are a picture of perfection, with teams of greens keepers and ground staff working on them seven days a week. So why the hell didn't anyone notice their graves, even a careful burial wouldn't go unnoticed, someone would have reported it, surely!

Right, get my phone out and ask Google.

"When was the Southport and Lancashire Golf Course first opened?"

"The Southport and Lancashire Golf Course first opened to members on the 5th of May 1920. It currently has one eighteen-hole course *(It is one of Europe's largest courses)*, one short nine-hole course,

3 putting greens, two driving ranges *(one of which is not used due to flooding)*, a Pro Shop and large clubhouse with many facilities"

Google rating 5.0 ***** (456 reviews)

Wait a minute, 1920, I was totally awake now! That meant all the burials happened when this place was open, how the hell did that happen? No chance, someone would have reported them or at least the disturbance in the course. I sat back on the bed, was this that little chink I had thought about, a tiny opening that might lead to bigger and better things? I got back into bed, Southport and Lancashire Golf Course first thing, see the club secretary or anyone who might want to talk to me.

Southport and Lancashire Golf Club.

I steered my car through the huge cast iron gates. They were painted gold and black in the shiniest paint I had ever seen. This place was like something from a Hollywood film set, massive gates, perfect gardens, flawless lawns and a wide sweeping driveway leading up to a magnificent white clubhouse on a slight rise above the surrounding area.

I passed a top-of-the-line Jaguar, two Lexus and a Lotus Exige, that car alone has got to be close to 80k. Made me feel a little embarrassed in my metallic silver Ford Mondeo, never mind, at least it was all paid for. I was just about to move into the large car park marked VISITORS to one side of the clubhouse, when I was nearly blindsided by a bloody white transit van. I wondered how the hell such a monstrosity had been allowed within a hundred miles of this place.

Anyway, I picked one of the empty parking spaces, got out, straightened my clothes and made my way to the entrance. I wasn't surprised to find sweeping stone steps, huge light oak doors with oversized brass furniture. To be honest, this whole place seemed just a bit over the top. I hate to think what the membership fees were each year, probably more that I earnt.

I just about reached the top step when one of those huge doors opened inward and a very smart looking chap in a dark suit, white shirt and black tie came out to greet me. He reached out his hand but never took his eyes off mine, he certainly had that security staff look about him.

"Good morning sir, and welcome to Southport and Lancashire Golf Club, how can I help?"

I wondered how the hell he knew I was visitor and not a member? I must have missed the CCTV cameras, I guess they will have spotted my lowly Ford as soon as it entered the main gate.

"Good morning, my name is Lee Hunter, I wonder if I might speak to the club secretary or any of the officials of the club"

"That won't be possible sir, not without an appointment"

I could have said that I had an appointment, but I guess he already knew I didn't.

"Thing is, sorry your name is?"

"My name is Francis Marks, deputy head of security"

"Yes, the thing is Francis, I will only take a few minutes, nothing too serious you know, just a question about the age of the course"

"You can find that out on the internet Mr Hunter. As for seeing one of the committee members, that will not be possible today"

I wasn't going to get passed this man, not without trying a little harder.

"That's a shame Francis, you see I am working with DI Smith, Southport Murder Squad. I guess I can get her to phone you, if necessary, if that might help?"

I hoped this would get him thinking a bit more. Does he want a local Detective Inspector chewing his arse, or will he stand by his guns and still refuse. If it was the latter, then I was truly sunk, as there was no way DI Smith was going to help me!

He stood there for what seemed like an age, he then gave a wry smile, I hoped this was a positive sign.

"Right Mr Hunter, please follow me. You can wait in reception, and I will see if anyone is available. If not, I suggest you follow my original suggestion and make an appointment"

The entrance hallway was vast, opulent and again rather over the top with its gold painted statues and large paintings of former grandees of the club. The stairs leading up to the first floor were white marble with dark veining, and light oak panelling covered the walls.

I was seated opposite the large reception desk on a rather comfortable red leather settee, there was a coffee table in front of me with several golfing magazines placed on it. Francis sprinted up the stairs and disappeared as they turned to the right. I settled down for a long wait, they would certainly not be rushing to see to my needs, and I knew it!

As I sat there a woman came gracefully down the stairs and disappeared into an office behind the reception desk, I thought how similar she was to Jan Talbot my office PA. It was then that I realised I hadn't heard from Jan all morning, and that was very unusual. She never ever forgot to phone me in the morning, just to say she was in, or maybe would be late, or a client wanted to see me. I looked at my watch, it was just past ten thirty, odd that I hadn't heard from her.

I pulled out my mobile, opened the screen and selected 'office' from my saved numbers. It started to ring, this wouldn't take long, she always left it for three rings and then answered. Not this time though, it just rang and rang with no answer. Ok, perhaps she's not in, got the flu or something, so I went back into my phone list and selected, 'Jan mobile'. Again, it connected but with no response, I wasn't unduly worried, maybe a client had popped in and she didn't want to answer. She will ring back soon I am sure of that.

I was just about the send her a WhatsApp message when a rather distinguished gentleman came slowly down the stairs. Perhaps in his seventies, in a very expensive dark blue suit and glossy black shoes, his white hair and moustache was set off with a suntan and the brightest blue eyes I have ever seen. He came serenely over to where I was sitting with a gentle and very relaxed smile on his face.

"Good morning Mr Hunter, my name is Charles Brightling, I am the General Manager of the Southport and Lancashire Golf Club, how may I help you?"

I stood up and reached out to shake his hand, his voice was as gentle as his grip, my old boss would have said "it was as wet as a rainy weekend in Brighton". I wanted to make some witticism about his surname, but I thought he had probably heard them all before, so I didn't bother.

"Thank you for seeing me sir, I am involved in the case regarding the recent finds on the course, I wonder if you might answer a couple of quick questions for me?"

"Mr Hunter, are you a member of the local constabulary?"

"No Mr Brightling but I am working closely with them, and I also represent a client who has a personal interest in the case"

"Oh, I see, you are a private detective Mr Hunter. Well, I have given several statements to the police already, but I am happy to answer your questions. I am rather busy though, so I can only spare you a minute or two"

"That's fine Mr Brightling, a couple of minutes should just about do it. It's concerning the bodies and the dates they were deposited"

This set a huge response off in Charles Brightling, it was if I had just accused him personally of murdering these eight people. He looked around with a very concerned look on his face, checking that no one had overheard what I had just said.

"Mr Hunter, these matters are not something we would want to discuss, they might cause some upset to members. If you insist on asking your questions, may I suggest we move to the office behind the reception desk?"

Without waiting for my response, he turned and briskly walked off, moved in behind the reception desk, and with me in hot pursuit, entered the office. There were four desks, numerous filing cabinets, a large conference call tv on one wall, and several CCTV screens on the other. The lady who resembled Jan was sitting at one of the desks busily working on her computer.

"Susan", he announced, "I wonder if we might have five minutes privacy?"

She looked up, smiled and left the office without speaking, leaving just Mr Brightling and myself.

"Right Mr Hunter, as I have already said, I have given several statements to the police, so I am not answering any more questions"

"I understand sir, but this won't take a minute"

He huffed, looked about the office and then looked back at me.

"Very well Mr Hunter, what is it you want to know?"

"Thank you sir. I understand that the course goes back to May 1920. Forgive me for my unfamiliarity, but how was it possible to bury eight bodies close to the ninth hole and no one noticed?"

"Well firstly Mr Hunter, the 'course' as you put it doesn't go back to the 1920's, but the club does. The course is where the members play, the club is the whole, including the clubhouse where we now stand.

Now the Southport and Lancashire Golf Club was inaugurated on the 5th of May 1920 by Colonel and Mrs Edward Frobisher. The land was gifted by the Creighton-Ward family and work started on the first course thereafter. It took two years before the first eighteen holes were fully open to members.

The layout of the course has changed several times since then, including the ninth hole which was originally some half a mile to the west of where it is now. Despite the sandy soil, we do have problems with laying water in the winter, so the course in general has been modified over the time it has been in use"

"That's very helpful Mr Brightling, but can I ask when the ninth hole was moved to where it is today?"

"If memory serves, that was the 1970's. It was moved from its original position in order to facilitate the laying of a new mains electric cable to the clubhouse. The line of the cable would have been right across the green and down the fairway, so it was decided to move the whole ninth hole, rather than trying to repair the damaged to the existing ninth"

"That's interesting sir, given the problems you have with standing water in the winter, can I assume there was extensive drainage work undertaken on the new ninth hole, before it was opened?"

"There would have been Mr Hunter, forgive me but that relocation was before my time here so I can't say for certain. You are right about the extensive problems we have with flooding and drainage, it's a constant problem here"

"It just seems strange that the eight bodies were not found when all that work was done Mr Brightling, very strange"

"Sorry Mr Hunter but I can't help you any more I am afraid, perhaps they weren't digging deep enough"

"You see Mr Brightling, one of your greenskeepers was recently tasked to put another bunker in adjacent to the ninth green. That kind of job does not require extensive or particularly deep excavations, but he managed to find the graves. How come the groundworkers who moved the hole and installed the drains found absolutely nothing, forty years earlier?"

The room fell into silence, I stared at Brightling, trying to read his mind, trying to ascertain what he might say, would it be the truth or lies. The silence went on for several more seconds.

"Sorry Mr Hunter but I must go, I have a very important meeting, so forgive me, but I must see you out"

Now that was a flight or fight response if I ever had seen one. He couldn't think of what to say next, so he was off. An experienced criminal or someone used to lying their way out of trouble would have come up with some kind of answer, no matter how unbelievable. They must have discussed this exact conundrum at management or board meetings, they were intelligent people, I was certain someone would have thought about this, just the same as I had!

"One last question Mr Brightling. You said the land was gifted by the Creighton-Ward family, can you remember who the head of the family at that time was?"

"Yes, in fact his portrait hangs in the member's bar. It was Edward Creighton-Ward"

"Oh yes, I have spoken to his family, shame he died a few years later, an air crash I was told"

"No Mr Hunter, that wasn't Edward Creighton-Ward, he died here on the course, heart attack I think, no wait, a stroke. Mind you he was 94 so he had a good old life"

"Wait a minute, you are talking about Edward Creighton-Ward?"

"Yes Mr Hunter, the one and only. A ladies' man, gambler, alcoholic, occasional bare-knuckle fighter and some might say a loose cannon, but you can't overlook his generosity, especially when it comes to the club"

"Did he have a relative, cousin, someone else who might have the same name?"

"Mr Hunter, ask anyone around here, there was only one Edward Creighton-Ward, trust me, there could never be another. Some might say, thank goodness for that!"

I stood there, mouth open rather like a goldfish in a tank. This was getting more complicated by the day, who the hell was 'this' Edward? Was he the grandfather of James, or someone completely different? Given the account of his character outlined by Mr Brightling, perhaps he had been ex communicated from the family.

That wouldn't have been the first time this kind of thing had happened. A powerful and very wealthy old English family would not be able to stand the embarrassment and shame of such a man. Like the lady of the house having an affair with the gamekeeper, or the young son running off with the chamber maid. So, with some made up story about the end of his life in an air crash, he was erased from the family!

This didn't explain why James hadn't simply denied all knowledge of Edward in the first place. Perhaps I had taken him off guard somewhat. That would certainly clarify why there was no trace of Edward in the family crypt, or in the parish records. I needed to find out a little more about the errant Edward Creighton-Ward, but who to turn to? Mr Brightling was already turning to walk out of the door, in a few seconds time I would be back in the carpark. Had I learnt anything, well yes, was I any the wiser, probably not!

I said my goodbyes to Mr Brightling and made my way down the steps towards my car. I pulled my phone out of my pocket, I hadn't heard anything from Jan yet, where the hell was she? I tried the office again and then her mobile but with no luck at all. I left a message for her to get back to me as soon as possible.

A Windswept Place.

The early dawn had broken gloomy and cold, a fine drizzle blowing off the Irish Sea, whirling around in the air like a million liquid diamonds, soaking everything it touched. Grey scudding clouds raced across the sky like a heard of wild horses, some dark grey some almost white. Occasional gusts of wind made standing uncertain, the grass slick and treacherous with the rain.

The two men pulled up in their white transit van, the gloom was their cloak, covering them and hiding their presence from prying eyes. They looked through the windscreen, the idea of carrying out their allotted task in this weather was not something they were looking forward to.

"Why the hell are we burying these two now, we could dump them anytime we like, they didn't go through any ceremony, what a waste of time"

"I am not sure, the man tried to escape, don't know what the final cause was with the girl, I guess we will never know now"

"Could have fuckin waited until this weather improved, we are going to get pissed wet through"

"Yep, but you know what the boss is like, if he tells someone to jump the only thing to say is, how high? You can't mess with him, he is likely to put a knife between your ribs just for looking at him the wrong way"

"That man is going to get us all into trouble, he's a psycho, no mistake"

"Yeah, but in the meantime, let's get these two in the ground, do you know where we are supposed to bury them?"

"Yep, the boss said next to the old oak over there, the burial map shows a bit of space"

"A bit of a space, how many bodies are in here?"

"Don't know but it's been used for quite some time, certainly before I started"

The van cab fell into silence, the only noise was the wind howling around them. Without another word the two men exited and opened up the back doors. They pulled out their tools and the two black body bags and set to work. It didn't take long to dig the graves in the sandy soil, there was a time limit to complete their work, it had to be finished before the dog walkers and any other people sallied forth.

By the time they had buried the two bodies, the dawn had started to break fully. The wet and windy weather had persisted though, keeping any other persons warm and dry at home.

"At least we didn't need to bury them in the traditional way, it's easier just throwing them in a hole"

They didn't go through the ceremony, they just died so no traditions for them, just chuck them in and fill in the hole"

"When is the next ceremony, I hope the bloody weather gets better by then?"

"The boss said they already had another woman, now they were after another man. He said it would be in the next few weeks, apparently some of the members are ill with covid so they have to wait until that's sorted out. They need to get it sorted as they are already behind, so there might be a couple more ceremonies before the year is out, so things look busy"

"Well, I don't give a fuck so long as they keep paying me. The more the merrier, this is a good little earner for me and you, keeps me in clover that's for sure. What's with all the ceremonies, dead bodies with their throats cut, burying them face to face, like the radio said, lovers in the sand"

"Don't ask me and I suggest you don't ask anyone else. It's some kind of cult, kill a man and a woman, bury them naked with fancy rings, goodness knows. It doesn't make any sense to me, but the money certainly does. I have recognised a few people though, certainly several from the big house, they are all mixed up in this make no mistake"

"They are all rich twats from that place, lords and ladies for sure, ruling class, they treat people like you and me as scum"

"No doubt"

He started the van, the windscreen wipers swished back and forth, moving not just rain but also some white sleet from the windscreen. They carefully moved off and headed back towards the road, their days work done, at least for now.

Where is Jan?

Just as I got back onto the main road my phone rang again. I looked at the screen on the console of the car, it said, 'call from Alicja'. She was the office cleaner, a rather stocky woman from Poland who had set up her own cleaning company. She was very good at her job and someone I had come to rely on. I pressed 'accept' and wondered exactly what she was going to say?

"Yes Alicja, what's up?"

"It's the office Mr Hunter, it's locked, no one here, do you want me to clean today?"

That shook me back to reality, away from puzzling about the 94-year-old, bare knuckle fighting Edward. I dropped down a gear, tapped the break, I needed to slow my mind as well as the car.

"Are you sure Alicja, she should be there by now"

"No one here Mr Hunter, I have been knocking for half an hour. Phone was ringing in the office, but no one answer. I am sure Jan is not at work today"

Now I began to panic, where the hell was she? I had known her for quite some time, and this was the first occasion she had gone missing. Jan had many attributes but two of her strongest was her time keeping and her meticulous organisational skills. If there was ever a problem, she wouldn't hesitate in telling me about it.

"Look Alicja, don't worry about cleaning today, the office is closed, I will ring you tomorrow if I want you to come in"

"Thank you Mr Hunter, I will wait until you call tomorrow"

Right, I knew where Jan lived so I would call in there before I went into town. She had probably got some terrible dose of food poisoning. I keep telling her to leave those kebabs alone. I guess when you have been out with the girls and had a few too many vodkas, your whole sense of food safety changes.

Right, get to her place quickly, if she needs help, I can get things sorted sooner rather than later. It didn't take more than ten minutes to find her house, in fact it was the top flat of a rather grand Victorian villa. The kind of place where a very wealthy family once lived, servant sleeping in the eves, in tiny little bedrooms, and working all day in the kitchen and gardens below. Those days were long gone but the magnificent houses still remained, most of which had by now been turned into flats.

I parked the car on the street, walked up the long path, up five sandstone steps and arrived at the large blue front doors. There were two door answering systems to the right, one marked, 'ground floor T Perkins' and the other, "first floor J Talbot'. I pushed the bell for Jan, expecting to hear her voice at any second but nothing happened. I pushed it for a second and then a third time but with no response. In an act of desperation and perhaps even panic, I pressed the one marked 'T Perkins' and stood back.

A rather slow and what sounded like an aged voice mumbled into the speaker.

"Just before you ask for anything, I can see you and this system also records your image. My son comes over every weekend to look at the pictures, so be warned"

I was kind of taken aback by that, I wasn't expecting such a long introduction, a simple 'hello' might have sufficed.

"Good day madam, my name is Lee Hunter, I work with Jan who lives above you, she is my PA. I am trying to track her down, I don't suppose you have seen her today?"

"She went out last night, some noisy women called about eight pm. They made a terrible racket, please tell them to be more respectful in future"

"Yes madam I certainly will. Just to be clear, did she come home last night?"

"They went out and I haven't seen her since, they were so noisy, went off in a taxi"

"Thank you, if you do see Jan, please ask her to contact Lee, it's very important"

There was a click, I don't really know why I made that last statement, there was next to no chance that she would ever pass my message on. I felt a rising tide of anxiety about this situation. Ok, she probably got blind drunk and was now sleeping it off at her friend's house. The thing is, it just wasn't Jan, she never got that drunk, never went missing no matter what.

One horrific thought wormed its way into my mind, like some disease-ridden maggot. Was this something to do with the 'lovers in the sand' case? Surely not, I am just imagining things, get real Hunter! Thing was, I had already received death threats, maybe they had decided to ramp things up somewhat, take a hostage to ensure my compliance!

So, what the hell do I do next? I don't know who made the threats towards me, but I guess that was something to do with James Creighton-Ward. I couldn't go storming into his place, I was likely to get shot, or worse get Jan harmed. The only thing I could think of was going to see DI Smith, maybe, just maybe she might be able to help.

"So, let me get this straight Lee, your PA Jan has gone missing, you think James Creighton-

Ward has got something to do with it, and you want me to go poking around his place?"

"That's about it Deborah, I can't think of any reason why she would just go missing, it's not like her, she is very reliable"

"Hang on a minute, so where does James Creighton-Ward come into all of this. Why the hell would he organise the kidnapping of a private detectives PA, it doesn't make sense. You are going to have to try harder Lee, do you honestly think I can send a couple of uniforms over to the big house on a whim, just in case she has been kidnapped. Or even worse, try and get a search warrant because 'Jan is reliable, and she might have been taken after a night on the piss'. You are an ex-cop Lee, so you know that those allegations are very serious, but also the Creighton-Wards are very influential in these parts. If you go making accusations like that, you better have dam good evidence to back it up, or you end up in court being sued back to the bloody stone age!

Do you actually comprehend how many people go 'missing' for 24 hours after a night out with the girls or boys? Almost all of them are found sleeping it off on a friend's settee, in the bed of someone they don't really know, or on a bench in a local park"

"I know Deborah, but trust me this is very different"

"Ok Lee, tell me why this is so very different"

It was then that I realised exactly what I had done. I had managed to paint myself into a corner with DI Smith, I would have to tell her about the death threats otherwise she would escort me out of the station with a 'don't be such a silly boy' slap on the back. I took in a deep breath, do I say nothing, and risk Jan being harmed, or tell Deborah everything, and risk a court order telling me to keep my nose out?

"Right Deborah, I am telling you this as a friend, and not reporting it as an official police matter, do I make myself clear?"

She looked at me with a frown on her face.

"Not quite sure what you mean Lee, but go on"

"What I mean Deborah is this is unofficial, it's not meant to be recorded as anything formal"

"Ok Lee, let's have it"

"A short while ago I received death threats about getting too close to whoever is at the centre of these murders. I record all my telephone calls, it makes sense in my line of work, here is the recording of the call I received a couple of days ago"

Hunter, we know what you are up to. We know why you are looking around but stop or we will stop you. You won't find anything and even if you do, it won't be of any use to you when you are laying dead at the bottom of the Irish Sea. You are dealing with forces beyond your control, people and things that you don't understand. For your sake and those whom you love, move on and forget everything you think you know. This is your only warning, take heed and move on Hunter.

"You see Deborah, I think these people are very serious and I am very worried that Jan has been taken in a move to stop me poking around in their dirty secrets. That's not all, when I told you about being warned off on the Creighton-Ward estate, well there was more to that incident than I mentioned at the time. Ken and I were warned off at gun point, and make no mistake Deborah, we both thought things would turn deadly if we didn't comply"

The room went quiet again, DI Smith looked down at the table, she was clearly thinking about her next move.

"Ok Lee, is there anything else you haven't told me, anything at all?"

"Well, yes there is. Tomorrow morning on the breakfast show, Russ Broadbent is going to mention that I have some vital evidence that will lead to the 'lovers in the sand' case being solved. Something that the police don't yet have, and proves exactly who is involved"

"Lee, that's tantamount to suicide, given what's happened to you already, you will be dead by lunchtime and Jan shortly afterwards"

"Yes, I know, but that plan was hatched before the death threats and Jan going missing. I thought it would be a good idea, perhaps flush someone out of the shadows, maybe get someone offering a deal for my silence. I just thought it might short circuit an investigation that was going nowhere for me, and to be honest for you also. This kind of approach often shakes things up just a little, you never know what drops out of the slime"

"I do know Lee, and that is someone is going to die, most likely two people come to think of it. You have to stop Russ Broadbent from broadcasting anything, it's too risky, especially if Jan has been taken. We need to find out what has happened to her, and we need to do that right now"

"Then you have to send someone to see the Creighton-Ward's before it's too late. They have her Deborah, I am sure of that, I even suspect where she is"

"Ok Lee, where might that be?"

"There is a huge estate building to the right as you approach the main house, that's where they are holding her. Come to think of it, they might be holding those other two youngsters that your colleague was talking about on the radio. Can't remember their names but one of them was an Italian backpacker"

"Yes, their names are Susan Forbes and Vittorio Bruno, I don't see that they are connected in any way Lee, that's just a coincidence"

"Trust me Deborah, they will be! You have eight skeletons, several missing youngsters, Jan has disappeared. I have been held up at gun point on the estate, issued with death threats, oh yes, and let's not forget the terrible experience Ms Greenwood just went through. This family are right at the middle of whatever is going on, cult ceremonies, sacrificial murders, call it what you will. If we don't act soon, there will be plenty more bodies to find, I promise you!"

The room fell quiet once more, DI Smith sat back in her chair and looked up at the ceiling.

"Listen Lee, let's just say for a moment that you are right, the Creighton-Ward's are holding several people at the manor, including Jan. Let's presume that these people are going to be murdered, for whatever reason, and then buried somewhere. It might all be connected to some long-lost ancestor called Edward, who isn't buried where he is supposed to be.

So, what the hell am I supposed to tell my boss when I ask for a search warrant and a team to carry it out? The Creighton-Ward's are sadistic murdering psychopaths, who are going to kill all these youngsters, who have gone missing recently. They will all be given a ring before they die, commissioned by a man who doesn't seem to have been buried, or in fact be actually dead. All this is the assumption of one Lee Hunter, but he has no real evidence at all!

You see Lee, that's not going to work, he is just going to laugh at me and tell me to come back with some real evidence, not some half-baked horror story"

"How about we let Russ Broadbent broadcast his 'exclusive news story' and then see what happens. You can have me watched, I can even wear a hidden microphone, if someone tries to snatch me, that's all the evidence you will need"

"Can't argue with that Lee, just one minor point. What happens if they just roll up and shoot you dead, blow a fucking great hole in your head? I will have absolutely no clue who did it, and yet another murder case to try and solve. I have enough on my plate with those eight sets of remains, we are still waiting for the DNA results, let alone finding out who the hell they are. No, it's too dangerous, there must be another way"

"Ok Deborah, what do you have in mind"

Silence descended once again, DI Smith scratched her head vigorously.

"Ok Lee, it's worth a try, only because I don't have a bloody clue about anything going on in this case, or about all your stupid accusations. You can carry a wire, we can tap your phone and DS Shacklady can watch you for the morning, and that young DC Stephen Burton for the rest of the day. Get here early, say 7am, and we can get you wired up and sort out where you will go and what you plan to do. No excuses Lee, no changing the plan, I am in charge of this, not you, do I make myself clear?"

"Crystal Deborah, and thanks very much"

"Don't thank me Lee, just do what I tell you to, understand?"

"Perfectly"

"If you have a god Lee, I suggest you ask for his help, the chances are you will need it"

I smiled but Deborah was right, there was more than a chance I wouldn't see my next birthday. This could all go very wrong indeed and very quickly!

Radio Rock n Roll Lancashire.

"Well good morning everyone, hey and thanks again for tuning into the northwest best and only number one radio station. My name is Russ Broadbent, and I am your host from now until 10am, but I guess you know that.

Once Maddy has read out the local bulletin and that so important traffic update, we can start to ease your day into life with some great mellow tunes, this morning we are concentrating on the 70's and 80's.

Also, I have some very interesting news regarding one of our local Detectives, and great friend of the station, Lee Hunter. He will be on the programme tomorrow morning at nine, and he has some exclusive info' about the skeletons found on the golf course. He can answer your questions on who they might be and why they were murdered, and those rings, what's that all about? Well Lee has some information regarding that as well, particularly concerning the mysteries of who commissioned them and when. So, tune in at nine tomorrow morning for an exclusive phone in with Lee Hunter, answering all your questions about the 'lovers in the sand' and much, much more, wow!"

I turned the radio off and sat down to eat my breakfast, two pieces of toast and a coffee, black one sugar. If Russ Broadbent's announcement didn't stir up a storm, then nothing ever will. Remembering also that I had a very serious death threat hanging over me I looked down at my toast, all of a sudden I lost my appetite.

I wondered if they would be able to resist the temptation to shut me up once and for all, given what had happened so far, I was pretty sure they wouldn't. Well, I had followed DI Smiths instructions to the letter. My phone had been tapped, I was wearing the wire, DS Shacklady was sitting in her car not far from here, and the rout for the morning was clear in everyone's mind. All I had to do was wait for a phone call from the perpetrators or see if they tried to get to me as I spent the day in the office.

I must admit to being more than a little nervous, in fact if I was being honest, I was bloody terrified. Also, what about Jan, yes it was possible that her disappearance had absolutely nothing to do with this case, but I was utterly certain that it was.

If there was any good news regarding her, the Missing Persons Team thought she was more likely to be a hostage, rather than a victim. She would be no use to them dead, that would serve no purpose. In fact, it might drive me on to dig even deeper into the case. So, I took some solace from that, it kind of made sense, but the question in my mind was, why hadn't I received some communication from them, why hadn't they told me that they had her, and to back off?

Right, dump the pots into the sink and let's get off, see what the day brings, some good news, I hope. I gingery opened the front door and slowly walked toward my car, all the time wishing that I hadn't asked Russ to broadcast that message! It wasn't long before the phone went off, I looked at the display on the dashboard, 'call number withheld'. Expecting the worse, I thumbed the 'answer' button on the steering weel and hoped beyond hope that the phone tap was working the way it should.

"Lee Hunter"

"Hunter, we have heard your plan to spread scurrilous lies about us tomorrow morning. That will not happen, we have your PA, and she will die if you even attempt to do such a thing. Just in case you doubt that we have her, just listen to this recording"

"Lee, Lee it's me Jan, they have me, they are threatening to kill me, and I believe them, do as they say Lee, please"

"Now you are in no doubt about what will happen, you need to follow these instructions. You will go on that radio station tomorrow morning and tell the whole world that you don't really have anything. It was all a huge mistake, and you won't be looking into the case anymore, do I make myself clear Hunter?"

I pulled over to the side of the road. I wanted to give them a piece of my mind, tell them if they hurt Jan, I would track each and every one of them down. I wanted to shout out that I don't back down to threats, I never have, and I never will. I couldn't though, I wanted to, but Jan was now in their hands, and I had no doubt what they would do to her if necessary. I sat there, took a phew deep breaths and allowed the red mist of hate to dissipate.

"Why have you taken her, your fears are based on what I know, not her. Why didn't you take me, then all of this could have been avoided? Why don't we do a swap, my life for hers, then you can be assured of my co-operation"

"Because if we had taken you, it would have confirmed people's ideas about the remains, the rings and the lies you have spread about us. No Hunter, there was only one way, take Jan, get you to retract everything you have said and so everyone could forget and move on. So, do as I have instructed and tomorrow morning things will change for us, you and your PA"

The line clicked and went dead. I sat there in the car, head pounding and sweat running down the sides of my head. I had to decide what to do next, I knew the police would be monitoring my call and somewhere around would be DS Shacklady, so I couldn't just go off and sort this out by myself.

I was shaken out of my melancholy by a knocking on the side window. I looked up, it was DS Shacklady, she was gesturing me to wind down the window.

"I heard that phone call Lee and I don't want you going off and trying to sort this yourself, like some twenty first century charge of the Light Brigade. That's not going to work, do I make myself clear?"

"What can I do Sharron? I wanted to swap, but he wasn't listening, I feel so responsible, this is all my fault and Jan is paying the price"

"This is their fault Lee, whoever 'they' are. They started this, they are murdering people not you. Just sit tight and we will plan to catch them. Jan will be safe I promise you. She is no good to them dead, it only reinforces what you suspect, it makes your case, they won't kill her"

I knew that last part about Jan being safe was meant to calm me down. DS Shacklady had no more clue about Jan's safety than I did, and there was no way she could guarantee me anything at all.

"Ok Sharron, thanks for the warning and don't worry, I won't go rogue on this one, not after Ruth and the murderess end she came to! One unnecessary death is more than enough for me, that won't happen again"

"Right Lee, well keep going to the office, I will stay out of site. Remember I will be in the vacant office below yours, any problems and I will be with you in a flash, ok?"

I sent the electric window back up and into place. DS Shacklady was absolutely right, stay calm and carry on. They will make a mistake at some point, all I could do was to wait until that chance presented itself.

I had to think, there must be something I had overlooked. Perhaps there was a clue, something so obvious it was hiding in plain sight? My mind whirled back and forth, my inner sense told me that there should be, there often is, but I couldn't quite put my finger on it. I reviewed the conversations with Ms Greenwood, James Creighton-Ward, Tom Tock but there was nothing.

It wasn't until I started thinking about the golf course and that general manager, Charles 'the watch' Brightling that I suddenly began to feel something. Maybe that thing hiding in plain site was not so camouflaged after all. I turned into the car park behind the office, turned off the engine and started to think in earnest.

What was it about that golf course? What did I know but didn't realise it, something we had discussed? I sat there for what seemed like an age but whatever was bouncing around in my useless mind just wouldn't come to the fore. I slammed the car door shut, pressed the key fob, listened to the bleep confirming the doors were locked, and set off for the back entrance to the office.

I reached the back door and stared at the code entry door lock. I had set up an easy entrance code, something I couldn't possibly forget. Being an ex-cop, I thought 999 would be a good one, after all, it was the emergency number in the UK.

As I reached forward, that thing hiding in plain sight came rushing forward like an express train in the night. How the hell could I have overlooked that, it was so bloody obvious. I had to get inside and call DI Smith, this was potentially big, very big!

A Dark Place.

Jan shivered in the damp cold cell. There was a LED bulb hanging limply from a short flex, it gave off a bright piercing light. The drowsy feeling was beginning to wear off but was only replaced by disorientation and terror.

She was laying on her back on a hard wooden surface, it creaked slightly as she attempted to move. She became aware of her nakedness, groping into the darkness for her clothes but there was nothing there. She wanted to scream, call out for help but something deep inside told her to be quiet, remain hidden in the shadows.

Still disorientated, Jan began to review the events of the last few hours. Things came into focus, then scattered again. Isolated memories, broken recollections, conversations, laughter. Nothing seemed to make sense, she remembered getting into a taxi, arriving at the club, her friends, joy, drinks, then blackness.

There was a noise, someone walking outside, heavy footsteps on a stone floor. Next the sound of a key, a lock being turned. Thump, thump as someone drove their shoulder into the ill-fitting door, then a blinding light. She closed her eyes, as a pain shot through them and into her brain. Remembering that she was naked, she thrust her hands down over her crotch, and then up to her breasts in a vain attempt to cover herself. A man's voice came out of the dazzling light, she tried to focus on the image but the drugs and the shooting pain forst her to close her eyes once more.

"Listen luv, I was the one who stripped you naked when you first arrived so there is no need to try and cover yourself. My name is Richard, I will be looking after you until the ceremony. If you do what I say you will be ok, if you don't, I will kill you myself.

There is no escape from here, some have tried, none have lived to tell the tale. I will feed and water you as required, and I will ensure your safety until they call for you. There are several processes to go through before your eventual most glorious ascent from this imperfect life.

In addition, the ritual you will be participating in, is the installing of our new Principal Brother, the first to have taken place in this millennium. The extra elements in this ceremony will be celebrated by the members with great eagerness. You must count yourself beyond fortunate, indeed blessed to be part of this observance.

You are truly fortunate Jan Talbot, so it's time to reflect on your sacred place as the next representative sent to meet our master.

Now, I understand that most of what you will undergo will seem very strange and indeed frightening, but you must trust in the members and the glorious new Brother Principal on the rising to that exalted office. Put your fears behind you Jan Talbot and look forward to the next and higher level of your existence. Many will envy you and all will wish they could be in your place. So please reflect on this as the newly made Principal Brother slices into your throat with the new blade, made specially for this event"

The terror of those words crashed into her brain, she felt like a road traffic victim just as the lorry hit her square in the chest. "Cut into my throat, newly made blade", what the hell did all that mean? She wanted to sit up, run for the door, and leave this place but she was unable, the drugs had taken her strength, immobilised her. She opened her mouth to scream but nothing came forth, her dry and desiccated throat would not allow any sound to be formed.

"Listen Jan, I can see you are somewhat panicked by what I have just said, but try and relax, fighting it will only make things worse. You need a little more time before those drugs leave your body. I have left here by the door two large bottles of water and some bread. I strongly urge you to consume the lot, you will feel much better once you have done that. I will return in a few hours, we can talk some more and don't fret about your nakedness, you are a fortunate woman, the members will enjoy looking at you"

"Let me go you bastard"

"Now, now, Jan Talbot, just relax. Your fate is sealed, and you are truly honoured as well. Try not to think of this world anymore, imagine the higher level and what will await you there. Your passage will be much easier if you just accept what is to come.

The pain won't be short lived but the senior members in the ceremony are indeed experts at what they do. I accept that terror will undoubtedly overtake you at some point and panic will certainly tear at your mind. You must discipline yourself, train yourself to appreciate and enjoy what is happening all around you.

Try to forget everything that you know, family, friend's, familiar things, they are all gone now. Remembering them will only add to your pain, so delete them from your thoughts. You belong to us now, as does your life and your body, you exist to facilitate what we do, no matter the fear and pain"

The door slammed shut, an overwhelming tidal wave of panic washed over her, at last she was able to scream, her body convulsed, as she shouted "no"

A Phone Call to DI Smith.

"Wait a minute Lee, what are you talking about, it's been moved, what's been moved?"

I have just had a major realisation, it's been staring at me all this time, it's so bloody obvious. The ninth hole Deborah, it's been moved, I asked the General Manager of the club, Charles Brightling. He informed me that the ninth hole was moved in the 1970's after some cable was about to cut right down the old fairway"

"That's very interesting Lee, thanks for that, still not sure what the hell this means?"

"They have been burying bodies on the course for a very long time Deborah, we know that. Goodness knows how many they have buried out there, just because the archaeologists say there was nothing else near the ninth hole, doesn't mean there are no more bodies elsewhere"

"You have a point Lee, but that course is one of the biggest in Europe, we simply can't scan the whole thing, it would take weeks, maybe even months and what evidence do we have to undertake that mammoth task, they seem to think we have everything"

"There isn't any extra evidence, but I do have a hunch. I think they had been burying bodies in a corner of the course, nice and private, out of the way, never to be found. By a twist of fate, that quiet corner turned into the new ninth, over forty years ago. That was after they had to move the original ninth due to the cable laying work. That screwed up their little cemetery, after all, you can't bury bodies next to a green where the bloody members are tapping in their par score. Someone would have something to say about that, I am sure! How on earth no one picked that error up I will never know. Perhaps the burial plan was mistaken, got the bodies in the wrong place, that's why the new 9th green was placed where it was, they thought it was clear to do so, who knows?

Anyway, if you can't bury your victims anymore because the new ninth hole is too close to the original burial ground, where the hell can you bury them? My guess would be on the old ninth hole, the now spare ground where the old fairway and green used to be up until the 1970's. If that's the case, that would explain why the burials appeared to stop, or at least why the bodies on the 9th are dated only up to 1970. It might also explain why there were fifty rings commissioned and only eight found"

"Yes, but it was decided that these killings were done every ten years, 1940, 1950, 60 and 70. It all seemed to make sense, why would there be any more killings?"

"Because it's 2022 Deborah, another five decades have passed since 1970, that's another ten bodies. That's always presuming that you were right, and the killings took place every decade. What happens if you are wrong, what happens if they are done every five years, or even every year? I know killers die, get thrown into jail and the killings stop, that would explain the last one being in the 70's, but what if they haven't, what if this is a cult thing and the killings are still happening?"

"So, what are you suggesting?"

"I suggest you get a warrant and send that county archaeologist over to the old ninth to see what she can find. That would also lend some credence to the Creighton-Ward involvement and might lead to a warrant to search the big house. I know this is a shot in the dark Deborah, but I am sure I am right on this. There are more bodies on that course and James Creighton-Ward is right at the centre of it"

"Ok, I will have a word with Adele and see if she can get her archaeology team out to the course. I will try to explain to the local magistrate why I want a search warrant, let's hope he goes for it. As for the Creighton-Ward's, I still think we are wasting our time. They are too well-connected Lee, one phone call from them and whatever we are planning will be blocked. Even if Adele finds a hundred bodies out there, chances are, nothing will connect them to that or any other family for that matter. If you are determined to continue with this theory, then you will need to get me some irrefutable evidence, and it needs to be absolutely watertight. If you ask me Lee, when dealing with the Creighton-Ward's, that evidence will simply not exist. Even if you do find it, I am certain that it will quickly disappear"

I stopped to think, she was right of course, my dad used to say, "It's not what you know, it's who you know". I had dealt with families like this, mainly criminal gangs, who had important people in their pockets, 'on the pay roll' so to speak. Trying to bring them to justice was like banging your head against a brick wall. Every turn was blocked, all the evidence would suddenly vanish, orders from superiors would call you off.

There must be a way, there must be one piece of information that no one would be able to erase, a bit of evidence that could not be disappeared. There has to be something that I could get my hands on, something that would link all of this together. The trouble was, it didn't exist and even if it did, where the hell was it and how do I get to it?

I was really beginning to think that I would never get to the bottom of this case, there were too many bridges to cross and most of them had armed guards at both ends. I was shaken out of my melancholy by my phone going off in my pocket. I reached in and pulled it out, I had to concentrate, whatever I did next might well prove critical.

"Hello, Lee Hunter, how can I help?"

"Oy boss, it's Ken, what you up to mate?"

That 'mate' thing always meant that he wanted something, normally money, but I was too tired to argue with him, so I just played along.

"What's up Ken?"

"Nothing boss, just wondered if you had any work for me, bit skint if you knows what I mean. Got to pay the man for me fix and I am a bit short"

As I made my way into the main office, the predicament of Jan struck me again. Where the hell was she, what was going to happen to her? It was all my fault, the waves of frustration and guilt washed over me. To be honest, talking to smelly Ken was the last thing I wanted, especially when it involved fuelling his drug habit.

"I don't have anything at the moment Ken, I have loads on my mind and I just can't think of what to do next"

"Oh man, you sound fucked up, why don't you come over to my place, we can have a bottle of vodka, get pissed like, take your mind of things"

That offer did make me smile, in fact I started to laugh out loud, it was the first time I had done that in some time. I know Ken had a million indescribable habits, most of which were illegal, and all would lead to his eventual early demise, but he had a deep and undeniable humanity. He was a victim of his childhood, parents who didn't give a toss, left alone to fend for himself when he should have been loved and cared for. This hadn't stopped him developing an inner kindness and compassion, perhaps borne out of his own neglect and loneliness as a child. I had known him for a long while now, he never stopped surprising me. If only I could turn him around, help him become a better person, not much chance of that though!

"You know Ken, that sounds a bloody good idea, getting pissed might just help, at least for an hour or two. Trouble is, I don't fancy your place, I would need a complete decontamination afterwards"

"Don't know what else to suggest boss, there is always one of the old garages opposite my flat, we could break into one of those. Hey that might be fun, never know what you might find in one of those"

Something flashed across my mind, I went through what he had just said, it triggered a memory in me, what the hell was it?

"What did you just say Ken, tell me that again"

"Just thought we could bust into one of those garages opposite my gaff, might find something cool, then we can get pissed, if you bring the vodka"

What the hell was it, what had smelly Ken sparked off. I stood in the centre of the main office and scratched my head. Then, like an unexpected crash of thunder, it hit me.

"Ken, you are a fuckin genius, where are you, we have a job to, and it doesn't mean getting pissed either"

"Oh, that's a shame boss, what you thinkin, doing some shop liftin, could be fun"

"No Ken, we are going to break into a garage, or more appropriately, a grave digger's shed. There are a few documents in there that could prove very useful indeed. I will pick you up from the soup kitchen in half an hour and don't worry, I will slip you twenty quid"

"Yea boss, up for that, see you in half an hour"

I put the phone back into my pocket. This might just turn out to be the break I needed. The trouble was, how the hell was I going to get rid of DS Shacklady? I don't suppose she would be happy with what I was just about to do. I had to come up with a story that might allow me to slip away, but what?

I grabbed my mobile again and called DS Shacklady, it was going to be a lame excuse, but it was the only thing I could manage at such short notice.

"Hi Lee, what's up?"

"Listen Sharron, I have to nip to the bank, it's only down the road a bit, so I will be back in five minutes, no need to trouble yourself"

"I need to keep an eye on you Lee, you know what DI Smith said"

"I know but it's a public place, no one will be stupid enough to try anything"

"Five minutes Lee, and I want a phone call as soon as you get back, understand?"

"Yep, no problems"

I stuffed the phone back into my pocket and left the office before DS Shacklady had a change of mind. I expected a phone call from her at any moment telling me to wait but it didn't come. I ran to the car, started it and I was off, just as quickly as I could, driving like a maniac to the soup kitchen to pick up smelly Ken.

By the time I got there he was waiting, lurking in the shadows like some cold war spy. I never quite understood why he did this, after all, he was waiting for me, not some KGB Colonel. Perhaps it was the modus operandi of the drug user, stay out of site, and away from the cops?

As soon as he spotted my car he came sauntering over, a big toothless grin on his face.

"So, what's this job boss, breaking into some grave diggers place and boosting some books?"

He slipped into the car, slamming the door behind him so hard that it made both my ears pop.

"I guess that about sums it up Ken. A load of bodies have been dug up on the golf course, I guess you must have heard about that, 'lovers in the sand'? I think it may be the work of a cult, headed up by a local family. Trouble is, I can't prove a thing, maybe these books might help, names, dates, places, you know what I mean"

"Why would anyone leave them in some shed, wouldn't they want to hide them away? I think those books boss will just be a load of receipts for work done and tools bought"

"That's a distinct possibility, maybe the books are not what I think they are, but we won't know unless we try"

"Let's go then, best done whilst we have some light, don't want to be messing about in the dark"

I slipped the car into gear and pulled away. I must admit that I was feeling very unsure about the whole thing. I had death threats hanging over me, I had lied to DS Shacklady, and goodness knows who might be following me. The next hour or so could be a turning point in the case, or it could be that last few moments of my life, and to be honest, I wasn't sure which it would be.

It didn't take long to reach the old church, it seemed quiet enough, no cars parked, no people wandering about. I parked some distance away and Ken and I made our way towards the lane at the back of the church.

I decided to make our approach through the old graveyard, trying to remain as inconspicuous as possible, dodging between the graves and the many Yew trees. The grass was wet and very slippery, but we managed to get down to the little lane and down towards the grave diggers shed.

It was gloomy and somewhat intimidating, perhaps due to the proximity of the graves, but the feeling was real enough. We slowly made our way to the front of the shed, it seemed larger than I remembered it, grey concrete and an up and over steel door, with peeling and cracked green paint. It stood like a sentinel at the end of the track, in the semi darkness, blocking the way of anyone who might pass this way.

I stopped, and looked up, I could see the edge of the asbestos roof, covered in algae and dark green moss. My mind was screaming, begging me to turn around and get back into the car. I wanted to run, this place felt evil, perhaps it was just the setting, or maybe there really was a malevolent force at play. I looked over at Ken, he seemed more at ease, he was certainly used to a degree of criminality. I reassured myself that my feelings of nervousness were due to being on the wrong side of the law for once, not to any malignant force.

"Right boss, what's the plan, just bust the lock or is there a window somewhere?"

"There is a window around the back Ken, but we can't bust anything. We need to get in and have a look, not destroy any part of this building. If anyone thinks we have been here, any other evidence will be destroyed. We have to be careful, in and out, no trace, do I make myself clear?"

"Crystal boss, leave it to me"

We carefully made our way around to the rear of the building. The brambles ripped at our clothes, clawing like the fingers of some hateful demon. I pushed through, several insects flew up and away, no doubt shocked by the intrusion into their quiet and peaceful existence. It wasn't long before we were looking through the dirty and streaked window at the rear of the building. I had failed to notice on my previous visit, but on the inside of the window was a steel mesh, bolted to the frame.

"Not getting through that boss, not without breaking something, I am sure. Might be better trying to force the lock on the door at the front"

"We can't damage anything Ken, we need to get in and out without them ever knowing"

"Well, that's exactly what I am going to do boss. That lock on the front door, it's just a simple garage lock, I can pick that in an instant. When you live the life I do, you need to get into the odd garage, stay out of the winter cold, if you know what I mean"

"So, you can open that door without any damage"

"Piece of piss boss, two-minute job. Come on, let's get doin', then off to the pub"

We scrambled back to the front, Ken squatted down at the door, pulled out a couple of pieces of wire and began to pick the lock. It took him no more than thirty seconds before he turned the handle and began to open the door.

"Done, told you it was a fuckin easy job. You leave it to Ken, winner every time"

I couldn't help laughing, I often wondered what a life Ken could have had, if only he had the breaks.

"OK, well let's get in there and see what those files contain. I don't want to hang around here any longer than is necessary. Right Ken, you keep a look out, any sign of anything at all and we scarper, understood?"

"No problems boss, leave it to me"

I made my way under the half open up and over door and into the building proper. It smelt of petrol and oil, old machinery, and weedkiller. It was full of machinery, ride on mowers, two chainsaws, some kind of mechanical roller and a small tractor. The walls were covered in hangers from which dangled spades, forks, hoes, and rakes. It was a proper workman's hideaway, there was a long table at one end, with a kettle, several mugs and a box of half used tea bags.

Under the window sat the dirty woodworm infested desk. It was once the pride and joy of some office worker, local solicitor, or medical receptionist, but no more. Stacked on it were several box files, I rushed over to examine what, if anything they contained.

The first one was labelled, 'fuel and oil', that contained several recent invoices and till receipts but nothing more than that. The next two were empty, apart from old spiders' webs and a copy of Playboy.

The fourth contained a register, thick and heavy with a red leather cover and gold edged pages. I opened it up and examined the slightly off-white pages within. They were divided into columns, 'date of burial', 'instructed by', 'place of burial' and total buried.

The dates ranged from about ten years ago up to the present day. The 'instructed by' column contained mainly the name Richard. Totals were always even, two or occasionally four. It was the 'place of burial' that intrigued me most. That column was exclusively annotated, 'plot 19'. I counted the numbers in the 'total buried' column and that totalled twenty-four. I ran my fingers through my hair, twenty-four people buried in the same plot, perhaps it just meant the same graveyard?

Also, why always even numbers, people do die together, a car crash, suicide, house fire, but all these burials were even numbers, that seemed a bit odd to say the least. Was I just trying to make a story, connecting two and two together and coming up with five? Could these burials be the next group of lovers in the sand? Were the even numbers a man and a woman buried in a perpetual embrace, each naked apart from a ring made by Ms Greenwoods father? I searched the rest of the files and a couple of manky draws beneath but there was nothing else of interest, just the red leather-bound register.

I stood there for a few moments, contemplating what to do next. I couldn't take the register, that would alert the group. I could take some photos on my phone, but would DI Smith be persuaded by that? Ok Lee, do something, make a decision, I decided to take the photos, it was all I could do. As I pulled my phone out of my pocket it began to ring. Without checking the screen, I put it to my face and answered.

"Lee Hunter"

"Lee, where the hell are you, you said you would be back in five minutes, that was an hour ago"

"Ups, sorry Sharron, erm, I met one of my informants, he has some hot news about the case, you know, bodies on the ninth"

"I don't care if he knows the location of the Arc of the bloody Covenant, get back to your office now"

"Yep, on my way, don't worry DS Shacklady, I am in a public place"

I pressed 'end call' and stood there, not exactly a public place I had to admit. However, I did have some information, so I took loads of photos and placed the register back into the box file and Ken and I carefully left.

We hadn't got ten yards down the little lane when I heard the approach of a vehicle coming in our direction. I couldn't see anything through the gloom, but it was certainly approaching and at a rate of knots.

"Boss, get off the road, into cover"

I didn't need to be asked twice. I threw myself into the laurel bushes at the side of the road and scrambled down into a shallow ditch. Ken appeared next to me, panting and looking a little scared.

"Just a coincidence boss or have we triggered an alarm?"

"I think it's just a coincidence Ken, I can't imagine anyone would go to the trouble of fitting an alarm and in any case, how the hell did they get here so quickly?"

It wasn't more than a few seconds before a white Ford Transit van went rushing past, throwing up dust and small stones as it did so. Whoever was inside was certainly in a rush. Unfortunately, I didn't get the chance to see who it was, but I guessed it must have been Tom Toc and his assistant.

"Right Ken, let's get the hell out of here whilst we have the chance"

Ken sprung out of the bushes like a gazelle being chased by a lion. He turned and started to run up the lane in his green parker coat, dirty grey track suit and old trainers. I followed not daring to look behind me just in case we were being tailed. My heart was pounding, and I soon realised just how unfit I had become. We had to reach my car though, or at least get off the lane before the van returned.

"Boss, it's coming back, that bloody van, we need to get off the road again"

I turned to look back down the lane, Ken was right, that crunching noise made by the tyres on the ground was getting louder. I looked to my left and right, this time we hadn't been so lucky. All up and down the side of the lane was impenetrable brambles and wild roses, there was no chance we could jump into that lot. Should we run up the lane in the direction we were going, or try and make it back to the laurel bushes and relative safety.

"Boss come on for fucks sake, we need to get out of here and quick"

I turned to see Ken at least another ten yards further up the lane. He was in full flight, sprinting away from me. I took off after him but almost immediately stumbled over a rock and my ankle turned over, sending a burning pain raging through my body. I fell to the ground and rolled over a couple of times. The dust engulfed me, making me cough and splutter.

I tried to get back to my feet but as soon as I put any weight on my damaged ankle, I folded and fell back to the ground. Ken stopped and looked back, he then began to move back in my direction.

"Boss, what's happened, we need to get away and quick"

"It's my ankle Ken, I can't put any weight on it, it's really screwed up"

"Get up boss, I will help, let's get as far as we can"

He pulled me to my feet, and we hobbled away, but it was not going to be fast enough. The van was approaching with incredible rapidity, it was almost upon us. My head was pounding with the fear and my ankle with increasing pain.

"Ken, just go, take my phone and show it to DI Smith, show her the pictures"

"I am not leaving you here, no way"

"Ken, we are not going to make it like this, at least you can get the evidence to the Police. If you stay with me then nothing gets out, and all of this will have been in vain"

"Fuck that boss, we both get out of here, so let's keep going"

He dragged me to my feet again, we stumbled up the lane but in only seconds the white van would be upon us and discovery would be certain. I fell a couple more times but, on each occasion, Ken hauled me upright. I could sense the van only yards away, we needed to get to cover right now, there was no more time.

I wasn't aware of any great changes to the brambles and hedgerow either side of the track. Without warning however, Ken pulled me towards the tiniest gap in the green and brown tangled web. He shoved me through, brambles, spines and wild rose thorns slashing at my skin. I felt a strong shove between my shoulder blades, propelling me deeper into the morass and chaos of the unfettered undergrowth.

Before I could protest, I found myself face down on the moss-covered ground. I tried to look behind me, attempting to find out where Ken was, but he was nowhere to be seen. At that precise moment, I heard the white van arrive. It stopped just beyond the undergrowth where I was laying. Two doors opened and then slammed shut, a familiar voice rang out, it was Tom Toc the grave digger.

"Oy you, what the hell are you doing down here, this is private you know"

"Sorry boss, I got lost like, I was looking for somewhere to sleep for the night. Don't suppose you have a few quid to spare, just for some food"

That voice was undoubtedly Ken but then another voice, it sounded familiar, perhaps the man who questioned me the last time I was here, I think his name was Richard.

"Listen you dirty twat, I don't know what the hell you are doing out here, but you best fuck off before we do you"

"Just looking for somewhere to sleep, that's all"

"Well just piss off, and do it now"

"Will do boss, on my way"

Then I heard Tom Toc speak again, this time his tone was more menacing.

"How the hell did you get out here anyway? It would take a couple of days to walk here from the centre of town"

"People like me are always on the move boss, it's what we do"

"I understand that, but why walk out here, into the middle of nowhere?"

"I don't know the area, like I said, I just got lost"

There was the sound of scuffling, feet being dragged, muffled cries. Then the sound of punches being thrown, material tearing. I needed to get out there, Ken was obviously being attacked, he didn't stand a chance being faced with two fit men.

"Now fucking tell me what you were doing out here. There will be more of that if you don't, or even worse"

"Told you boss, I was..........."

There was more sounds of fighting, thuds and slapping, Ken was paying the price for my stupidity. If only I had done what DI Smith had told me to do, if only DS Shacklady was standing here with us. It was time I did something about this situation, wholly of my making. I pulled the phone from my pocket and quickly called up DS Shacklady.

"Lee where the hell are you? Deborah is doing her nut, she will have me back on traffic patrol tomorrow if you don't come back"

I whispered in a low voice, "Sharron, I am on the old lane at the back of the parish church, near to the Creighton-Ward place. My life is in danger, get here now. I have some photos, evidence of murders and mass graves"

There was a long silence, "What, how the hell……"

"Never mind Sharron, get someone here now otherwise I am a goner"

I didn't get the chance to say anything more, I felt a strong hand wrapping itself around my ankle and dragging me out of my hiding place. I tried to kick myself free, but the iron grip was way too strong.

"Well Tom, look what we have here, another tramp looking for somewhere to sleep, or a bloody meddlesome private detective?"

"Looks like the later Steve, I think we load them both into the van, take them to the big house, see what the boss says"

"I think that's a great idea Tom, maybe we kick them half to death first, might be fun"

"So long as you don't kill them, we can't question two dead interfering bastards now, can we?"

I looked up, Tom Toc and his accomplice were standing directly over me. Tom was holding what looked like a spade handle, and in my mind, he was prepared to use it, without hesitation,

Behind them was the white van and leaning up against it was a blood-stained smelly Ken.

"Now fuck whit, what are we to do with you? The boss is going to beat you badly, no doubt about that, even if you tell us what you were doing here. I have seen you before, nosing about, don't know what you think you are going to find. It's a graveyard and an old church not the Kremlin, no state secrets in that place"

With that he levelled a kick into my rib cage. The pain was extreme, my breath seemed to disappear. It was replaced by an overwhelming panic as I gasped to re inflate my lungs. Another kick smashed into me, I tasted blood, coughed violently, I tried to roll away, but I couldn't move.

"Go on Tom, smash his face in with that shaft, let's see him get up once you have hit him a few times"

Tom Toc took a step towards me, and without hesitation, brought the shaft down at me. I was able to move just enough to prevent the blow from hitting my head, instead it thudded into my shoulder. He swung the thick shaft upwards once more, this time he wouldn't miss.

"Go on Tom, let him have it, smash his fucking head open"

He started to bring the shaft hammering down, but before it hit, I caught sight of a familiar green parker coat appear behind him. It was Ken, blood streaming from his nose and a cut above his right eye. There was a glint of something shiny in his hand, he pushed it into the back of tom Toc. This caused my assailant to scream, stand upright and drop the shaft. Ken struck again and again, plunging the knife into the back of Tom Toc, bright red blood flying in all directions.

There was a moment of silence, almost like someone had pressed pause as everyone apart from Ken was taken aback by what was happening. Ken pushed the now critically injured Toc to one side and launched himself at his accomplice.

He fell backward as Ken crashed into him, they rolled away towards the other side of the track. This was my opportunity to join in and fight for my life and the life of Ken. It was probably the adrenalin, but the pain in my ankle was no longer affecting me, neither was the pain from my damaged ribs.

I stumbled upright, picked up the now bloodstained shaft from the lifeless body of Tom Toc, and made my way to where Ken was fighting for his life. By the time I reached the two men, Ken was laying on his back with the other man sitting on his chest, with a small rock in his right hand.

There was no time to think, no time to consider the implications of my next move. I swung the shaft as hard as I could, catching the man on the back of the head. There was a sickening crack as it impacted, he shook just for a second, and then fell limp on top of Ken.

Ward 4F, Southport Hospital.

I opened my eyes with a jolt, there was a blinding light, people standing around me. What was that smell, it smelled like, like a hospital, how the hell did I get here? My eyes started to focus, my hearing began to return. I blinked several times, a man with a stethoscope around his neck was on one side of the bed, there were two other people on the other side.

"Nice to see you back with us Mr Hunter, my name is Doctor James. When they brought you in, we had to carry out an emergency operation on you. Seems you had a couple of broken ribs, both poking into your lung. Dam lucky chap if you ask me, but you will be fine, bit sore for a few days, just take things easy"

I stared back at the young man, I was trying to comprehend what he had just said. I think I kind of remembered a fight, an old church, rolling around in the undergrowth, or was that just adream?

Then one of the other people spoke, I looked straight at her, it was DI Smith. Whilst the aftereffects of the anaesthetic and the morphine pain relief were still fuddling my brain, I could completely understand the look on her face.

"Lee Hunter, I am sick of visiting you in hospital, the last time I came to your bedside you had been shot. This time you were nearly beaten to death, and all because you didn't do what I told you to do. You are a menace to yourself, my officers and to my job prospects. You have no bloody idea what problems you have caused me, the rollockings I have had, and none of it was my fault"

I looked up at DI Deborah Smith, my head had certainly cleared somewhat after that broadside. Standing next to her was DS Sharron Shacklady. I must admit to feeling somewhat embarrassed, and very guilty at the trouble that I had inevitably caused her also.

"Deborah, look I am sorry……"

"You shut up and listen to me Lee bloody Hunter, from now on you are under my strict and complete control at all times, do I make myself clear? You will do as I say, you will never deviate from the plan, no matter what the consequences might be. If you dare do anything without telling me first, I will throw you in jail for obstruction, attempted murder, assault with a deadly weapon and anything else I can cook up"

"Wait a minute Sharron, did you say attempted murder?"

"Yes, that dam fool mate of yours stabbed one Mr Tom Toc in the back. He isn't dead but the medics tell me that it is a bloody miracle he is still alive. He is going to need another operation or two before they dare let him out of hospital. As for his friend, you managed to crack his skull and give him a severe concussion.

Now I am willing to believe what Ken told us, you were assaulted and were just defending yourselves. As for what I do about that, let's wait until the other two wake up and hear their stories. This could get very messy for you two Lee, very messy indeed"

"How's Ken?"

"He's fine, a broken nose and several bruises and cuts, but he will be ok. We took him into custody straight from A and E. He is locked up in the cells, we have de contaminated him in the showers, and given him his methadone, he is sleeping like a baby"

"He was defending me Deborah, no more than that"

"Ok, let's see what happens when the other two wake up. Now, Sharron tells me you made a phone call just before the gunfight at the OK corral scene on the lane. You mentioned something about photographs and evidence of murder and burials. Can I assume this is in connection with that lunatic theory of yours re' the Creighton-Wards?"

"It's not some lunatic theory Deborah, I am certain in my own mind what is happening. The Creighton-Wards are killing, they have been burying them on what is now the new 9th hole, but since the cabling work in the 70's, they have now swopped to the old 9th. That's where you will find more bodies, I can assure you of that. If you pass me my phone, I will email all the photos I took, that should secure you a search warrant, I am sure"

"Look Lee, if those photos say, the Creighton-Wards buried ten people here in this hole, then that might get me permission to dig. If it's just a load of entries in a book without any specifics, then they will shut me down before I even make the call to Adele and the county archelogy department. If you think that you are going to nail them, without any indisputable evidence, then you are pissing in the wind, they are powerful Lee, very powerful indeed"

She was right of course, I needed something more substantial, but what? The photos from the red leather-bound register were important, but they were part of a picture, not the whole story. So, what would open this case up, how could I get some real traction in the investigation? I needed that 'indisputable' link as DI Smith put it, that photo with a face, the CCTV image, a piece of DNA. It had to be absolutely watertight, incontrovertible, absolutely certain.

The Committee Room.

"I would like to bring this meeting to order if I may"

The room fell into silence, those present, around forty men, all sat down. The leader of the meeting remained standing, fingering the large gemstone at the centre of his collar. From his place on the low podium, he presided over the assembly.

"By now you will all be aware of the meddling of one Lee Hunter. He has managed to disrupt our organisation and hospitalise two of our most valued employees. Hunter has been warned on numerous occasions about his interference. We have even taken his PA into our care and made it abundantly clear what will happen if he doesn't back off. This however seems to have had little effect on his conduct to date.

I am informed he is presently in Southport Hospital, and due to be released in the next 48 hours. The question is what do we do next with this loathsome worm? Do we leave him to wander around in our affairs, probably with little or no affect. Do we warn him again, in all probability that will be a waste of time. I would like to gain the thoughts of the members before any decision is made"

A low mumble spread amongst those present, conversations moved about the room, angry words, stern agreements. Two men stood, they respectfully waited for the leader of the meeting to call them to speak.

"Yes, Brother Forbes, what have you to say?"

"Brother Principal, I thank you for the opportunity to speak. After consulting with some fellow brothers here, the most appropriate action would be to get rid of Lee Hunter, once and for all. Whilst he has no evidence or real information about us, eventually he will happen by luck or judgement upon something of note"

"I thank you Brother Forbes, before I ask for a show of hands, I would call upon Senior Brother Jones to speak"

"Thank you, Brother Principal. The conversations I have had would concur with those of Brother Forbes. Get rid of Hunter before he finds out something that might prejudice our organisation and its members. We all agree that this should be done without delay and in a manner that would not lead to any suspicion falling upon us"

The Principal smiled and nodded his head. He bent down and quietly discussed matters with the other men sat on the podium, before standing upright once more.

"I thank you all for your input and to be honest, concurring with my own thoughts. I will ask for arrangements to be made this very afternoon for the removal of Lee Hunter. I will ask for this to be completed in a timely manner, so as not to interfere with the ceremony of raising my successor in two days' time.

Further to that, since a raising is very rare, we have decided to use Jan Talbot, Hunters PA as the main participant. We feel that this will enhance our reputation with the master upon high, demonstrating to him our utter obedience. For those who have not witnessed a raising, in order to seal the appointment of your new Brother Principal, a human sacrifice is carried out.

This is not the same as our normal ceremony where a marriage is carried out between a man and a woman. A raising involves the sacrifice on just one person. This alternates between a man and a woman, and since at my raising twenty years ago, it was a man, this time it will be a woman. Extra glory will be gained from the sacrifice of Jan Talbot because of the pain her death will cause Hunter and any associates he has.

I will therefore reiterate the need for all participant to ensure that you are well versed in the ceremony, and your parts therein"

The meeting was then brought to order before being officially closed. The members broke off, with an air of excitement and anticipation, regarding the raising in just two days' time. Once the room had emptied, the Principal took his Samsonite brief case from the floor and placed it carefully on the desk in front of him. After clicking the two latches open, he removed his mobile, opened it up and selected the name Kevin Stone.

"Good afternoon sir, what can I do for you?"

"Good afternoon Mr Stone. I have a little job for you, concerning one Lee Hunter"

Kevin Stone laughed, he had been expecting this call for the past few days, especially after the incident involving his old friend, Tom Toc.

"Let me guess sir, you want him disposing of?"

"My thoughts exactly Mr Stone, and a soon as possible please, I know how expert you are at these things"

"Don't suppose you know where he is now?"

"Ward 4, Southport Hospital. I have been told he will be there for another 48 hours or so"

"Might be a bit tricky getting rid of him in a hospital sir, it's a bit public. If I can confirm when he is being discharged, I will follow him and undertake the task soon after"

"I will leave it up to you Mr Stone, you are the professional at these things. I would like it done before the ceremony if possible. Also, I need you to explain to Hunter exactly what will happen to his PA during the raising of my successor. Don't spare any elements, none of the details, he needs to know why she died and the agony she went through"

"Don't worry sir, I will make sure he is cognisant of all that will happen, down to the tiniest detail. The last thought that will go through his mind before I kill him will be, it was all my fault"

"Excellent Mr Stone, I trust you will be at the raising"

"I certainly will sir, and I will bring the video of the vary last moments of Hunters life"

Ms Greenwoods Residence.

Ms Janice Greenwood looked back at the middle room where all her father's and grandfather's documents were stored. She was now confident that everything was back in its place, and the only thing missing was the main payments ledger.

Whilst she was deeply shocked and very depressed at the events surrounding the break-in and the loss of such a valuable document, there had been some benefits from putting the storeroom back together. For example, she had found a scrap book she had assembled whilst at school. It had fallen behind one of the large bookcases. Looking through it brought back many fond memories from her childhood. There was a file containing some notes and memos from her grandfather. She had found this stuffed into the back of an obscure folder named, second hand rings.

There was also a small manila envelope found behind one of the drawers in her father's desk. It must have been inadvertently pushed out of the back of the draw many years ago, never to be seen again. There was no title or writing on the envelope, but it contained several faded black and white photographs. There was a couple of faces, she turned each one over, the writing was very discoloured and indistinct. She would need to get them under a stronger light to see if she could decipher what they said. There was a bleached photograph of a large building under construction. The faded writing on the reverse looked like, 'a new beginning' or perhaps, 'a new building'.

There was a picture of what appeared to be a Mayoral chain of office, a grand creation, and one of great cost. It had an ornate and heavy gold chain and at its centre was a bright platinum star inset with diamonds and what looked like a huge green emerald. She turned the picture over. Again, the words were faded, almost indecipherable but this time readable, at least in part.

MADE   PRINCIPAL
IN   ACEME   OF THE PREVIOUS
COLLAR.

She stared at the photo for a while, nothing in her records suggested such a commission. The cost of this work would have been huge, tens of thousands, or more likely hundreds of thousands of pounds, even back in her father's time. The emerald alone was three or four inches across and then there were the diamonds. Why hadn't her father recorded this, there were many records of work for just a few pounds, so why not the collar?

She put the photos back into the envelope and dropped them into her bag. She had promised to visit Lee this evening. It was truly miserable being in hospital, so a few chocolate treats would help him pass a few more hours.

Ward 4, Southport Hospital.

"So, my father's records store is back in one piece Lee, it's been a long job but well worth it"

Whilst I was very pleased to see Ms Greenwood, the story of her girlhood scrap book and her grandfather memos were not exactly thrilling me. I was really appreciative of the chocolate and packets of Pringles though, now that had really cheered me up.

I was glad to see her, she had been through a lot, most of which was of my doing. It wasn't that long ago since she had been sitting in a similar hospital bed, after the break in at her house. She seemed more relaxed now, she was a strong woman and not one to bend in the face of adversity.

"Find out anything new Janice, any more details about the case?"

"Nothing new Lee, found some old photos but I can't decipher what is written on the back though. Oh yes, and some old keys, I don't have a clue what the keys open, I will try and find a lock, might be something about the house. More than likely the lock which they once opened has long since vanished. As for the photos, I brought them over, perhaps you could have a look, might keep you busy whilst you are confined here in the hospital"

She reached into her dark brown leather handbag and brought out the tatty manila envelope. She showed me the photographs one by one, handling each one with reverence and care.

The first one she showed me was of a huge collar, the photo was black and white, but I could tell it was gold with a white gold or platinum centre incrusted in diamonds. It was set with a huge gemstone, which Janice assured me was an emerald.

"I can't quite make out what it says on the back Lee, 'made principal in aceme of the previous collar'. I thought perhaps it means, made in principle in replacement of the previous Mayoral collar?"

I looked at it for quite some time. Her father must have been a very well-educated man, that English didn't make a lot of sense. Also, that most certainly was no Mayoral collar. To start with, everyone I had ever seen had the town or city coat of arms proudly emblazoned on it, there was no such emblems here.

"What makes you think it's a Mayor's collar Janice?"

"Well, who else would have the money to commission that sort of thing?"

"That's no Mayor's collar Janice, I would put money on it. I think that's some sort of badge of honour, maybe an officer of an organisation, the chairman, something like that. What else have you got?"

"There is this, it's a half-completed building, I think it says a new beginning, or perhaps a new building"

She handed me the photo. As soon as I saw it something triggered in my mind. I stared at it for several seconds, I had seen this somewhere before, but where?

"Have you any idea where this building is Janice?"

"Sorry Lee, I have not seen it before"

Next came the two photos of men, very Victorian, dressed in their high collars and dinner jackets. The writing on the back of the first was impossible to read, maybe it said Sir John, perhaps not. The second was a little better and in the bright lights of Ward 4, I could make out some of the writing. It said, Brother Principal, then there was a name, it was indistinct, perhaps Edward, at his raising. It was then something struck me, I looked back at the photo of the collar. The words on that and the last photo were similar. Putting my rather laughable crossword powers to good use, I started to make a little sense of the missing words.

"Janice, could the wording on the photo of the collar read, made for the Brother Principal, in replacement of the previous collar? I know it's a bit of a long shot but this last photo, I think it reads, Brother Principal Edward, at his raising"

"You have lost me Lee, Principal Brother, raising?"

"I think these photos are linked, not just a random collection, stuffed in an envelope one hundred years ago. What if they are to celebrate the new collar, made in replacement of the old damaged one. It was made for the raising of Brother Principal Edward, and also the commencement of the new building, or new beginning"

"That's a rather random connection Lee, are you sure? They may have just been some odd photos at the end of a roll of film"

"I don't think so Janice, why put these photos in their own envelope, no I am sure they are connected. What if, and I know this is a bit of a stretch, that photo is Edward Creighton-Ward, at his raising to Brother Principal. That collar is for some kind of organisation, I would put money on it being a cult, a very secret organisation, bent on murder and sacrifice"

"Lee, I think they have been pumping too much morphine into you. You are hallucinating, you need to de-tox and as soon as possible"

"No Janice, I have never been more lucid, and another thing, that building, I know where I have seen it before. It's the bloody Southport and Lancashire Golf Course club house, just after construction began. It doesn't say 'a new beginning', it says, 'a new building'.

It's all starting to make sense, the burials on the ninth hole, the Creighton-Wards gifting the land. This is certainly Edward Creighton-Ward, the missing man at the centre of all of this dam mess. We need to show this lot to DI Smith, I am certain she will get her search warrant now, she has to!"

"Lee, they are just a random collection of old photos. They don't mean anything, there is no specific context or explanations. They might have been my father's friends, the local wine tasting club, a load of old golfers, who knows, I certainly don't. If you passed this story on to Detective Inspector Smith, she would throw you out of her office.

My advice would be to sit tight, continue your investigations and see what else crops up. I am sure you will crack this case sooner or later. If you try and make something out of nothing, then any help you might be looking for will simply disappear"

Talk about throwing a bucket of cold water over me. It took me a few minutes to calm down and see the reason in what she was saying. Ms Janice Greenwood was absolutely correct, if it wasn't credible, it wasn't going to fly. I had to find more, it had to be indisputable, beyond any reasonable doubt.

We passed the next hour or so chatting, speculating on the keys and a safe they might open containing a million pounds worth of jewels. Oh, yes, and eating my chocolate and drinking the coke, with a little scotch added that Deborah had brought me. It was rather pleasant really, a nice distraction from the order and routine of Ward 4. Eventually she said her goodbyes and left, with a promise of a nice home cooked dinner when I got out, nice!

I was just about to wander off to the TV room when a familiar figure entered the small six bed ward. He wandered over to me sporting a very large grin and holding a huge bunch of flowers.

"Well as I live and breathe, Lee Hunter, so glad to see you alive and well"

I couldn't believe who I was looking at, the shock on my face must have been obvious.

"Don't worry Lee, I am not here to ask for my money back, I just wanted to see that you were doing ok. I heard all about your fight with those two idiots at the back of the church. I used to go down that lane when I was at school, drinking cider and smoking Rothman's fags. Listen, if I can do anything for you, all you need to do is ask, you know that don't you"

I couldn't help but laugh, the man standing in front of me was Tony Bianchi, or fat Tony. The very same gangster who was going to kill me not that long ago, unless I paid back the 30k I owed him.

"Sorry Tony, you have taken me a little by surprise. I didn't expect a visit from you, nice as it is to see you"

"Oh, don't mention it Lee, ever since you rumbled Mr Brau and the bent cops, life has been wonderful for me. They all got life, all his business ended up in my hands, and I am making a bloody mint, sweet.

So, you are my most favourite person right now, well if you don't include my wife. Anyway, she won't be around much longer, and neither will that bloody gym instructor she's shagging. Did you know what they do together on the parallel bars?"

"I don't Tony and to be honest, I am not sure I want to"

"Yeah, good thinking Lee, mind you, I wish I was young enough to do that. Anyway, I have a plan for the both of them, and it doesn't include getting divorced"

He leant back and laughed, I wasn't absolutely sure what he meant by that comment, but I could certainly guess!

"So, I brought you some flowers and, in my pocket, I have a bottle of eighteen-year-old Oban single malt. It costs a bloody fortune, but you get what you pay for, that's for certain. I will slip it into your bed side cabinet, don't want those nurses taking it off you, do we?"

"Thank you so much Tony, I really appreciate that"

I can't really remember how long we chatted for, the Oban slipped down very nicely. The bottle was half gone before Tony decided he had to leave.

"Listen, my driver will be getting pretty bored outside Lee. Sitting in the Rolls is very comfortable, but the view when you aren't moving can get a bit tedious. So, is there anything I can do for you, all you need to do is ask? I can have those two idiots who put you in here disposed of if you want. I can have them taken out into the Irish Sea and dumped overboard. See how well they swim with a concrete block tied to their ankles"

I did laugh but I knew Tony was deadly serious, he was a man of his word and that was not always a good thing. Violence and intimidation were his stocking trade, fortunately I was in his good books, at least for now.

"There is something you could help me with Tony, and if we get it sorted out, it would be worth a million brownie points for you in the local community"

"Sounds interesting Lee, what's the proposal?"

"Well firstly, I have some pretty serious death threats hanging over me. I am certain that someone will have a pop, sometime in the very near future"

"Oh, that's easily sorted Lee. I will have a man looking after your every move within the hour. One of my own bodyguards, carries a vintage Walther PPK, knows how to handle himself. Nice guy by the name of Chris Davis, no one is getting past him"

"Thanks, I appreciate that. The next problem I have is persuading the local Police to get a search warrant. I am certain that bodies are being buried on the Southport and Lancashire golf course"

"I am a member there Lee, we don't go around killing members you know"

"No, I am sure you don't, but this goes back nearly one hundred years, and maybe more. I have information regarding the Creighton-Ward family and their involvement in numerous murders. They are disposing of the bodies on the course, and more recently, on the old ninth hole which was moved in the 70's.

The Police won't even try to get a warrant, they say the family will simply block anything they attempt to do. I guess I can sympathise with that, but it doesn't help solve the problem, how do we get to dig, legally, on the old ninth hole?"

"Why was the hole moved in the first place Lee?"

"I was told that a new electricity mains cable had to be installed. That cable was going to run right down the ninth fairway and green. It was decided to move the hole to another part of the course, rather than trying to work around the installation"

"Ok, I see your problem. I assume you don't have any cast iron evidence, otherwise the Police would be able to get a search warrant"

"Well not cast-iron Tony, but I know I am right on this. If only we could dig that old fairway and green, I am certain we will find bodies and plenty of them. Once that is done, getting a second search warrant for the Creighton-Ward house will be easy. That's where the killings are taking place. I am sure they are ritualistic, so somewhere on that estate will be some kind of shrine. A killing place, where their sick perverted rituals are carried out"

"Lee, if you don't mind me saying, this is one fucked up story. I am not surprised the Police won't try to get a search warrant, they will get laughed out of court. Next you will be telling me of some errant relative of the family who is running all of this from some turret at the top of the manor house"

"Not quite Tony, but there is a missing person in all of this, Edward Creighton-Ward, I can't find him anywhere"

"Lee, you need to listen to what you are saying. This is like some cheap horror film you can watch on a Saturday night on Channel 4. Missing family member, mass murders, ritual killings, next you will be telling me there are vampires involved"

Tony was right of course. It did sound a little far-fetched, but he wasn't involved, he didn't have all the facts. He hadn't seen Ms Greenwood's files, he didn't know of the break in at her place and the missing ledger.

Also, the rings and the connection with the family, that was beyond doubt! He didn't know that my PA, Jan Talbot had been taken. Additionally, there were the death threats, if everything I had was just nonsense, why had someone gone to the trouble of threatening my life?

"I can see from your face Lee that this is something you believe in. So, who the hell am I to run you down, if I can help, then so much the better. Especially if I can get some kudos from the local community, might even lead to some big contracts"

"Thanks Tony, that's a big lift, I was beginning to think I would never get any movement on this. How do you think you can help, what can you do that the Police can't?"

He leant back and laughed again. "Lee Hunter, I am a man of considerable resources, and some might say, cunning criminality. Now, one of my, how can I put it, mainly legitimate business involves ground works. You know, digging trenches, laying drains and cables.

How about I write to the golf club, say that the mains gas pipe has been leaking. The one that runs just outside the west boundary of the course. That land is common land, so we can pitch up, park a couple of vans, get some guys walking around in hi vis jackets"

"So, how's that going to help?"

"That west boundary of the course is where the old ninth fairway and hole will have been, I am sure of that. There is no other place it could have been sited, nowhere, there isn't any room. It could have been closer to the club house, but that would have been out of sequence as you moved around the course. The north side backs on to a large housing estate and railway, it can't possibly be there. The eastern side of the course is where the ninth hole is now. So, the western boundary is where it used to be sited, simple"

"So how do you know that the gas main is leaking?"

"It isn't, because there isn't one, well not for a couple of miles further inland. Thing is, I am guessing no one else knows that either. My dad you to say, 'just act daft and no one will question you'. If my guys turn up in proper company vans, work gear and a few hi-tech gadgets, no one will even notice them, believe me"

"And how does that find any bodies on the golf course?"

"This time of year, it goes dark very early. By five it will be pitch black, one of my guys can jump the boundary fence, go and poke around, dig a few exploratory holes, just like Time Team. If he finds any bodies or parts thereof, we report it to the local cops"

"That's a bit risky isn't it, trespassing, obtaining evidence and obtaining proof without a search warrant. They aren't freely allowing access to their land, and there is nothing obvious that might lead to a search"

"There you go Lee, thinking like a cop again. You need to think like a villain from time to time, it's liberating you know.

My men aren't searching anywhere, they are just checking the pipe, simple. Oh yes Officer, we were checking for leaks and came across these suspicious looking holes, maybe graves, so we thought it best to inform you"

"But there is no gas pipe"

"Lee, please, you need to think beyond the obvious. There is no gas pipe and no leaks, but no one will ever check. If those bodies are there, the cops will have a bloody field day, and leaky gas pipes will be the last thing anyone will be questioning"

"And if there is nothing Tony at least no harm done, and I can move on"

"Precisely, but if you are right, we just sit back, act daft and let the local Murder Squad help themselves. They will be so bloody excited, you won't hear a word from them for months or even years to come.

They will pin a medal on you for your ingenuity and perseverance. I will get a multi-million-pound contract for my hard work and diligence on the 'gas main'. Lee, what could possibly go wrong, just don't mention how we got the contract to investigate the leak in the first place!"

I looked down at the floor, this was madness, there was no way it was going to work. The thing was, I couldn't think of any other way, and Tony was just the man to actually pull something like this off. I drank the last of the Oban in my glass and looked back at Tony.

"Right, get your gas crew together, the sooner we go looking for leaks the better"

Tony started to laugh, I couldn't help myself, I joined in. His huge frame shook, his rosy cheeks wobbled. We laughed until we cried, well until the Ward Sister came storming in. That laser like stare soon put a stop to our joviality.

"Right Lee, looks like I need to leave. Chris will be here as soon as you are discharged, just call me when you know for sure. I will get a team together, hopefully we can wrap this up in a couple of days"

We chuckled again, Tony turned and left. That visit had been very interesting indeed and I still had half a bottle of 18-year-old Oban in my locker, wonderful.

The Derelict Pub Car Park.

The night had closed in, it was already frosty and very cold. Kevin Stone stood at the side of his classic bright red Alpha Romeo GTv6. His breath was turning to great billows of steam as he exhaled. His contact should already be here, he felt agitated standing in the car park, and very vulnerable.

He had a job to do, his boss had instructed him to get rid of Lee Hunter. He had not been specific, but Kevin was fully aware of the connotations of those instructions. He was also aware of what would happen if Lee Hunter did not disappear, and very soon. Kevin enjoyed all the privileges and frills of his employment, but it came at a cost. That cost was absolute obedience, failure would result in replacement and probable death.

He rubbed his hands together and blew hot breath on them in a futile attempt to keep them warm. If this guy didn't turn up in the next five minutes he would leave. The car park was quiet and dark but subject to the occasional visit from drug dealers and users. The pub, once the centre of the local community, was now derelict and vandalised. It stood like a dark and empty shell, waiting for the next futile attempt to turn it into a successful business.

He was just about to leave when an Audi A8 pulled into the car park. It drove straight to where Kevin was parked. This was his man, and he had done business with him on several occasions in the past. He wasn't the cheapest, but he was reliable and very discreet.

The passenger window slowly descended, the smell of cigar smoke wafted out into the night sky, classic FM playing quietly on the car's stereo. The dark figure of the driver remained motionless, whilst awaiting the arrival of Kevin from his place in front of the old pub.

As he bent down by the open window, he could see the man, sitting in the driver's seat. He was wearing a sheepskin coat, silk shirt and tie, and dark leather driving gloves. He didn't turn to look at Kevin but stared straight ahead, as is still driving the car.

"I didn't think you were coming, it bloody freezing out here"

The man didn't speak, he just held up his left hand.

"Bach's Brandenburg Concerto, it's a three-movement orchestral work. It was completed in around 1721 for the Prussian Royal family, wonderful. It brings tears to my eyes every time I hear it"

Kevin squatted at the side of the car whilst the music played and finally faded away.

"Now Mr Stone, I have a selection of what you requested, have you got the money?"

"I have, just a simple 9mm is all I need, nothing fancy"

"I don't do fancy, just good value for money and confidentiality at all times"

"Then let's do the deal, I want to get the hell out of this place, it gives me the chills just being here"

The man didn't speak again, he slowly got out of the car and went to the rear, pressed the button on the cars key fob and the boot sprang open. Inside was a blanket, once removed it revealed six handguns.

"You know the price Mr Stone, we have already agreed that. I would recommend the Berretta, it's very nice, it's not been used before. I can't do you a discount, these types of clean firearms are always in demand, but I will throw in a box of 9mm ammunition, just for good will"

"The Berretta will do me fine, and the box of ammo'. Will you buy the gun back once I have used it?"

"I am always interested in preowned weapons Mr Stone. The price I will pay you will of course be significantly lower than the price today, you do understand that"

"Yeh, no problems, my boss is paying anyway, so I don't give a fuck. Aren't you interested in what I am going to do?"

"Nothing to do with me my friend. If you want to kill someone, rob a bank, or blow your wife's lover to kingdom come, that's your choice, after all, it's a free world"

"Well, this joker is out of hospital tomorrow afternoon. I will follow him home and do the fucker in his house. I will give you a call after that, no need to have the gun in my possession any longer than I need to"

"You know my number Mr Stone, just give me a call"

A Dark Place.

Jan Talbot had been sitting on the hard wooden bed all night. Sometimes crying, occasionally falling asleep, but always shivering with cold and fear. She was naked, apart from a dirty old beach towel that she kept wrapped around herself.

She had lost all sense of time, it could have been the middle of the night or mid-morning. The only illumination was a bright LED bulb hanging centrally from the ceiling, on a short electrical cable. It blazed a clear white light, irritating her eyes, it never went out, never varied in intensity.

The only person she saw was a man by the name of Richard. He opened the door three times a day, checked her over, left some food and water and then left. He hardy spoke and never showed any sign of compassion towards her. This was a truly miserable place, it stunk of despair and death.

She thought back over the past few days, leaving the office, talking to her boss Lee Hunter on the phone, meeting her friends. Much of what followed was blurred or confused. A night out, maybe birthday celebrations, meeting a couple of guys, but in truth, nothing really made sense. She tried to wring some logic out of it, why she had ended up here, but there was nothing. It felt like a nightmare, an episode inserted into her life. It was like watching a horror film, this couldn't be real, but it certainly was.

"Right Jan Talbot", she spoke firmly and in a slow and controlled manner. "You need to get a grip, sitting here wondering what day of the week it is, is not helping. I am sitting in a cell, somewhere, naked with a smelly beach towel wrapped around me. I have been told some story about getting my throat cut, and some ceremony for a new principal. Well, I have no intention of just letting that happen, no way"

Those words, 'throat cut' made her feel nauseous, the terror rose up in her like a wildfire on a dry and dusty moorland. She started to shake, talking to herself wasn't helping, she was at the mercy of whomever came through that door. She began to cry, there was nothing she could do but wait for the inevitable end.

She didn't hear the key turn in the lock, the first thing she noticed was the door open. In walked Richard, a large smile on his face, his eyes glowing with excitement.

"Right Jan, not long now until your ceremony. I need that towel though, the last thing we want is to find you hanging from the light. So, hand that over, there's a good girl"

She looked down at the dirty yellow towel but before she could react, it was ripped away from her, the friction causing her back to burn slightly. She wrapped her arms around herself, trying to cover her nakedness but to little avail.

"I wouldn't worry about being seen naked Jan. When you enter the ceremony, you will be uncovered for everyone to see. When you are tied to the table, they will all gather around. They will be excited to see your body, especially when it's covered in your blood.

Trust me, being naked will be the last of your worries. Just lay back and enjoy the whole thing, especially when that blade slices into your flesh. The brother executioner is an expert. He can make it last hours, cutting into your soft skin, removing parts of your body. They tell me you stop screaming after an hour, the burning pain and the endless torment cause your mind to shut down"

He laughed again turned and moved towards the door.

"Just relax Jan, no one can help you now, your end is set, and nothing can change that"

The door slammed shut. She sat there on the hard wooden bed, hyperventilating, her mind swirling, her whole body shaking uncontrollably. He was right, this was the end, the only thing she had to look forward to now, was an agonising death.

The worst part of all was, in that ceremony when she cried out in terror and pain, no one would even care and no one would come and save her.

Outside Southport Hospital.

The night was cold and windy, I didn't want to go outside, I could see the trees blowing from side to side, the wet carpark glowing in the yellow streetlights. It was one of those 'stay by the fire' nights with a brandy or a hot coffee.

Tonys henchman, Chris Davis was standing right behind me. He was huge, he didn't speak too much but he didn't have to, one look from him and you felt fear. He was well over six feet, powerful shoulders, a rounded chest and with piercing blue eyes. He had very closely shaved dark brown hair and beard. He clearly took his job very seriously indeed, checking every detail of every move I made.

"There is no way we are falling into a trap Mr Hunter", he said in a low and very deliberate manner. "I will check all the routes before we proceed, remember the six 'p's. Perfect preparation prevents piss poor performance. Before we go outside, I am going to check the cars, the route we will take to my vehicle, make sure no one is waiting for us, you wait here"

I didn't have much choice really, I was sitting in a wheelchair and Chris was the man pushing it. I must admit to feeling very alone when he walked through the sliding doors. I wondered if I was actually scared, or all this cloak and dagger stuff had unnecessarily spooked me?

It took about two or three minutes for Chris to return, he didn't have any expression on his face, just a calm and in control demeanour.

"There is a man waiting in a car just outside and to the left. He could be waiting for someone to come out, but he could also be waiting for us. Given that you have had credible death threats, I will assume he is a risk, and we must therefore be very careful. We will move out and to the right, keep your coat over your head so that he cannot readily identify you, do you understand?"

I quickly agreed and covered myself with my coat. It felt somewhat exciting, like playing cops and robbers when I was young. I could feel my heart pounding in my chest, after all, I also took those threats seriously, this situation could be very real indeed.

My destination was a small bungalow just on the south side of the town, near to lane ends. It belonged to fat Tony, probably in payment of a debt. At least it was anonymous and couldn't be connected to me, so I should be safe there, at least in the short term. I just needed time, allow Tonys men to do their work near to the golf course. If they could find some evidence, then DI Smith could get her search warrant and the case would be blown wide open.

We made our way across the carpark. The fine drizzle stung my eyes, I tried to gaze under my coat and into the darkness but to little effect. Whomever was waiting for me was somewhere out there, but it was impossible to see where. It seemed somewhat surreal as we made our way to Chris's waiting car, a huge Mercedes Benze G-Wagon that was parked near to the main exit. It was like some cheap action movie, I had convincing death threats but surely no one was actually going to carry them out. Like DI Smith had said, 'in all probability, they are just trying to scare you". The trouble was, fat Tony was less relaxed about the whole thing. That's why I had one of his heavies pushing my wheelchair, that told its own story, I guess.

We were almost at the G-Wagon when the action started. There was a noise from somewhere behind, Chris stopped and looked around. The noise got louder, a revving engine, perhaps sliding tyres on the wet carpark. It wasn't what you would expect to hear in this type of environment, something was definitely wrong.

He took up station standing right next to me and reached inside his black puffer jacket. Crouching slightly, Chris pulled out a small handgun, stuffed it into his outer pocket and began scanning the night scene.

"What can you see Chris?"

"Nothing as yet, could just be some local yob trying to provoke the security company. They come bombing into places like this, just to see if they can get a reaction from them or even the local police. Seems to have stopped now, let's see if we can get closer to my motor, once inside we will be fine"

His calming words certainly helped my blood pressure settle somewhat, but that was compensated for by the site of that handgun. There was no way that was a legal weapon, and just being near someone armed like that could mean big trouble. I wanted to say something but thought better of it. The last thing I wanted was to distract Chris, especially on this very dark and wintery night.

"Right, let's get a move on, we leave the wheelchair in the carpark, are you capable of getting into the car?"

"Leave it to me Chris, I can manage"

He moved back behind me once again, I could feel the power in his muscles as he pushed me towards the waiting car. I wanted to shout out, make him push faster, the closer we got, the more frightened I became. It wasn't more than a few moments, then we reached the side of the dark grey Mercedes Benz G-Wagon.

The locks clicked off and the internal lights came on. Chris opened the rear passenger door and beckoned me inside, never taking his eyes off the scene, staring deep into the inky blackness. Despite the pain in my back and ribs, I pushed myself out of the chair and up into the leather clad vehicle. The door closed as I sat down, with a satisfying thud, oozing quality and strength.

Chris moved quickly to the driver's door, and despite his size he slid into position with consummate ease. The internal lights dimmed and went out as the engine purred into life. He clicked the gearbox into drive, checked all sides and gently moved off.

"Right, hold tight, I don't intend hanging about"

As he moved towards the exit, I caught site of some lights, somewhere out in the darkness. One minute they were there, the next not, and then once again. Without warning they appeared right next to my door. Chris swerved the vehicle to the right and then to the left. I hung on for dear life, assuming that this might be more than one of the local thugs.

I was pushed back into my seat at the G-Wagon accelerated with some considerable force. The lights appeared once more, this time somewhere behind us. Chris swerved to the left, and then accelerated, I was thrown about, like a child's rag doll. I grabbed at whatever I could, the leading edge of the leather seats, the door handle, whatever came to hand first.

The vehicle swerved again and then stopped violently, I found myself pushing on the passenger seat in front of me. Before I had time to react, I caught site of Chris as he turned and looked backwards out of the rear window. The vehicle accelerated once again, but this time in reverse. This threw me into the footwell between the rear seat and the front passenger seat.

I desperately tried to regain my position but to no avail. The G-Wagon stopped once more and then surged forward, continuing to accelerate, swerving to the right and then away once more.

"Are you ok Mr Hunter? We are out of that carpark now and onto the main road. That twat missed the turn. I think he crashed into one of the lamp posts near to the exit, bloody amateur. What the hell made him think he could get close to me, when will they learn"

I managed to push my throbbing body upright and onto the back seat, this time fastening my seat belt! I couldn't even guess what speed we were doing, but it certainly was way above the speed limit. Strangely I trusted Chris, I desperately hoped that trust was well placed.

"Don't worry Mr Hunter, we will have you at the bungalow in twenty minutes, don't think that clown will be troubling us again"

"I bloody hope not, shit I thought I was going to die"

He laughed, a deep and powerful laugh, "Die Mr Hunter, not with me to protect you, not a bloody chance"

It was then that the situation changed once more. I felt a bump and then a heavier impact on the rear of the vehicle. This caused us to swerve from right to left but Chris managed to gain control over the situation.

"The bastard is back Mr Hunter, he must have seen which direction we took. Hold tight, looks like we have a chase on our hands"

The Mercedes Benze G-Wagon lurched forward, the engine roaring into life once more. Then heavy breaking as we swerved to the right. For one second I thought we were going to turn over, but Chris brought the vehicle back under control. Another burst of acceleration before Chris applied the brakes to maximum effect. It felt like we were going to end up on our nose. I thrust my hands forward, but the seat belt mechanism activated and pulled me back into the seat.

I instinctively braced myself, any moment now I expected an impact from behind, but nothing occurred. We came to a shuddering stop, the anti-lock brakes kicking in, clicking as they did so. Chris opened the side door and turned to me, a look of anger on his face.

"Wait Here Mr Hunter, I am going to deal with this prat, I will be back in a second"

He jumped out of the car and disappeared into the night. I tried to turn in order to see what was happening but the glare of the lights of a vehicle behind us dazzled my vision. I could hear shouting, a car door slamming, there was some movement behind the light, but I couldn't tell what was going on.

Then it happened, two shots, loud cracks ringing out in the night. Did I just hear that, surely it wasn't what I thought it was? This was just a car chase, we just wanted to get away. I wasn't some gangland boss, or international terrorist, things like this didn't happen to people like me, did they? I felt firstly cold and then somewhat nauseous. A few days ago, I was a happy go lucky private detective, things were looking up, all be it in a fairly mundane way. Now I might be part of a fatal shooting, or maybe on the verge of being shot myself.

I braced myself for what was to come, even if Chris had managed to secure the situation, there was no getting away from the fact that I was now part of this. No police detective, magistrate or judge would ever think otherwise. How had it come to this, any moment now I would find out. I would either be an accessory to murder or have two bullets driven into my brain. Either way, I was finished and all for what, some bloody stupid idea and a load of decade old records. Next time, if there was a next time, just keep your dam nose out Hunter, stick to the boring stuff, it's safe.

I sensed someone at the side window, just a few inches from where I was sitting. I wanted to turn and see who it was, but I was frozen to the spot. It felt like I was sat in that position for minutes, not seconds, but I slowly turned, who was the winner, what would happen to me next?

Dusk, next to the Southport and Lancashire golf course.

The afternoon had started to darken as the early winter sunset approached. It was typically cold for the time of year but dry. The pale red and blue sunset had begun over the western rim of the Irish Sea. It was striking in its majesty, a portent of a frosty and freezing night to come. There was a calm descending over the pine woods, the animals of the daylight had now ceased, and the creatures of the night had awoken.

Four white Ford Transit vans sat in a clearing in the trees. They were parked on National Trust land, no access to the public, so no dog walkers to interfere with what they had to do. Each van had a large sign on its side.

NORTHWEST GAS SERVICING - EMERGENCY GAS LEAK TEAM

They were no more than fifty meters from the post and wire boundary fence of the golf course. The vista was one of remote beauty, bracken, young trees, and an abundance of low growing scrub. There was no sign of humanity this far out, just the rustling of the pines and the occasional bird. It was secluded, almost detached from the hustle and bustle of the world beyond. Half a dozen men milled about, all dressed in bright yellow high-vis clothing, carrying shovels, and other equipment.

"So, let's me get this straight boss. We need to cross that boundary fence and start to poke about in the rough ground?"

"That's about it Henry, as I explained, we are looking for potential graves, bodies buried anywhere in this area"

"I don't get it Mr Bianchi, who the hell would bury bodies on a bloody golf course? Someone would see them, it's a stupid idea, they would never get away with it"

"They would get away with it Henry because no one would expect it! Respectable and very old golf club, lots of millionaire members, and this area is miles out of the way. Why the hell would anyone come this far off the main course? It's a long way around the 18 holes anyway. It's one of the longest in Europe, why make your round of golf a hell of a lot longer?

No, when you stand back and just look, it's a perfect place to bury someone. I bet no one has been out here for months or even years. The only guys ever to venture out here will be the groundsmen. Who's to say they aren't the men burying the bodies anyway?"

"Still don't see it boss, why not just take them out into the Irish Sea and throw the bodies overboard?"

"Because Henry, it's ceremonial, these murders are ritualistic. The bodies need to be buried according to their sick rules. That's why they found all those bodies on the other side of the course. Couples buried embracing each other, gold rings, and goodness knows what else"

"Ok, so you think there are graves here, why?"

"It's a long story Henry, but it's a friend of mine, Lee Hunter, I kind of owe him one, but don't ever tell him that. Just get the guys over that fence once it goes dark and start poking around. Use the metal detectors, grub about in that long grass and those brambles. If anyone comes over just say you are looking for that mains gas pipe, that should suffice. My money is on finding something, Lee Hunter is a clever man, and he has a nose for things, you know the kind, he just seems to come up with an answer. Anyway, it's the only real option, Hunter tells me that most of the spare ground around here is marshy and tends to flood, or at least that's what he had been told. So, it's here or nowhere else, easy really"

"Ok Mr Bianchi, leave it with us. As soon as the light goes, we will be over there. I will give you a call if we find something"

The night drew in, covering the men and their machinery in a dark blanket, hiding them from the world. Henry led the group over the wire fence and onto the golf course, the bracken clinging and tearing at their clothes, wrapping it tendrils about them like some alien life form.

They had been told to limit the use of flashlights, but the almost impenetrable undergrowth meant using them became a necessity. Henry looked about, the tangle of mother nature almost reached to his waist, young trees arched above his head.

"Listen guys, there is no way anything is buried out here. You couldn't drive a spade into the ground, let alone dig a bloody grave, it would be impossible. Let's spread out a bit, you never know, we might find a clearing, but I think it's an early night and a pint down the pub"

The guys laughed as they moved off in different directions, hacking away the scrub, pulling the brambles and thorns from their clothes. It was a full two hours before they met up back at the white vans. They were exhausted, some bloody from entanglements with mother nature and all looking forward to a couple of pints and a Chinese takeaway on the way home.

"Right guys", Henry wearily announced, "what have we found, anything suspicious?"

There was a long and uninterrupted silence from the group. It was immediately obvious that they had nothing to report.

"Right, I will ring the boss. To be honest, I didn't think there was anything here, it's too far out of the way and a bloody wilderness. Before I ring him, has anyone got anything else to add?"

"Yeah Henry, I have"

"Go on Simo"

"Before joining Mr Bianchi, I did a load of work around here. I contracted out to the National Trust, planting trees, building footpaths, loads of stuff. I overheard you talking to the boss, saying about flooding on the course. Well Henry, I can say from personal experience that that's far from the truth.

The land around here is sandy and bone dry, even in the winter. Yes, there has been some marshy ground in the past, but that was drained and sorted years and years ago. There is no flooding around these parts, why the hell do you think they built the course here?"

"Well, there must be some flooding, they have been seen doing drainage work, must have cost a fortune?"

"They didn't do any drainage work Henry, trust me. I have been working in these parts all my life, and so did my dad, there is nothing to drain. I can't say what they were doing, but it wasn't drainage work"

The men stood there in the yellow light of their headtorches in complete silence. There were questions starting to emerge and nothing seemed to make sense.

"Also, why have they closed one of the driving ranges Henry, I have heard it's due to flooding, but that's total nonsense. The members would not put up with that without good reason, believe me. They have two driving ranges, my dad helped build both of them, fantastic facilities. They are way out on the western side of the course, a five-minute walk from the clubhouse"

"Mr Bianchi said it was closed due to flooding, so it must be genuine. One was closed and one open. I don't know which one though, do they have names Simo?"

"They do Henry, one is called 'the eighteenth' and the other 'the ninth', kind of makes sense given it's a golf course and all of that. It's the shorter 'ninth' driving range that's closed. I have seen the sign, plain as day"

CLOSED DUE TO FLOODING. DANGER-
MARSHY GROUND.

"The boss was certain there was something going on out here, where we are now. He wouldn't have gone to all this trouble if he wasn't certain or at least suspicious. We must be careful not to jump to any conclusions though, making stories up"

"Not sure what you mean Henry?"

"Well Simo, the boss was certain of bodies being buried, his mate Lee Hunter said so. Trouble is, you would need a truck full of dynamite just to clear the bloody ground around here, you can't even see the soil for the brambles and undergrowth. If I was planning to do something like that, I certainly wouldn't do it here, no way.

Now, you tell me that the ground in these parts is bone dry, it doesn't get flooded. So why is the 'ninth' driving range closed, that doesn't make sense? Is that just a cover story, is that where they are burying bodies? There is no way anyone is burying anything here, it would be impossible"

"I see your point Henry"

"Also Simo, the boss and this Hunter guy were certain the bodies were being buried on the old ninth fairway. Maybe Hunter got it half right, but it's not the old ninth fairway, it's the 'ninth' driving range"

"This is getting a bit complicated Henry, who's to say they were burying anything? Has anyone got any proof?"

"To be honest, I would always take Mr Bianchi's word on anything. He is a clever man, got where he is today because of it. If he says there are graves out here, then that's good enough for me.

Trouble is, where the hell are they, certainly not here, no way!

If they are burring victims, it has to be somewhere else. Could be that closed driving range, might be a bit obvious if you ask me. Thing is, we can't just go digging holes everywhere, easy enough here, our cover story is plausible enough. What story do we have next time, and the time after that? Eventually we will get rumbled and thrown off the whole bloody area. We need to make sure what we are doing is correct, next time will be the last time"

"That's if we have a next time Henry. This gas pipe deception won't work over by the driving ranges, there is no way anyone would put a gas main over there"

"You have a point Simo, time to phone the boss, let Mr Bianchi sort this out"

Outside the Mercedes Benze G-Wagon.

There was a tap, tap on the side window, if it was Chris, I would live, if it wasn't, I would certainly die. Those death threats came rushing back, I kind of dismissed them at first, perhaps I had been in denial. The only two people who really took them seriously were DI Smith and of course Tony Bianchi. What made me think I was beyond such things? I was dealing with forces I couldn't possibly understand.

Now my cavalier, devil-may-care attitude to my own and other lives was coming to a head. In the next few moments, I would live or die, and I hadn't really taken any of this seriously, well it was too late now. If Chris was dead, I would soon follow, no one would go looking for Jan, the Creighton-Ward's would get away with everything. Who was next on the hit list, Ms Greenwood, smelly Ken, Tony Bianchi?

It was easy being a cop, huge teams around you, money in the budget, intelligence, computer analysis. That was all behind me now and I hadn't really come to terms with it. I was bowling along as if the whole world owed me a favour. No one would mess with Lee Hunter, I was a private detective. Yeah right, in truth, no one gave a fuck. I was just a small fish in a very large pond. The sharks out there, fat Tony, Mr Brau, the Creighton-Wards were much, much bigger and stronger than me. I just hadn't thought about that, when I was a cop, we were the big boys, now I was just the little minnow hiding in the weeds.

I needed the think like that minnow, stay in the shadows, away from the big jobs. Of course, it might be way too late now. Funny how you have these bursts of reality, just when it's too bloody late.

There was another tap on the window, I slid around to see who was standing outside. The darkness dimmed the picture, but there was no doubt, this was not Chris Davis. I felt like someone had blown a freezing cold breath over me. My throat dried and my hands began to shake. I had seconds to live but try as I might, I couldn't think of what to do.

"Ok Hunter, get out of the car, do it now"

I wanted to stay where I was, it felt safe in the vehicle, but of course I was not. A couple of bullets through that glass and I would be no more. I didn't want to die, I still had things to do. I wanted to call out, but there was no one to call to. It was him and me, we were the only two people left in the world.

"Get out of the fuckin car Hunter before I empty this shooter into you"

Why didn't he just shoot me where I was, why waste time? Strange how your thoughts wander in times of stress. Just do as he asks, maybe someone will drive past, might even be the boys in blue. Maybe someone heard the two shots, the armed response team might be on their way, right now. I just needed to play for time, keep him occupied, that's the only chance I had.

"Right, I am getting out"

"Stop talking and just do as you are told"

I pulled at the door handle, it clicked with a reassuring noise. Slowly I pushed it open. I thought about ramming it right into him, but my broken ribs would have prevented me from using all but a minimum amount of strength. I slid my legs around and stepped out onto the road.

The man facing me had a lifeless look in his eyes, as if this situation was one he had played out many times before. He was a little taller than me, dressed in a heavy leather coat, dark jeans, and a beany hat. He was holding in his right-hand what looked like a Barretta 9mm pistol. I had no cause to think it was not real, to be honest, did it really matter, he was going to kill me anyway even if it wasn't.

"Kevin is my name, I thought I would tell you that before I killed you. Before I do, why the hell did you decide to stick your nose in? You were told on numerous occasions to butt out, so why didn't you? Does all this really mean that much to you? They are just people without names, victims to be used. They don't really mean anything to anyone, after all, there are billions of people in this world"

I laughed, it wasn't funny, not in the slightest. It was just that speech about them not being missed. Who the hell did they think these victims were, tailors' dummies, sprites in a video game? I felt a surge of morals, I wanted to remind him that they would be missed, they were loved by someone. I of course knew that would fall of deaf ears, he clearly wasn't interested in that point of view. He had a job to do, and he simply got on with it, no matter the cost in lives.

"I must have got pretty close to your organisation Kevin"

"What makes you say that?"

"Well, I haven't really found anything, no proof, it's just supposition on my part. I must be pretty close though otherwise you wouldn't be standing there in front of me"

"Look Hunter, I truly haven't got a clue, I just do as I am told. You have a point though, you have certainly pissed someone off. That person is very high up in the organisation though, he gave me this job personally"

"So, what are they doing then? Ritually killing victims, burying their bodies on the ninth? How long has this been going on, my guess is a century or so? It's the Creighton-Ward's right, they are at the centre of all of this? Oh, and another thing, what's the story with Edward Creighton-Ward? I can't seem to find him anywhere, other than in Ms Greenwoods fathers records. Did he really exist, why did James tell me some cock and bull story about Edward dying in an aircraft accident and being buried in the family crypt?"

"I think you are way off with the time Hunter, it's been a lot longer than a century. I don't know exactly to be honest, but this thing goes back, way, way back. You need to think holistically, it's not some piss ass group of men killing a few hikers and young teenagers.

This is huge, surrounded by ritual and history, it has a long tradition, written laws. The men who control it are way beyond anyone you could stop Hunter. These men control everything, politics, the press, big business, even the police. You wouldn't believe who I have spoken to at these meetings, it would take your fuckin breath away.

Listen, I know you tried, I even admire your courage, I really do, but you had no chance, no chance at all. You might as well of taken on the whole British army by yourself, with both hands tied behind your back. You really would have stood a better chance of winning, that's how big and powerful this is Hunter"

That kind of stopped me in my tracks, was it really that huge, that powerful? DI Smith had warned me off, she said that I wouldn't get anywhere with the Creighton-Wards. Seems she was right, perhaps I should have taken more notice of what she told me. This still left me with so many questions and no real answers. I felt my time was very short, perhaps I could get him to answer just one more, before he ended my life in this cold and lonely place.

"So, what's the story with Edward Creighton-Ward, why can't I find him in the family crypt of the church records?"

"Can't help you there Hunter, I know he existed, I have seen his portrait. He is often mentioned by the members, and in the history of the society. He must be buried somewhere, he was born a long time ago, you might even meet him in hell sometime soon"

He laughed, reached over with his left hand, pulled back the slide on the gun and pointed it right at my head.

"Ok, I guess this is goodbye. Any more questions before I pull the trigger?"

It was strange how calm I felt, I wondered if this was some kind of self-protection. The minds way of washing away fear in those last moments.

"Yeah, just one. Have you got my PA, her name is Jan, Jan Talbot?"

"We do, and she will form the centre of the next ceremony, she will enjoy that"

"Where the hell are you holding her?"

"That's a fuckin stupid question, you will be dead in a few seconds, why do you want to know that?"

"Because the man standing behind you has a gun, and he is pointing it directly at your head. If you tell me where she is, he might not pull the trigger"

Kevin laughed, "that's the oldest one in the book Hunter, you really don't expect me to fall for that"

The was a silence, before a voice came out of the darkness.

"He is not expecting anything Kevin. When you shoot at someone, better make sure they are dead. That was a schoolboy error on your part, you really screwed that one up. Did you truly expect me to do a job like this without a bullet proof vest on? Unlike you I am not a rank amateur, ok you got the drop on me back there, but now things have moved on. So, be a good boy and drop that pistol before I unload my weapon into you, there's a good lad"

Kevin slowly raised both hands, he smiled at me as he did so.

"Listen you two, there is no way I am giving in, my life is over no matter what I do. If I surrender to you, the organisation will kill me by noon tomorrow. The rest of my family will be dead by the end of the next day. These people don't mess around Hunter, remember that. They are meticulous, thorough, nothing escapes them Hunter, nothing! I guess I could turn, might get a lucky shot in, who knows, chances are you will get me first. So, you see, I am not simply going to drop my gun and come like a good boy, as you put it.

All the best with your work Hunter, you have stirred up a bloody huge hornets' nest I can assure you of that. However, you will never get to the bottom of it, I can promise you that, it's too deep, too well controlled"

"Listen Kevin, you could help us, break this sick organisation open, save lives…….."

I didn't get time to finish, in the blink of an eye Kevin levelled the gun to his right temple and pulled the trigger. I will never forget the look on his face as he realised his end had come. Was it fear in his eyes, I am not so sure, it looked more like relief, the end of a lifetime of torment, I guess I will never know.

Later that night.

The bungalow was warm and dry, the smell of freshly made coffee wafted in from the kitchen. I sat on an old leather settee in front of the gas fire, still shocked at what had happened. I couldn't stop thinking about Kevin, at how much fear he must have felt. He thought it preferable to blow is own brains out rather than not do as he was told.

I was shaken out of my melancholy by a knock at the door. My heart jumped a couple of beats, I wanted to get up and run, but the comforting voice of Chris calmed my raging fear.

"Don't worry Mr Hunter, it's just the boss"

Tony Bianchi swept into the living room with some alacrity. He sat next to me on the settee, a look of astonishment on his face.

"So, tell me Lee, what the hell happened?"

"We were ambushed by someone called Kevin. He chased us from the hospital carpark. Eventually Chris blocked him off and went to sort it out but got shot. However, because he was wearing a bullet proof vest, he survived. Anyway, after a long conversation this Kevin character put the gun to his head and pulled the trigger, game over"

"Bloody hell Lee, so what did the old bill say, did you call them?"

"They turned up anyway, someone must have said they heard the shots. We were away out of town, maybe it was a local farmer. Anyway, we just said we found a man standing in the middle of the road, pointing a gun at his head. We tried to talk some sense into him, but he said he was depressed and couldn't cope. The next thing he pulled the trigger and that was that. Well, that was partly true I guess, let's just hope no one asks the farmer how many shots he heard, perhaps three might be a little excessive for a suicide!"

"So, what was the conversation all about, did he tell you anything concerning the bodies?"

"He was in the middle of all that when Chris re-appeared. That's when he decided it would be better killing himself rather than letting the organisation torture him to death. Dam unlucky, I think he would have told me everything, but fate jumped in and changed all of that.

He did say that the killings are ritualistic, and the organisation goes back many years, perhaps even centuries. It is run by men who control all the levers of power, at the highest level. He did mention Edward Creighton-Ward, he said he had lived, and he had seen his portrait, but he couldn't expand on that any further.

Worst of all though, they have Jan, and they are going to use her at the next ceremony, as a fuckin sacrifice. We need to find her Tony and find her very soon. This ceremony could happen any time"

"Look, I will ask around, I know a little regarding these men he spoke about. He is right, they do control everything, and everyone of any importance. They use money, blackmail, bribery, death threats, anything they can, and they are very good at it. They don't ever appear anywhere, never rise to the top in any organisation, they just exist, behind the scenes, in the shadows.

It's going to be tough Lee, no one will ever admit they know them, or that they work for them. Look what happened to that guy Kevin. He thought it preferable to blow his own brains all over the road than disobey his orders. That's how powerful these men are, that's the level of fear they engender"

"You don't sound too optimistic Tony"

"Don't get me wrong, I am a criminal, I know and have done things that would make your hair curl and land me in jail for a thousand years. But I have to be honest Lee, I am not hopeful of finding anything out. As for finding your PA, that's not going to happen, the only person who might have been able to help was Kevin"

"Tony, there must be something we can do. Surely this organisation is large enough to be visible. Human sacrifice, innocent victims, we need to find someone who is part of all this, someone sickened by what they know or see"

"I am sure there are such people, just like Kevin and look what decision he came to! Where do we start, they are ghosts in the system Lee, faceless, nameless men, to all intent and purposes, they don't exist. I can't over emphasise it, they don't have jobs, email accounts, they aren't of Facebook or Twitter. They don't have criminal records, they aren't company chairmen or some kind of celebrity"

"But they do exist Tony, and that makes them vulnerable, that gives them a presence, even if they don't want one. You can't just lead a non-existent life, you need to live, earn money, interact with society, eat and drink"

"You are right Lee, but the problem is trying to find one of them! Then once you have, trying to get them to talk, that's never going to happen"

"Well, I might just know where to start, it's possible that I do know one of these men"

"Really, who the hell is that?"

"It's the man who kicked all of this off. After those bodies had been found on the golf course, wearing the rings, I was contacted by a Ms Greenwood regarding her father's records. It seems her father and grandfather had been making these rings for many years. They had been commissioned by the mysterious Edward Creighton-Ward. So, I went to see his family and met his grandson, a man by the name of Charles Creighton-Ward.

He told me that his grandfather, Edward, couldn't have commissioned the rings as he had died many years previous to them being made. He sent me off on some wild goose chase looking for his grandfather's burial place and date of death, neither seemed to exist.

This annoyed me, I don't like wasting time and I certainly don't like people lying to me. Anyway, myself and smelly Ken went poking around on the estate and got chased off at gunpoint. Not long after, the death threats started. Ms Greenwoods house was broken into, and important documents were taken that related to the rings. Then Jan went missing, seems she has been taken because of me digging into this case. You know about me and Ken getting into trouble on the lane behind the old church, and then Kevin the assassin turned up.

I have been certain from the start that Charles is at the centre of all this, he is the man heading up the organisation. If we can get him to talk, then the whole thing will start to come into focus"

"Oh come on Lee, what do you expect, just pop over there and have a chat, get him to confess?

That's not going to happen, you have more chance of becoming the next king of England"

"Listen, that's where this case leads to, Charles Creighton-Ward and the big house"

"The big house Lee, does he play golf?"

"What the hell has golf got to do with it?"

"You said the big house"

"Yes, it's what people have been calling his manor, the big house"

"No Lee, that's not the big house"

"So, what the hell is the big house then?"

"The big house is the club house of the Southport and Lancashire golf course"

"What?"

"Yeah Lee, have you never been there? The place is bloody huge, stands on top of the hill. That's why people call it the big house. It's the main club house and administration centre for the course. You can even hire rooms there for weddings, birthdays, and stuff like that, they have even done TV programmes from there. You can hire office space with reception staff, WIFI, parking, desks, the bloody lot"

A wave of realisation washed over me. I had heard that phrase, 'the big house' so many times, I had always presumed it meant the manor. My mind whirled with possibilities. Maybe I was wrong from the start. Was it possible that Ken and I had squandered our time wandering about in the grounds of the manor? Should we have been poking around at the golf course?

Was that where they were holding Jan? We wouldn't get a second chance at this, I had to choose. Concentrate my efforts on the manor or the golf club house. If I chose the wrong site, we would run out of time and Jan would die for certain, but how to make that choice.

"So, what are you thinking Lee?"

"They are holding Jan somewhere, more than likely at the same place where they have the meetings. We have a choice, the manor, or the golf club. Choose the right one and the case is solved, make a mistake and we lose Jan and the whole organisation disappears for ever"

"Well, I am a member at the golf club, and I can assure you there is nothing untoward going on there"

"Yes, but that's exactly as it should be. Men in the shadows you said, never appearing anywhere. A ritualistic murdering cult based in the local golf club, who the hell is going to believe that? It's exactly what you wouldn't expect, it's laughable even thinking it. If Jan is there, then we need to get to her, and do it very soon"

"Ok Lee, so what do we do next?"

To be honest, I couldn't think of a sensible answer. There was no way the club would allow us to have a look around. It took me all my powers of persuasion just to get to see Charles Brightling, the General Manager. I dug deep, there must be something, a way to see what was going on, but what?

"Tony, I forgot to ask, how did your guys get on with the search of the old ninth hole?"

"No luck I am afraid. The whole place was a bloody jungle, you couldn't have dug a hole there if your life depended on it. Henry did mention a few things though, especially when it came to the driving ranges.

One of his guys did a load of work around there, as did his father. Seems there is no flooding or marshy ground, there hasn't been for generations. He couldn't understand why I even thought that. Also, why anywhere was closed because of it. So far as he was concerned, the whole area was bone dry, even in the winter"

"No Tony, I was told by the General Manager about the flooding, it must be right"

"That's not what Henry was told. The guy who works for him, Simo, has worked around there all his life, knows the place like the back of his hand. Seems like someone is wrong, or has been spinning you a line, and I bet I know who that person is!"

"We need to get into that club house Tony, we need to get someone on the inside. A person who isn't known, not you or me, an anonymous face. They can poke about, see what turns up"

"Yeah, but who the hell is going to do that, it might turn out to be a bloody suicide mission?"

"I have an idea, let me make a phone call"

I reached into my pocket and pulled out my phone. Flicking through the saved numbers I eventually came up with the name I was looking for and pressed call.

"Hello, Detective Constable Steven Burton, can I help?"

"Hi DC Burton, it's Lee Hunter here. Are you still attached to the Murder Squad and DI Deborah Smith?"

"I am Mr Hunter, why do you ask?"

"I need you to do a little poking around, shouldn't take long. I will of course ask your boss, might be fun, are you up for it?"

"To be honest Mr Hunter I would relish it. I am sitting behind a desk at the moment, checking statements and reports, it's bloody boring. I hate paperwork and looking through files, I know it's important, but I need to get out, not tap away on a keyboard. Yes, it has to be done, good policing and all of that, but it's a shit job.

The trouble is with these murders on the golf course, it's just hopeless. No matter how many reports I check, there isn't one credible lead to be had, it's bloody impossible"

"Right, well I will have a chat to Deborah, see if we can get you from behind that desk for a few days. I will get back to you soon"

The Bold Arms Southport.

"You what Lee, you're having a bloody laugh right?"

Deborah spat bits of her double cheeseburger across the table towards me. The look of complete horror on her face made me laugh, but I could tell she was not amused. I had seconds to recover the situation before she got up and left.

"No Deborah, I just need to borrow DC Burton, just for a few days"

"You can't borrow a serving police officer, they aren't for hire to the general public you know"

"Listen, I can explain, I need an anonymous face, someone who doesn't usually work around here. We think this cult is operating in the Southport and Lancashire golf club. You can hire offices there, if we can get DC Burton inside for a week or so, he can have a look around, see if there is anything suspicious.

Don't forget, my PA Jan is missing. I have been told that she has been taken by this cult and that she will be killed very soon. She will be being held where they operate, if that's the golf club, then that's where she will be"

"I know she is missing Lee and we are using everything we have to find her. The trouble is, we have no leads at the moment but trust me, we are looking and looking very hard. We will find her Lee, and very soon"

"Thank you Deborah, but time is short, I beg you please help me, I think I know where she is. I don't know who else to turn to, if we don't get to her soon, they will kill her"

"Lee, you said 'we' think this cult is operating in the Southport and Lancashire golf club, who is we?"

"Mmmm, I thought you might ask that. If I tell you, promise not to leave?"

"Go on"

"It's Tony Bianchi, he has been asking a few questions, seeing if anything pops up. I know he is the local racketeer and gangster, but he is really trying to help. Deborah, I have no one else, Jan is going to die and it's all my fault. Please, please help, just for a few days, that's all I ask.

Get DC Burton inside that golf club, he can hire an office space, act as a local business guy. It's all kosher, you are looking for Jan anyway, he is acting on an anonymous tip off"

There was a long silence between the two of us. Deborah turned and stared out of the window. It was bright and sunny outside, but that sunny vista hid the effects of the cold wind blowing in from the north. She turned back but didn't look at me, she just scanned the whole area, wincing as she did so.

I could tell that the events of the last few weeks had begun to drag her down. There must have been huge pressure on her from above to get this case solved. No one wanted to see a case of multiple murders splashed across the local and national press, especially a holiday town like Southport. The trouble was, she had absolutely no leads at all, nothing and there didn't seem to be any change for the better coming up on the horizon.

"Listen Lee, I can't just go and order surveillance jobs, it takes time, paperwork and permission. I will go and see my boss, but I wouldn't hold out any hope"

"I bet he says yes Deborah, he wants this case clearing just as much as you. Getting that young DC in there on the pretext of business won't do any harm. With a bit of luck, it might even lead to somewhere, but if we don't try then we will never know"

"Ok, I will go and ask but on one condition"

"Just name it Deborah"

"Tell me everything and I mean everything you know. Including why you just happened upon a man standing in the middle of the road, with a Barrette 9mm pointing at his head"

"Look, I have had death threats, I believed them to be valid, so Tony Bianchi said I could stay at his place for a few days. I was on my way there when this guy suddenly appeared"

"I am not sure I am totally convinced by that Lee. What else do you know, what has Bianchi been doing to help?"

"He has had men looking about the golf course, just to see if there are any more graves out there. One thing he has been reliably informed about is the condition of the ground. From the start I have been fed a load of rubbish about the ground around the course being marshy and waterlogged. I was speaking to Charles Brightling, the general manager of the golf club. I asked him why no bodies were found when the drainage work was undertaken around the course, especially the new 9th hole. He couldn't come up with any reasonable explanation, I wondered at the time if this was just bluff!

I could never come to terms with the fact that the greenskeeper had found those bodies. He was only digging a shallow bunker, any drainage work would have been a lot deeper than that. Also, why has one of the driving ranges been closed due to flooding? There has been nothing like that in the area for generations, it doesn't make sense.

They are covering things up Deborah, I am sure of it. That greenskeeper found those bodies and panicked. He rang 999 straight away, I bet if he had reported to Brightling first, the whole thing would have been hushed up"

"There is a lot of assumptions and make believe in that Lee, and why would they close a driving range when they didn't have to? I think you are trying to fit things into the narrative, and it doesn't completely make sense"

"It does make sense Deborah, they have to get rid of the bodies somewhere. Not only that, it has to be done in accordance with their rituals. Maybe they can't just be dumped in the local canal, or in an anonymous pit on the edge of a construction site. Perhaps these bodies have to be kept close by, who knows? But I will lay a bet that the eight you have found are just the tip of the iceberg. This has been going on for generations, there could be dozens of bodies out there.

I am certain it all started with Edward Creighton-Ward, his family gifted the land and he saw the club into existence. I bet it goes back even further. The gift of the land and the inauguration of the golf club was just one episode in this sorry story. It had always been somewhere safe to enact their sick games, a place to bury the dead. The trouble was it all got out of hand. The golf course expanded, became ultra-successful and increased way beyond its expected boundaries, now it's an international success, not some quiet little place for Edward and his mates.

Meantime, the killings continued and the whole thing started to derail. They were running out of room to bury the bodies, and the locations of some of them got lost. Added to that, the course expanded in all directions, it was bloody chaos, a disaster for the organisation and impossible to control.

That's why those bodies were found on the later ninth hole, perhaps they were lost, or they were miss located on the burial plan, maybe they didn't think their graves would ever be disturbed when they moved the ninth green. Well, they were right, they were safe, that was until some bloody hapless greenskeeper dug a new bunker or two, in the wrong place!

Now Jan has become entrapped in it. She will be next Deborah, we need to find her and do it now. If we don't, there will be another and another, they won't stop. They are protected by privilege and power, they feel safe. Tony Bianchi is going to poke about, see if he can find out who is really running all of this, but he doesn't hold out any hope. We need to crack it Deborah, we need to find Jan, stop this sick game of theirs"

There was another long silence, DI Deborah Smith was looking straight at me, but I could tell her thoughts were elsewhere. She ran her finger through her hair, looked down at the table and then back at me.

"Listen Lee, you have become a real bloody nuisance. I have to say though, you generally come up with the right answers. You certainly helped with the last case and nailing those three bent cops. Maybe you are barking up the wrong tree this time, but I can't just ignore what you have said, just in case you aren't. I will set this surveillance job up, might only be for a couple of days, but it's better than nothing. If what you say is right, then we need to act quickly and carefully. If these powers that you talk about get wind of what we are doing, then we will be shut down in the blink of an eye"

"Thank you Deborah, I am right, I just know it. If Tony comes up with anything, I will tell you straight away, that's a promise"

"I will throw you in the cells if you don't, now that is a solemn promise"

We drank the rest of our drinks and munched away at the remains of our cheeseburgers. It had been a productive meeting, at least I felt something positive was now going to happen. As Deborah said, we had to be quick and very careful indeed.

A Dark Place.

She could hear someone coming down the corridor. That familiar noise on the worn grey stone floor. This would be her food and water, she didn't know what the exact time was, but her stomach suggested afternoon.

She gazed about her, the sterile whitewashed walls and the terracotta floor felt bleak and lifeless. A smell of damp rotting things filled her nostrils. The whole cell exuded a bland and sterile air. The pure white LED light hanging from the ceiling banished any shadows or contrast. It was a depressing place, not just because of her predicament but the lack of anything natural. There was no disenable passage of time, no sense of hope.

She had tried to gain some impression of where she was. No one was willing or able to assist. Looking over his shoulder as he entered each day didn't help either. All she could see was the wall of the corridor, it was just as bland and lifeless as her cell. As for the age of the place, it was clear that it was very old indeed. The worn floors, cracks in the walls, the smell of corruption in the air. This place was not just years old, it was decades old. She could be anywhere, it might not even be in Britain. She started to cry again, they would never find her, she would die alone, and no one would ever know.

The key went into the lock, it was a familiar but also a chilling noise. The crunching rusty lock turned over, and the door began to open. Much to her surprise, a new face appeared, a woman about fifty years or perhaps older came into the cell. She had a large bottle of water in one hand but no food. She threw the bottle onto the bed, it landed just to Jan's right, bouncing, and then hitting the wall before it came to rest.

"Richard won't be with us again, well he won't be anywhere for some time to be honest. You don't need to know my name, you just need to follow my instructions. You can drink the water, but you won't be eating again. The ceremony requires that you are purged of food and sustenance, so you don't need to concern yourself about feeling hungry. Stand up, and follow me, you will be washed tonight and every night before the ceremony"

Jan Talbot felt a rush of anger, even hatred, how dare she or anyone else order her about. What gave anyone the right to dictate to a person when and how they eat. The anger boiled over, the pressure built in her until she couldn't control herself any further.

She lurched forward, intent on doing as much harm as possible, damaging this woman in front of her. The vengeance and loathing in her soul exploded in a wave of violence. It was if the whole world slowed, colours became indistinct, as she assailed her captor.

The first few steps went so well, her retribution was clear and sharp. She grabbed the anonymous woman by the shoulders before swinging a right fist directly into her face. It landed with a satisfying crunch, blood spraying from the woman's nose. Jan swung again, this time a punch landing on the woman's right eye, forcing her to stumble backwards. Jan took a step forward, ready to strike once more but the woman lurched headlong, stabbing something into Jan's stomach.

She felt a sharp and excruciating pain rip through her body. Her whole brain began to shake, and she had a pronounced feeling of insects crawling all over her. Unable to move or function in any way, Jan fell to the floor, struggling to breathe, shaking, and convulsing.

The woman looked down at her and laughed, Jan could do nothing but stare. She felt detached, as if gazing from behind a glass screen.

"You stupid bitch, did you really think I would come in here without some kind of weapon. Tasers, I love them, they really have a wonderful effect don't you think? Anyway, after some

Italian kid tried to escape, the committee thought it a good idea to equip us all with these things, what fun. Thank you for giving me the opportunity to use it, if you feel like trying to escape again, please feel free. Now get up, take off that filthy towel and come with me.

Jan obeyed, she was still not in full control, it felt like a dream as she was shepherded into the white tiled shower room. The pain of the freezing water was unbearable. Its force knocked her to the floor, the spray stung as it fizzled on her naked skin. All the time the woman laughed, drenching her continuously.

"Don't worry dear, I will be back tomorrow, and we can do the whole thing again. I will bring the scrubbing brush next time, well actually it's the old stiff yard brush. Let's see how beautiful that white skin of yours looks after I scrub you down with that. Now lie still, I need to spray you down some more"

The torture seemed to go on for ages, at times Jan thought she would surely drown. Her tormentor seemed to delight in spraying her face. The intense jet forcing water into her mouth and up her nose. She choked, held her hands in front of her face but to no avail. The relentless suffering was remorseless, she tried to scream but it was useless. She held herself tightly in a ball, the hard and cold tile floor only adding to the misery. She lay there, the cold jet playing on her naked skin, slashing at her body, imparting pain wherever it landed. Eventually the pain relented as the water jet ceased.

"Right dear get up and dry yourself, the towels are here, just outside the door. Don't worry, the ceremony is in a few days, so you won't be doing this for much longer. The trouble is, once they get you into that room all your fears and nightmares will come true, believe me. I have seen what they do to people, it's my job to help clear up the bloody mess. I still don't believe just how much blood is in one person, and the smell, all those bodily fluids, it's a terrible mess you know.

I don't know how long the ceremony takes, but I bet they take their time. At least you will be on your own, maybe that's not a good thing. All that violence and agony focussed on just you. I can honestly say I am glad it's not me going in there. Apparently, it's some sort of ritual for the new Principal, they haven't done that for a few years, covid messed that up.

Anyway, if you have a god, I think you should start praying, the next few days are going to be hell my dear. Then they will end in pain and torment, and eventually your death"

Jan just lay motionless on the floor, she quietly sobbed to herself. This nightmare in the shower would soon be over, but only to be replaced by another. She was alone and no one would come to save her. She would be buried in an unmarked grave and remain hidden from everyone she knew for the rest of time. She had thoughts of family and friends, if only she could reach out to them and say goodbye.

The Office of DS Deborah Smith

"You want me to do what boss?"

"Listen DC Burton, it's simple, you are going to hire some office space at the golf club, move in and have a poke around. See if anything is out of place, we suspect that the missing PA of Lee Hunter might be being held there. I have already spoken to DS Shacklady, she will meet you in the carpark at 09.00 tomorrow morning"

"Yeah, I got that bit, but why the hell would they be holding a kidnap victim at the Southport and Lancashire golf club? People go there to relax and chill out, not kidnap women"

"It's a long story Stephen, but the tip off I got was credible, so we need to follow it up"

"Ok, you're the boss. What about money, they will want to pay"

"Right, this is the pack from Finance. All the details are in here, your false name, bank details and the code the golf club need to use to get their money. You will be taking DS Shacklady with you, she is your head of finance and co-director. She has made an appointment to see the business manager there, you two get that office booked and get to work. You need an office for ten working days, you are new to the area and are looking to expand the I.T. department. As I have already mentioned, get to know the place, see if anything looks curious. You and Sharron are to spend as much time as possible digging about the place. If you even suspect anything untoward, then get in touch as soon as possible, do I make myself clear?

This has the potential to turn very nasty indeed Stephen so no risk taking. If there is any doubt, then back off, Sharron is in charge, she can make the critical calls. If the tip-off is right, these people will not flinch from killing anyone who gets in their way"

"Right, I will do some research on the place and expanding an I.T. department, they will certainly ask me questions"

DC Stephen Burton turned and left the office. Deborah sat staring into the distance, drumming her fingers on the desk. Lee Hunter might well be right, but equally it might turn out to be a fantasy based on nothing more than gut feeling. The thing was, Hunter had been right before, in truth he was right almost all of the time. He had a natural nose for things, she simply couldn't ignore what he was saying. If Jan Talbot was being held in the bowels of the golf club, her life was in imminent danger. They had to get to her and do it soon before it was too late.

Her mobile began to ring, buzzing and pirouetting around the desk as it did so. She caught site of the caller ID, it was Marcus. She smiled, this had been a troubling day, a chat to Marcus was just what she wanted.

"Hello, DI Smith, murder squad"

He laughed, "Inspector Marcus Cooke here, Thames Valley CID"

She smiled, it was good to hear his voice again. They were both so busy, time seemed to slip away without notice.

"How's your day been Debby?"

"To be honest Marcus, it's been shit. I have just committed two very good officers on what will probably turn out to be a wild goose chase. On the other hand, if it isn't a waste of time, they could find themselves in the hands of a group of demented serial murderers. So, one I loose and two I loose, like to swap jobs?"

"I guess that's the privilege of rank Debby, you get to decide, the trouble is, it's not always a nice choice. The job we do is 59 minutes of normality and one minute of bloody terror. One thing's for certain though, it has to be done. There are millions of people out there depending on us. I guess working in a burger bar would be safer, but you'd soon get bored"

"You are right Marcus, but sometimes that burger bar sounds a very tempting proposition"

The Bungalow

To be honest, I felt relaxed in fat Tony's bungalow. He had someone parked outside, we had takeaway delivered and the fridge was full of beer. All of the problems I had become embroiled in seemed a million miles away. Trouble was, they weren't, and Jan was still missing. It might already be too late, but I had to think there was till time, the question was, how much?

The real fear was that I had got this completely wrong. It wasn't the golf club, they had nothing at all to do with it. The big house was some place I had never heard of and turned out to be an old stone building in the wilds of Scotland. Edward Creighton-Ward was simply an outcast 'black sheep' of the family, who no one claimed owner ship of anymore. If I was wrong, where the hell was Jan? She wouldn't stand a chance, and no one would ever be able to rescue her.

A cold sweat rolled over my skin, a knot of acid forced its way up my throat. In truth, no one had a clue, I was the only person with any sense of direction in the case. I had to believe I was right. The thing was, if I wasn't, I would end up blaming myself until my dying day, and not for the first time!

I could hear someone coming up the path, a key being pushed into the Yale lock. It was fat Tony, I knew it was him, he always turned the lock the wrong way. After a lot of rattling and some muffled swearing, he finally got the door open.

"Lee, how the devil are you? I have some news, some good and some bad"

"I am fine thanks Tony, let's have it"

"Well, my guys went over to that closed driving range, 'the ninth' I think it's called. It didn't take them long to spot the masts with the CCTV cameras. The question is, why all the security, no one is allowed in there? Apparently, there are loads of cameras, they look in every direction and Henry assures me that they are also night vision.

Now I have to admit to knowing a thing or two about CCTV. In my business it pays to understand such things if you know what I mean. I can honestly say that I have visited many a warehouse with less surveillance than that place, a lot less!

Trouble is Lee, there is no way of getting even close to that driving range without being seen. I can't think of a way around this, trying to disable those cameras will be impossible. They are all interlinked, getting close to one will simply get you spotted on a dozen more"

"Can't we disable them another way, perhaps your boys could pose as the maintenance engineers"

"Good thinking Lee, but these kinds of systems are on national contracts with big time security companies. You can't just turn up in a van with a fake ID. You need access codes and security clearance from the company you are visiting. Security at the golf club will have photos of all the maintenance people who visit to fix the cameras. There is no way you are getting within a mile of them without being legitimate, no way at all"

"Then we need permission to go there, if we can't do it illegally, then we need to be authentic"

"Yes Lee, but how the hell do you expect to do that? The security company most certainly won't help, and the golf club will just laugh in your face.

Even if they aren't burying bodies out there, they won't let you near the place, just out of principal. It's private property, very private, as soon as you step on the land, they will call the police and you will spend the night in the cells"

"Ok, can you get close enough to see if anything has been going on there?"

"Nope, the place is surrounded by trees and bushes. Even if you get to the fence line the grass is a meter high, you can't see anything of the range itself. Whatever they are doing out there, if they are doing anything at all, is all very well hidden"

"Right, then we need to get some kind of proof, at least reasonable suspicion. If we can do something, anything, then DI Smith can go and get that warrant"

"Ok, but what?"

"Good question Tony, a very good question indeed!"

The Southport and Lancashire Golf Club.

DS Sharron Shacklady and DC Stephen Burton walked up the steps of the prestigious club house. It was surprisingly warm for the time of year, perhaps spring was making an early appearance. They had an appointment to see the business booking manager at 11am. The time was now 10.55, so they had five minutes to wait for the enthusiastic Miss Bellingham-Wood.

"I can't see anything untoward happening here Sharron, can you? Look at all the activity, golfers coming and going all day, the bars and restaurants will be open until midnight. It would be impossible to hide anything, there are too many people about"

"Well Steve, the boss told us to have a look around and that's what we are going to do. Remember the old saying, if you don't buy a ticket, you won't win a prize. Not sure what kind of prize she expects us to win though. Like you, I can't see this being where Lee Hunters PA is being held. Of all those places out of the way, hidden in the woods, forgotten by everyone, why the hell hold her here?"

"I suppose it's big enough to hide her Sharron. You could conceal a bloody Battalion of soldiers in a place like this, no mistake. Look at it, four stories high and half a mile long.

I hate to think how much membership costs, I counted a dozen cars in the car park worth over 80k. Thing is, I bet someone would notice something out of place, hear a scream, see something suspicious. People who pay for this level of service and security like to feel special, safe and cosseted. You expect to see certain things at a place like this, expensive cars, celebrities, money, extravagance. You don't expect to see, or hear kidnapping, hostages and torture, you simply couldn't keep it a secret and if you didn't, the membership would fade away like a spring mist!"

They walked up to the first step, carved from stone, precise and geometrical. It was an impressive place, from the first step to the highest roof tile. They began to climb but as soon as they reached the top step, a young and very smartly dressed woman came bounding out of the huge entrance doors. She was tall, with short blond hair, and a smile so white you would struggle to look at it on a bright summer's day.

"Well hello, I am Miss Bellingham-Wood, the business booking manager, I guess you are Sharron and Richard"

"Hello Miss Bellingham-Wood, I am Sharron Shacklady, and this is my co-director, Stephen Burton"

She advanced towards the two undercover police, extending a hand of friendship. They greeted each other in a polite and business-like manner and agreed to proceed to Miss Bellingham-Wood's office. She ushered them into a bright and impressive space, modern but still holding traces of the traditional.

The meeting itself went well, as the groundwork had already been laid over the phone. Miss Bellingham-Wood showed them several business spaces and undertook a complete tour of the building. Eventually they found themselves back in her office, ready to sign the 'short-term business opportunity' contract.

"So, welcome to the Southport and Lancashire golf club business suite. I am sure you will be very comfortable here, with all the tech and facilities you require. Should you need anything at all, you know where my office is and my mobile number so, please don't hesitate in contacting me, night or day. This is a very exciting opportunity for us, we welcome you with open arms and hope you will stay for as long as you require. Now for that coffee, if you forgive me, I will be back in a minute or two"

With that, Miss Bellingham-Wood stood up from the meeting table and left her office. The smell of her perfume wafted about the place as she exited. The office descended into silence apart from the gentle hum of the air conditioning unit.

"She does feign pleasure very well, don't you think Steve?"

He laughed at the remark. Miss Bellingham-Wood was certainly a very polished operator, well trained and focused on her profession.

"I bet she does this sort of thing a hundred times a week Sharron. Must be a bit tedious after a while. The same conversations with the same kind of people, but it pays the bills and looks good on the resume I guess"

DS Shacklady looked about the office, took in a deep breath and turned to face DC Burton.

"I agree with the comments you made before we came in Steve. This place is busy, very busy, people coming and going, it never stopped. The security staff are everywhere as well as CCTV cameras. Now you might say that they are all in on what's going on, but I doubt it. I counted five cleaners running around with trolleys, another half a dozen waiters, those two guys with sack trucks full of booze. I might accept some high-level managers, even a couple of security guys being in on the kidnapping, but all this lot?"

"Yeah, I think we are barking up the wrong tree here Sharron. I bet there are loads of rooms, offices maybe somewhere in the basement to hide her. The problem is, keeping it a secret, no chance, not a bloody hope. Can you imagine Miss Bellingham-Wood stumbling on some blood curdling ceremony, or a woman tied up in a darkened room. Not sure she would simply turn around and carry on with what she was doing, do you?"

"Ok Steve, we concur that this is a waste of time. We stay professional, complete the job and in the meantime report back to Deborah. I will tell her what we think and what we have seen. At least they can be getting on with finding out where she actually is, or at least coming up with a plan B.

In the meantime, we can go over to the bar, have a glass of vino, and try those panini's Miss Bellingham-Wood so strongly recommended, agreed?"

"Sounds like a plan to me Sharron, the first round is on me"

A Disturbing Truth.

It was just after dawn, not particularly early for mid-January but Ms Janice Greenwood had not slept well all night. Tossing and turning, as she contemplated her latest find, and it was something that deeply disturbed her.

It had all started a few days ago whilst completing the re organising of her father's files. Since the break in, life in general had not been settled for Ms Greenwood. She often awoke during the night, thinking that she heard noises outside the house. Feelings of fear and unease when recollecting the violent events of just a short while ago.

She had found some old photos at the back of a desk drawer and also a bunch of three rusty keys. She and Lee Hunter had tried to make some sense of the old black and white images whilst he was in hospital. The trouble was, it would be no more than speculation, guess work, without any specific text or explanation.

They might have been of Edward Creighton-Ward at some sort of ceremony, but nothing was certain. One picture could have been the early construction of the golf club house, but that wasn't definite. There was a photo of a ceremonial collar, it certainly looked very expensive, and had been made by her father, but for what or whom?

She had put such unanswered questions behind her by now, but the three rusty keys, she couldn't stop thinking about them. She tried to imagine where they came from, what lock they might fit, but to no avail.

It was on one restless night that the possible answer came to her. In the back of one of the cellars underneath the house. She remembered finding an old safe, covered in sack cloth and old carpet. She was very young and curious, every dark and secret place was a magnet to her.

She asked her father about the safe, he cleared his throat and made some excuse about it being there when they bought the house. She remembered him being disturbed by the conversation, almost shocked by what she had found. He gave strict instructions to leave the safe alone, and not to play anywhere near it.

This of course was too much of a temptation to such a young mind, and so every opportunity she could get, she would try to open the safe. It must have been years before she eventually gave up any hope of ever opening it. Finally, it's very existence slipped into her deepest memory, hidden away, like the safe, in the dark recesses of the past.

These memories only re surfaced when she found the three rusty keys on a simple wire ring. There was no indication of where the keys would fit, or even any mark from a manufacture. It felt like any connection between the keys and the lock they would open, would only ever be known by their long dead owner.

Eventually she decided to give up any hope of finding the lock. Perhaps it was a door or desk that no longer existed. Maybe a garden gate or even a garage long since forgotten by time and living memory. She had settled for this until one night, whilst tossing and turning, she remembered she had overlooked one possible place. Down in the cellar, underneath the very house she lived in.

The safe, the old half rusty relic from a time gone by. The very thing that her father had told her to leave alone. Was it possible, could these keys found in her father's old desk be the answer? Would they resolve a question that went back many decades, would they finally show her what lay within.

Nervously she swung her legs out of the bed. The nigh time air was cold and damp, maybe she should wait until later in the morning. Memories of her father ordering her to leave the safe alone rattled around in her mind. No, it was her house now, it was time to see If the keys were in fact from the safe.

Putting her slippers and dressing gown on, Ms Greenwood took the keys from the bedside cabinet and made her way to the cellar. The door was located under the stairs, set into ornate wooden panels. At first glance it could easily be missed, blending into the yellowing white gloss paintwork. Memories came flooding back as she reached for the round Bako-light handle. Ms greenwood had of course been down in the cellar many times since her childhood. However, these forays were for the mundane, collecting firewood, depositing old clothes ready for collection. There had been no connection to her father, the old rusty safe or former times.

She opened the door, flicked on the light switch, turned immediately left and began to descend. She could feel the hairs on the back of her neck bristling, hear her heart pounding. Why, she had been here many times before? The keys in her hand would probably not unlock the safe anyway, this was undoubtedly a waste of time. Finally, she reached the concrete floor below, screwing her eyes to gaze into the damp half-light of the cellar. There were several rooms leading off the main area, one was an old coal bunker, another had been used by her mother to wash clothes. Two had not been used in her lifetime but the fifth, that contained her father safe.

She pushed the button on the torch, these old rooms had no power of their own. The candles formally used to illuminate them would not suffice for the tasks she had now. The beam stabbed into the darkness, a shaft of pure white light striking forward of her. She followed, scanning back and forth, quickly locating a pile of colourless and dusty clothes and hessian sacks. This was it, under that bundle lay the safe and perhaps an answer to the question from years ago.

She stopped and looked about her. A child's voice whirled about the room, maybe her mother calling her for dinner. Memories washed over her, so many people, parents, grandparents, friends. A tear welled up, such happiness, the security of her family, she had been truly blessed.

She approached the bundle with some reservation. What creatures lay within, ready to bite, sting or scare her. She had no intention of finding out, so she kicked the bundle to one side piece by piece, eventually revealing an old square metal object.

It was dark grey, or black, standing around three feet tall and probably the same in depth and width. There was a discoloured brass plaque on the front, with a handle and key opening beneath. She rubbed away at the ovel plaque, the inscription read, 'W. WILLIAMS AND CO SAFE MANUFACTURERS'.

The whole object had an indestructible and immeasurably solid feel.

She stood back and looked down at this grey/black object. It was her fathers, a direct link to the past. Whatever lay within might bring back many memories, or more likely only set more mysteries loose to torment her mind.

With some trepidation she reached into her pocket, fumbling for the three rusty keys. At the same time Ms Greenwood shone the torch at the key lock opening on the front of the W Williams and Co safe. It was clear the key needed to open this would be long and substantial. Looking at the three keys in her hand, two were immediately rejected. They were brass and looked more appropriate for a small lock, perhaps that of a desk or display cabinet. The third however was made of heavy metal, black with a large round head. The shank was thick and around five inches long. The rust hid any writing or identification that might have been stamped anywhere on the key.

With shaking hands, Ms Greenwood gently inserted the key into the lock. There was some resistance at first, a metallic crunch as the dust and debris of ages came together. She tried to turn it, but it jammed, she tried again, this time with some success. After several attempts it finally turned, the safe was unlocked. Janice Greenwood pulled down on the brass handle, and with some considerable effort, the safe door came loose.

"I can't open this, what happens if I find something inside that I don't want to? I might find nothing of course, it's almost certainly empty. Just because my father told me to stay away, doesn't mean that he didn't empty the safe years afterwards. Yes, it will be empty, all this will have been for nothing"

With a renewed confidence she pulled on the handle and opened the door. A cloud of dust whirled into the air, the beam of the torch illuminating the particles as they spun in front of her eyes.

Shining the torch into the iron box, she took a breath and looked inside. There glistening in the half-light was a very familiar object. Made of precious metals and sparkling diamonds and most impressively, with a large green emerald at its centre.

Mounted on a creamy white alabaster bust was the collar from the old black and white photographs. She fell backwards onto the dusty cellar floor, gasping and with eyes blazing. She sat there for some considerable time, heart pounding, beads of sweat forming on her forehead.

She couldn't take her eyes of the bust and the collar, she wanted to slam the safe door closed and throw away the key. Was this the collar made for that sadistic murdering organisation that Lee Hunter was certain existed? Had her father made this for them, was he part of this sick cult?

There was a dark and dusty plaque at the base of the bust. The torch occasionally illuminated some potential writing engraved upon it. Moving onto her knees, Ms Greenwood crawled forward, she reached out in an attempt to clear the grime from the brass. At first the letters remained indistinct, simply filling with more dust and filth as she rubbed. Eventually, one by one the words cleared and finally the inscription became comprehensible.

MADE FOR THE NEW PRINCIPAL
JONATHON GREENWOOD.
IN REPLACEMENT OF THE PREVIOUS OLD
COLLAR GIFTED TO EDWARD CREIGHTON-
WARD

Those simple words shocked her to the core. She collapsed, prostrate on the floor. It was her father's name, there on the bust, Jonathon Greenwood. She heaved several times, the acid foamed into her mouth.

Things started to come into focus, the old black and white images with indistinct writing. Lee Hunter had thought it said, "made for Brother Principal Edward, at his raising, in replacement of the previous collar"

He was certain it was connected to Edward Creighton-Ward, that was correct it seemed. The horrific truth was, it was also connected to her father, Jonathon Greenwood!

How could this happen? Her father was a loving and caring man, he was always kind to her and her mother. This was impossible, there must be some mistake, maybe another Jonathon Greenwood. She would put it to the back of her mind, forget it ever happened. The trouble was, she knew that would be impossible, the question was, what would she do now?

Sat by the Fire.

I couldn't quite remember how many whiskies I had consumed. Tony had brought a bottle of Glenfiddich Grande Couronne. It said on the label it was 26 years old and fat Tony told me it cost him £260! I guess it didn't, he probably extorted it out of some client under threat of death. I must say though, he did have very good taste and a surprising knowledge of fine Scotch whiskey.

Anyway, he had a double and then left, there was some meeting he had to attend. Trouble was that the remainder of the bottle sat on the drink's cabinet, and I simply couldn't resist. So, I was pissed and most of the Glenfiddich Grande Couronne seemed to be missing. I guess Tony would have forgotten about it come tomorrow, so I should be ok.

Over the last couple of days, time had begun to slow. Despite Tonys best efforts there was no more news about my PA, Jan. The police had drawn a blank as well, I was beginning to think we would never find her. I had a recurring nightmare, the phone would ring in the middle of the night. I would answer it, "she is dead Mr Hunter". I would lay there for hours afterwards just thinking about her. This was all my fault and there was nothing I could do to put things right.

I was shaken out of my drunken melancholy by the ringing of the mobile on the arm of the chair. Shit, was this the phone call, had DI Smith found somebody in the canal? I looked at the screen, 'MS GREENWOOD', well I guess she wasn't dead, yet!

"Hi Janice, how's things going. I was intending to call in on you. I am in hiding, long story, but Tony recons it's safe for me to come out now, let's hope he's right"

There was a long pause, so much so that I looked at the screen to make sure I was still connected.

"Hello, are you still there Janice?"

"Yes Lee, still here. I have been thinking, you know, about this cult you insist exists"

"Yeah, I am sure they do, it would explain so many things"

"What do you think they do, have meetings and things like that?"

"Well, they must get together to discuss matters, carry out their ceremonies. The result of these assemblies' lays in the ground around that bloody golf course. Dead bodies Janice, posed in the ground, like lovers together forever"

The line went quiet once again. I thought I heard a gasp, perhaps crying, but I couldn't be sure.

"Are you alright Janice, you don't seem yourself. Is something bothering you?"

"No Lee, I just hate the thought of all those people being murdered, and for what? Your PA is missing, I wonder if she is a victim of these evil men? Perhaps there is more than one group. What do you think Lee? One group of men getting together for a chat and a second, well doing these terrible things"

I sat back in the chair, that was an odd thing to say, two groups? What was she trying to suggest? I couldn't think of what to say next, maybe it was my intoxicated state, I had probably missed the point.

"Sorry Janice, I don't understand. There is only one group, their victims lie in the morgue in the local hospital. They are a bunch of murdering sadistic psychopaths and if we don't stop them soon, they will kill again. This time it will be Jan, I have no doubt about that"

This time I was certain I could hear crying. Had I said something I shouldn't have? We had talked about this before, she knew my thoughts on the subject, why was she getting so upset? Perhaps it was the result of the break in. I recalled from my time in the police that the trauma caused by such an event could be extreme. Folks would often move house, even break up a relationship. She needed some professional counselling, I would speak to Deborah, they would have liaison staff ready to help.

It didn't quite sit right though. She had asked questions about the meetings, where there two groups? I wasn't a councillor though, perhaps the break-in had affected her in a different way. Maybe dreams of the group, nightmares of people losing their lives. She sounded very upset indeed. Janice Greenwood was a very strong and independent woman, this wasn't like her at all. I wasn't going to put the phone down until I had got to the bottom of this.

"Janice, is everything ok, don't just say yes if it isn't. I know you and you don't seem yourself"

"No, everything is fine Lee, I am just tired that's all"

I wasn't satisfied with that response. I could still hear that trembling in her voice. A slight delay in her reply as she composed herself. For one moment I wondered if she had suffered another intrusion into her home. Maybe she was being held against her will. I discounted that possibility. If that was the case, she wouldn't have access to the phone. Or if she did, it would be to make a demand on behalf of whomever held her prisoner. No, there was something else going on here, but what? I scanned other possibilities, but nothing seemed to fit.

"Janice, I am going to pop over now if that's ok. It's not late, it would be lovely to see you again"

"No, it's fine Lee, I am very tired, and I need to go to bed"

"Then why the questions about the group? I am not sure what you are trying to get at. You seem very upset about something and I don't want to leave you like that"

The phone went quiet again, I was now certain that something wasn't right. Most of the time I had spent with Janice was listening to her speaking. I had never known her go quiet like this, never, not once.

"Lee, I have found something, down in one of the cellars. It's in my father's old safe, those rusty keys, they opened it"

"Ok, so what was it you found inside?"

"It, it's the collar Lee, the bloody collar"

"What collar Janice, I don't understand?"

"The collar in the black and white photographs, the ones I brought to the hospital. We couldn't make out the words on the back, or what the collar was meant for. Now I know Lee and I am sick to the core, I just don't believe it"

I had to think before I replied, what the hell had she found? It sounded like the collar in the photos. Well, we knew about that, we have an old black and white photo of it. So, it was secured in her father's safe, waiting for someone to pay the bill perhaps. To be honest, he had made it, he had a safe in his house, seemed like a good place to store it. Maybe he was waiting for a delivery that never happened, who knows?

Perhaps the one in the photo was not the only example, there might be a dozen of these things out there, we had no way of knowing. In any case, the one in the photo didn't seem to have any inscription on it, so identifying its purpose or owner would be impossible. In truth, all we had was a very expensive collar, with a magnificent emerald jewel at its centre!

"Ok Janice let's not get ahead of ourselves here. It's a collar, sounds like the same as the one on the photos. It might be one of ten, fifty or a hundred of these things, who knows. Just because it's in your fathers safe, doesn't mean a thing. I guess he was waiting for payment before delivering it, I think that.........."

"Lee, it's not just sitting there waiting for someone to pay the bill, who never turned up. This collar belongs to someone, and I know who that is"

My mind started to race, she said she knew who it belonged to. If it was Edward Creighton-Ward, then the case was blown wide open. Surely DI Smith would have to take some action now.

We had proof, links, the information we already had about the rings. The old photos of the golf club house, the collar and the connection to the Creighton-Wards. Then there was the mystery about Edwards burial, the death threats from the family. What about the bodies on the golf course and the logbook from the old shed recording the burials. It was overwhelming and not just circumstantial. Any magistrate would be happy to issue as many search warrants as needed.

"Right Janice, I will contact DI Smith, tell her what you have and the connection to the Creighton-Ward's. We can get this thing rolling at first light, that murdering family will be locked up in the cells by teatime"

There was another silence, I could hear her breathing on the other end of the line. There was something else, I just knew it, something she hadn't told me yet. The silence was deafening, I wanted to ask but I was afraid of interrupting her thoughts.

"Lee, I said I know who the collar belongs to. There is an inscription on the alabaster bust from which it hangs"

The was another long silence, the tension was palpable. I instinctively knew something was not as I had expected to be.

"A name Janice, what name?"

"It's my father Lee. The inscription reads. 'Made for the new principal Jonathon Greenwood. In replacement of the previous old collar gifted to Edward Creighton-Ward'.

There is no doubt who this collar belonged to, who the principal of this cult was. Who ordered innocent people to be murdered and buried in the sand. It was my father, he was at the centre of the whole thing Lee, I can't believe it, why? He was such a kind and loving man"

I could hear her crying, this must have been a real shock. I needed to get over there immediately. This situation had to be attended to, things had changed and not for the better!

The Office of Chief Superintendent Watkins.

DI Deborah Smith replaced the handset, her boss sounded annoyed, and reluctant to speak on the phone. She went over the last few days, what could she have done that pissed him off, who knows?

She grabbed her phone and ID card, left the office, and made her way to the top floor, office number 403. His name plate adorned the door, Chief Superintendent Watkins, "maybe it would be my name on the door one day, then again", she thought, "pigs might fly"

She knocked, a muffled response came from within. DI Smith took this to be an invitation to enter and she wasted no time in complying.

In front of the window, sitting behind a large modern desk was her boss. A man in his mid-fifties, greying hair, tanned skin and deep blue eyes. He had a welcoming smile and an approachable and calm manner.

"Hi Deborah, take a seat, we need to have a chat"

"What have I done this time boss?"

He laughed, "nothing Deborah, it's just that I have had the gypsies from on high. Apparently, a local well-to-do family have made it clear that they don't appreciate us poking about in their private affairs"

"Oh, I see. Let me guess, the Creighton-Ward's?"

"To be honest I am not certain Deborah, but it's probable"

"To be honest boss, we aren't really poking around. Hunter has some cock and bull idea about a satanic group of devil worshipers. They have been killing people and burying them in the sand. He keeps trying to get us involved, but there is no way we are getting a search warrant, not on what he tells me. It's a load of speculation and fanciful dreaming. It might have a thread of truth, but I doubt it.

We have that surveillance job on at the golf course that you signed off, but nothing more than that. Lee Hunter is convinced his PA is being held there, I doubt it but it's worth a try. I won't be going beyond that though, not unless we come up with something. Anyway, what the hell has the golf course got to do with that family?"

"Not sure Deborah, but the fact is, the family are on our backs, big time! This warning has come from the very top, and I mean the highest places. Someone or some people are very pissed off"

"Strange, I know Hunter has been over to their country estate. He assured me that he had received some death threats from them. He got himself involved in a fight behind the old church, he gave me a load of photos of some burial register. It didn't make a lot of sense to be honest, so I filed it under, 'bollocks'.

Maybe they think Hunter is a cop, who knows? He has asked for our help, but I can't do much more than we have done already. Odd that they are getting all pissy about Hunter though. It was a bit of trespass and a fight at the old church. He hasn't done anything of real note. What the hell can some PI do to harm the reputation of that family?"

Chief superintendent Watkins sat back in his leather chair, glanced at DI Smith, then swivelled around to look out of the window. It had begun to snow, a light drift blowing around in the wind. It made her feel cold even though the office was warm and dry.

"Seems odd to me Deborah. A ne'er-do-well PI and ex-cop disturbing things to such an extent, that a local family go all the way to the top to put a stop to it. Don't you think that's a bit odd? And, if we are to believe Hunter, they have made credible death threats against him, why?

They are one of the most powerful families in this part of the country, how can Hunter do them any harm? He is no more than an annoying wasp on a summer's day, spoiling everyone's picnic. If it is the Creighton-Ward's and they are genuinely worried, they should get an injunction and shut him down, simple"

"So, what are you saying boss is give Hunter the option, back off or face the consequences?"

"Not sure Deborah. It just seems a big load of overkill, I wonder if Hunter has got something, hit that big red nerve. I have been in this service since before you left school. To say that I have seen it all is an understatement, there is more to this than meets the eye.

Big rollers like the Creighton-Ward's like to keep a low profile. They don't like to draw attention to themselves. They operate in the background, making money, dodging taxes, taking advantage of people, functioning just within the law. The last thing they want is a load of people like me knowing that they are pissed off with someone or something. They don't want any additional attention, not unless someone is being a really big fucking nuisance.

Hunter is an ex-cop, but he is also a very experienced one. People like him don't just go off on some daydream, a Disneyland fairy tale. He must have something, the family wouldn't want him gone if he didn't, the question is, what? Look, let's give him a chance, get him in here, we will listen to what he has to say and take any appropriate action"

"No problems boss, but what he has is mainly supposition and conjecture. I agree with you about Hunter being an experienced ex-cop, but this time I think he is way off base"

"Well, if that's the case, we can warn him off and tell him to wind his neck in"

The Home of Janice Greenwood.

The atmosphere in the house was black and full of pain. I couldn't deny the significance of the plaque on the alabaster bust. There was no doubt who this collar belonged to and what it had been intended for. I had no option but to state the obvious. Her father had been involved and perhaps even lead the group perpetrating these heinous crimes.

The question was, what do we do with this information? It was of historical significance for sure, but it bore no relevance to today's enquiries. The only thing it did confirm was a link between Janice's father and the group. Even if I took the bust and collar to DI Smith, it would prove nothing. It had no relevance to anything, it was a collar given to the new Principal, Jonathon Greenwood, so what.

Even the mention of Edward on the plaque proved nothing. I knew he had existed, even the family confirmed that. The only dispute was the date of his death, well that wasn't exactly the crime of the century.

"Lee, I don't want anyone knowing about this. My father was a good man, dragging his name through the mud won't achieve anything"

I wanted to open my mouth and state the obvious. Her father was the head of a murdering bunch of psychopaths, but that wasn't going to help anyone. Janice didn't deserve any of this, she had become a victim of circumstance. The only reason she had become involved was that her curiosity had got the better of her. She had seen the reports of the bodies on the 9th, recognised the rings from her father's records and contacted me. Janice Greenwood had no idea of what she was walking into, and I was certain she had no idea of what she would find.

"I don't see any particular advantage in broadcasting this info' Janice. What he did, whatever that was, took place decades ago. What we do have is a collar and the suggestion that the cult did really exist. What we need to do is connect that to something in the present. There must be a way of using this collar to flush out the current members"

"Good thinking Lee, but what? They will have new regalia for certain, no one will remember my father, why should they? I am not certain if there is anything we can do. There is no way anyone from the group will come forward to claim it, that would be stupidity of the highest order"

"Look Janice, I am bloody sick of all this messing about. I am going to take this collar and the bust straight to Charles Creighton-Ward and ask for an explanation. Let's see what that explanation is, gauge the reaction in his eyes. I know he won't say anything of significance, but it will certainly stir things up somewhat"

"And what happens if he has you dragged off and shot, or sacrificed at the next meeting?"

"Then we will have an answer, or at least you will"

As soon as the words left my mouth, I knew I had made a terrible decision. Going straight into the lion's den, and asking questions, not a good idea. Still, something had to be done, the case had to move forward, and this was the only thing I could think of.

I called fat Tony and told him what I was planning to do. He begged me not to go, he was right of course, but I had no choice.

"Listen Lee, I know people like this, they will have you dragged off and killed for certain. They don't give a fuck about you, the law or anything else for that matter. They are and always have been out for only one thing, and that's the family. They don't care who they tread on, or who gets harmed along the way. They don't think like we do, they live on a different level. They just don't care, leave this to me, there must be a better way"

"There isn't Tony, I have to go back and talk to Charles, he has all the answers, no one else. We can dance around this until hell freezes over, but unless I get Charles Creighton-Ward to talk, it all remains in the dark. I should have done this days ago, then Jan Talbot would be safe at home, Janice Greenwood would not have had her house broken into. There wouldn't have been a fight by the old church, no death threats, no more missing persons. This has to stop now Tony and I am the only person who can do this"

"Look Lee, let me send a couple of my boys over there with you, they can pull you out if necessary. They will certainly stop any harm coming your way. I can have it all arranged in half an hour"

"Thanks Tony, I really appreciate your concern and the offer. I have to do this by myself, and I have to do it now, before I lose my nerve. These bastards have to be stopped before they do any more damage"

I didn't wait for Tony's reply, I closed the call and turned my phone off. I didn't need any distractions or people trying to talk me out of it. This was all my doing and I was the one to sort it out.

"Janice, you wait here, I will be back, I don't know when, but I will be back. I need to take the bust and collar"

"So, what if Charles just takes it off you and denies all knowledge?"

"That's why we need photos, preferably with today's paper in the background for the date.

Photos of you and I holding the collar, plenty of proof that this thing does actually exist. Once we have done that, I will be off, please don't try and stop me Janice, this needs to be done"

I left her house with the bust and collar in the back of my car. If I was being honest, I was bloody terrified. I couldn't see any other option though. The police wouldn't entertain me, and fat Tony would simply land me in another shoot out at the OK corral, there was no other way.

I had tried my best to find some tangible links but to no avail. False trails, relatives that didn't seem to exist, burial registers that didn't prove a thing. Some old black and white photos with illegible writing on the back. Now the collar and bust, but that was just an artifact. It belonged to Jonathon Greenwood, the father of Janice and jeweller to the rich and powerful.

Then there were the bodies in the sand with the rings made by Janice's father. But trying to link them to anything had proven impossible. I knew in my heart what was going on, I was certain of the part of the Creighton-Ward's, but that wasn't enough. You can't go accusing someone without proof, a definite and incontrovertible link. I had nothing though, these people knew how to hide their tracks. Ok, I had exposed something, but they knew it wouldn't lead anywhere.

Their burials had been discovered by the 9th hole. It must have been a terrible shock knowing what had been found. They knew though, there was no link, and even if there were, a quick phone call would shut the whole thing down. They were bomb proof and they knew it, no one could touch them.

The thing was, I just couldn't let it go. Maybe it was the ex-cop in me, maybe I didn't like the idea of people getting away with things, just because of their place in society. Whatever the real reason, I was going to expose this and get my PA back. She didn't deserve to be tangled up in such a thing and I was going to get her out and sort this once and for all.

The Office of Detective Inspector Deborah Smith.

The smell of coffee drifted around the office. DS Sharron Shacklady and DC Stephen Burton sat opposite their boss. The snow had started to settle on the ground and as the night drew in, the cold increased, penetrating every soul to the core. The dark of the night turned the white blanket into a crispy sparkling carpet, stretching out in all directions.

"We need to keep an eye on this lot boss, we could end up getting snowed in"

"Yeah, we won't be long Sharron, I thought I would call you over to get an update on the golf course surveillance"

"Nothing doing boss. The place is busy, busy, busy all the time. The bars don't close until after midnight, cleaners are working all the time as well as the security staff. If you wanted to do anything even slightly dodgy in the club house, forget it, someone would notice.

Stephen and I have poked about, over every level, in all the dark places, it's a waste of time. She is not there boss, there would be nowhere to hide her. More importantly, why the hell would you? Just find an old barn out in the middle of nowhere, tie her to a chair, job done!"

"Ok, thanks for trying. I kind of guessed it but we had to give it a go"

Before DI Smith had chance to continue, her mobile began to ring. She looked at it buzzing on her desk, with a weary expression on her face.

"DI Smith, can I help?"

"Hi, it's Tony Bianchi here, listen I need to tell you something, it's about Lee Hunter"

"Tony, what the hell do you want, it's late and we are just about to go home"

"Inspector, you need to listen. Its Lee Hunter, he's off on a suicide mission and you have to stop him"

"Tony, what the hell are you on about?"

"It's complicated, but Lee is on his way to see Charles Creighton….., whatever his bloody name is. He is going to front him up, get him to confess, just like you do when you slap me about"

"Tony, I have never once slapped you. I would love to do so, but I haven't, well not yet. Get Charles Creighton-Ward to confess to what Tony?"

"The killing, you know, that devil worship shit. He really believes it Inspector, and he thinks Charles is the main man, you have to stop him. He has some jewel incrusted collar, he thinks it belongs to the big boss or someone like that. I don't know, it's just part of this crazy idea he has. Bodies in the sand, devil worshiping, kidnapping his PA, fuck knows what else. He has had my guys looking for buried bodies on the golf course. Found nothing though, just a load of nettles and hawthorn bushes"

"Hang on Tony, Lee is on his way to the manor house to see Charles. What the hell does he think that will achieve? They will have him thrown out into the snow, or just slam the door in his face"

"I know that Inspector, wouldn't surprise me if they gave him a bloody kicking just for the pleasure of it. I offered to help but he wasn't interested. You can't go fucking about with people like them Inspector, they are likely to just tie you up and throw you in the river"

"Alright Tony, are you sure he is on his way?"

"Certain of it, he's already left"

"Ok, leave it with me. If you hear anything else, get in touch straight away, do I make myself clear?"

"Yep, go get him Inspector, he doesn't deserve to be torn apart by that lot. He is a good guy, one of the few, trust me, I should know. He laid his life on the line for that little girl Brau had hostage. She would be dead for sure if it wasn't for Hunter. Then there was your CSI, he jumped on that bent cop to stop him shooting her, took a bullet for her. He cracked that case Inspector, three bent cops now in jail, he is a fucking hero.

Don't leave him to that bloody family, they will have him for breakfast"

DI Smith pressed 'end call' and looked up at her two colleagues. No one spoke, the office was silent, like Lord Street in the falling snow.

"This is all I need. Hunter is on his way to the manor house, he is going to front up the family. We all know how that's going to end, and not very well I can be sure. Also, if Hunter is right about his PA and they do have her, she will certainly end up dead"

"Let's go and stop him boss"

"It's not as simple as that Steve, we have been given an order from on high. Leave the Creighton-Ward's alone, that's from the very top. If we go charging in, we can kiss our job's goodbye, pensions and all"

"We can't just leave him Debs, you know what people like that are capable of. At least the likes of Tony Bianchi are visible, we know what they are up to, most of the time! That family have fingers in many pies, all kinds of folk in their pockets. They are dangerous because they operate in the shadows. No one would suspect them and if anyone did, well a quick phone call and you are told to back off"

"Yes Steve, but what are we supposed to do? Hunter is a grown man, he can choose what he does next. We can't go over there on any official business, we have been told to butt out. In any case, we don't have any kind of real intelligence, let alone a warrant"

"So we just leave him to his fate Debs. That doesn't sit right with me, he wouldn't do that to any one of us"

"I know that Sharron, if it wasn't for Hunter, Kaye Marie would have been murdered in that container in the recycling unit. Also, that girl and I would be long dead by now if it wasn't for Hunter"

"So, let's get over there, maybe we can get to him before he arrives"

"Listen you two, if we do this, we may end up flipping burgers somewhere. This family are the real deal, they won't stop until we are sacked and thrown out in disgrace"

"And if Hunter is right boss?"

"I know Sharron, the thing is, I am absolutely certain that he is not!"

"Then we go flipping burgers, at least we get free fries to take home"

The room fell into silence. DC Burton's attempt at humour was largely ignored. The next decision they made might well be their last in the police force.

"Hang on, Chief superintendent Watkins wanted to call Hunter in. He suspects Hunter has something on the family, why else would they want him shut down? I am going to call him, tell him what we are planning. He might just order us to stop being so bloody stupid, but I wonder if he might just let us go"

"I would be very surprised if he did Debs"

"I have known Mike for years Sharron, he was my boss when I first became a detective. He is more pragmatic than most and willing to take the odd risk. That's why he has risen to the top. Let me ring him, tell him what we have in mind"

"And if he says no?"

"Then we go anyway Steve. Hunter is an absolute pain in the arse, but I won't leave him to his fate, no matter how annoying he is, I owe him my life, as do many others"

DI Smith reached for the phone on her desk. She knew the speed dial for Chief superintendent Watkins, so pressed the corresponding keys without hesitation. It rang for several moments without reply. She then changed to his mobile number, she knew that he was bound to have that switched on.

"DS Watkins"

"Sir, it's DI Smith, I wonder if I can run something past you?"

"Go for it Deborah, always a pleasure to talk to you"

By the time DI Smith had finished, the tension in the room was palpable. They could tell by the look on her face that the conversation hadn't gone well.

"Deborah, if you do this, there can only be one of two outcomes. One, the Creighton-Ward's will ensure that you three are thrown out of the force for good. Two, you might, and I say 'might' get out of this with a level of credibility. I still think Hunter is on to something, but proving it is another thing altogether.

A least you can try and stop Hunter from making a complete ass of himself, or worse. This is completely off the record of course, there is no way the force can support you in any of this. Even if Hunter is right, there is no guarantee that the family won't take their revenge out on you anyway!

My guess is, you will end up being thrown to the lions by the top brass, no matter what the outcome is. Even if they cart a couple of members of that family off to jail, you will still pay a heavy price.

Doing what you have in mind is the right thing, that's for sure. Is it the best thing for you three, I guess it isn't. Will any good come of it, probably not. Will that family end up in the shit, I seriously doubt it.

The thing is Deborah, at least you will be able to sleep at night. You see, doing the right thing is not always the easiest path to take. I have been there, my partner died because I was too scared to get involved. I swore I wouldn't do that again and I never have. I still can't sleep at night though, you never forget those decisions, never!

You can't forget that look on his widow's face at the funeral as she gazed over at me. The still living partner of her dead husband. What was that look, was she angry that I was still alive? Did she wonder why I didn't go with him that night? Did she question why he was alone, whilst I was at home?

You see, he wanted to go and knock on the drugs dealer's door. He didn't have a warrant, there was no proof to arrest the guy. My partner wanted to 'rough him up', take his frustrations out on the little shit. He was fifteen years my senior, I was a fresh and shiny new detective. When he told me to "stay at home, leave it to me", I was more than happy to comply, because I was scared. I wasn't doing the right thing Deborah, I was taking the easy way out. Anyway, that was the last time I did that, doesn't make it any easier though. Not late at night when I wake up, staring at the face of his widow at the funeral.

Look, if it were me, I would go. I can't tell you that though, this is your future not mine. All I can say is, you don't want to lay in bed at night, like I do, staring at the face of someone who questioned why you didn't act"

She put the phone back onto the cradle and looked up. The two faces staring back at her were young in service, but willing to do the right thing. DS Watkins was right, she had to act. Hunter had laid his life on the line more than once for her and her colleagues, he deserved their help.

"Right, this is what I am going to do. What you decide is entirely up to yourselves, but I will never think any more or less of you, no matter what decision you make.

Hunter is on his way to the manor house to tackle Charles. We all know what's going to happen when he gets there. Personally, I think he is barking up the wrong tree, there is nothing that links the family to anything remotely like this.

He knows this woman, a Ms Greenwood whose father supposedly made the rings found on the bodies in the sand. There is no real proof of that though, just some dusty old records.

There is a missing Creighton-Ward, one Edward. Could have died in a flying accident in the 30's, might not have done! He isn't buried where he is supposed to be, big deal, I am not going to lose sleep over that.

Hunter is certain that there are more rings and possibly dozens of bodies still waiting to be discovered. The Archaeologists have been over the areas with a fine-toothed comb, there is nothing more to be found.

Then there is his PA, Jan Talbot. Hunter is certain that the family are holding her hostage, so that he backs off. The missing persons team have people out searching, knocking on doors, dogs, the lot. We have no information at this time about her whereabouts. So far as the force is concerned, there is no link between the family and her disappearance.

So, what the hell do we have that links the family to this? Nothing is the short answer. What does Hunter have, about the same, sod all! The trouble is, he is certain that he does and that's where the problem lies.

We need to get out there, grab Hunter, knock some sense into him. We also have to properly examine any evidence he has, or thinks he has. Let's put this bloody nonsense to bed once and for all"

The three detectives grabbed their coats and made their way down to the ground floor. There was no need for any further conversation, they were going to do the right thing, even if it meant losing everything that they held dear.

The night air was frigid, cutting like broken glass into their lungs as they breathed. The snow was falling much harder now, the signs weren't good, soon the roads would be impassable. If they were going to achieve anything, it would have to be soon, very soon.

At least DC Stephen Burton's Toyota Rav 4 had proper four-wheel drive. It may have been over a decade old, and much the worse for wear, but at least it would grip the snow. They would need every bit of help that they could muster, tonight would be one they would never forget.

Was this a good idea?

My car slid to a stop by the gates guarding the main lane leading up to the big house. The windscreen wipers were just about coping with the snow, but the cold was becoming intolerable.

By now, the adrenalin had worn of and the 'macho he-man feelings' were long gone. The reality of what I was about to do had well and truly struck home. Tony Bianchi was right of course, there was a real risk that I would end up at the bottom of the local canal. I had to do this though, everyone involved was entitled to an explanation and Jan had to be found.

The only way I could see to achieving everything I wanted was to confront the family and make them tell me what the hell was going on. So, I slid out of the car and into the cold night. I reached for the torch in my pocket and made my way to the ornate cast iron gates. They were over ten feet tall, at least the same in width and joined in the middle by a large electronic lock. The torch shone through the snow, illuminating the black and gold paintwork and to the right, a stainless-steel call box used to communicate to whomever sat at the other end.

As I approached, I noticed on each stone pillar a CCTV camera pointing directly at me. This wasn't going to work, they already knew I was here. When I pressed the red 'call' button, the security men would simply laugh into their coffee, and carry on watching the football on their TV.

I thought about turning and going home, whilst I still could. What the hell was I thinking, this was a complete waste of time. In fact, the whole case was a waste of time. The only thing I should be concentrating on was Jan and getting her back, not some stupid collar, with some spurious meaning and use!

No, I was here now, and I was at least going to try. I would press that button and demand to see Charles. If he told me to go, then at least I had tried my best. I approached that red button with some degree of trepidation. My fingers had started to go numb with the cold, as had my feet and legs. I reached out and pressed it, stood back and waited for a reply. Almost immediately the box crackled into life and a clear and commanding voice came forth into the frigid night.

"Mr Hunter, if I am not mistaken. I have spoken to Mr Creighton-Ward already, it seems he was expecting you. Please follow the road directly to the main house, you will be met there. Do not deviate from the track, do not stop or get out of your car until you reach the main house. Do you have any questions Mr Hunter?"

I was taken aback by the short message, I really wasn't expecting anything, let alone an invitation. Was this just a joke, I wondered for a few seconds?

"Thank you, I will proceed as directed"

As soon as the words left my mouth, the electronic locks clicked. I made my way back to the car and gingerly drove through the gates and up the recently cleared lane. It struck me that this little strip of tarmac on a private estate had been ploughed clear of snow, but the main roads outside were nearly three inches deep.

It didn't take too long to reach the main house. It was illuminated like a luxury cruise liner. There must have been fifty or more windows shining brightly into the darkness. It seemed much larger in the blackness, its edges lost in the night. Its imposing bulk matched the power and influence of the family it protected. I had not been able to ascertain, with any certainty, what exactly the family did. Some suggested oil exploration, other stocks and shares. The truth was, the Creighton-Ward's existed in a shadowy zone, not documented or official. Whatever it was that maintained their lifestyle, was certainly considerable.

I drew up to the front of the house, the huge circular driveway embraced a fountain as large as an Olympic swimming pool. There were subtle lights illuminating certain aspects of the building and surrounding area. By the time I stopped, I could see someone standing at the top of the steps leading to the huge oak doors.

I got out of the car wrapping my coat around myself and made my way up the steps. Each one felt icy and dangerous underfoot, perhaps a portent of what was to come. Looking up, I tried identifying who was waiting but the snow stung my eyes.

Eventually I reached to top of what must have been twenty or more sandstone steps. Waiting patiently and without any outward sign of emotion, was a man perhaps in his seventies. He was diminutive in stature, with a shock of white hair.

"Mr Creighton-Ward is waiting for you in the library, please come in. Can I interest you in a brandy or perhaps a hot beverage Mr Hunter?"

"A hot beverage with a brandy in it would be nice"

I expected this request to illicit some level of reaction from the man, but I was sadly mistaken.

"Very well, can I take your coat sir, I will ensure it is fully dried, ready for when you leave. Once I have shown you into the library, I will see to your beverage request Mr Hunter"

He led me into the brightly lit and very warm central hall. It was as huge as I remembered it, and very welcoming on this, the vilest of nights. Turning right we walked down a short oak panelled hallway, which terminated at a heavy looking door. The man politely knocked and opened it, beckoning me in first.

"Ah, Mr Hunter, I am so glad you came to see me. We have a lot to talk about, not least of which, that foolish notion you have about me and my family"

He stood up, his back to the roaring fire and offered me his hand. I walked towards him, gazing around the room as I did so. It was lined with books of all colours and sizes, the shelves must have extended ten or twelve feet high. The was a warm atmosphere, there was a faint smell of smoke and the sound of crackling wood.

I advanced and shook his hand. It felt like shaking hands with a lion, and any minute now it would be bitten off. However, his manner was warm and friendly, so I decided to make the best of the situation I now found myself in.

"Take a seat by the fire Mr Hunter, I have a rather fine brandy open, should be ideal on a night like this"

He nodded to the man who turned and made his way to a small drinks trolley. He poured two rather large brandies and brought them over on a silver tray. After placing the tray on the coffee table between the two armchairs, he left.

"Right Mr Hunter, or should I call you Lee? Please feel free to call me Charles"

"Call me Lee and thank you for seeing me"

"Lee, now how can I help you to clear up this misunderstanding about my family?"

"I don't think it's a misunderstanding Charles, I firmly believe you and your family are involved in the 'bodies on the ninth' case and probably more besides. More urgently, my PA, Jan Talbot has gone missing, and you are holding her, probably somewhere on this very estate"

He stared into the fire, whirling his brandy slowly around in its glass, the only sounds were the popping or the fire and the ticking of a mantle clock. Eventually, he turned back to face me.

"Lee, I need to explain something to you. I am not sure you are going to accept what I have to say, but I would ask that you at least give me the chance. I trust you will treat, in the strictest confidence, the whole of this conversation. I will of course deny all knowledge of this discussion should you ever repeat it.

There is far more to all of this than you might know Lee. This 'case' as you put it goes back many generations and involves the most extreme forms of sadism that you might imagine. It implicates many people from all walks and classes of society. Its evil coils reach out far and wide and not just to this country. My family has been implicated on several occasions, but we have managed to clear our names on each instance. It is very troubling to me that the name of my family is dragged into the cesspit once again. We are not involved in such things Lee, it is possible that there might have been some family connection to it many, many generations ago, but no longer. Hence the request that I made to have you warned off the case. Yes, that was me but not because we are implicated but merely to protect our good family name"

I sat there for a while before answering. He was obviously going to deny any involvement in the bodies, the kidnapping of Jan, the death threats and the attempt on my life when leaving the hospital. He wasn't going to sit there and confess all, I had never expected that. What I wanted was the release of Jan and an assurance that it would all stop. I knew the latter would be sheer fantasy, but I had to get Jan back and time was running out.

"Charles, I am certain that your family is implicated in all of this, and I know you have Jan. What I want is her release, please let her go, she has nothing to do with any of this. She is being punished for nothing more than working for me"

"Lee, there is nothing more I can do other than reassure you of our innocence. Of course, I don't expect you to believe every word I say, but I can't do any more than appeal to you. You are wrong about us, we have nothing to do with any of this.

I do however suspect who is actually responsible for your PA's disappearance. The trouble is, I am not sure that you are going to believe me"

"Go on, let's have it Charles, let me guess, it's the boogie-man?"

"I understand that you are working for, or perhaps with one Ms Janice Greenwood"

"Yes, she contacted me. She has some information regarding the rings found on the murder victims buried on the golf course, what of it?"

"I assume she told you that her father made these rings, assisted by her grandfather?"

"Yes, and she has all the documentation to prove it. Or at least until some of that documentation was stolen"

"I am not sure about the stolen documents Lee, but there is no doubt about what she has told you, thus far. Has she told you who her father was?"

"Yes, Jonathon Greenwood. It seems possible that he was a member of your group. Janice may have found the collar he might have worn"

"Very good Lee, has she told you the name of her grandfather?"

"No, why? I assume another Greenwood"

"Oh of course, on her father side. No, the name of her mother's father. Before she married Jonathon Greenwood, she of course had a different name"

"We never spoke about things that far back. Just her father Jonathon and her mother who died many years ago. We never discussed her mother's family at all, let alone her family name. Why is that so important?"

"Because Lee, her mother's father, was a name you already know. Janice Greenwood's grandfather on her mother's side was Edward Creighton-Ward!"

This revelation hit me like a huge tidal wave. I must have looked like a goldfish in the local pet shop, with my mouth gaping wide open. I looked down then back at Charles, had he lied and if so, why? I tried to assimilate the information, try to understand the dynamics of what he had said. If this was just a fabrication, what could he hope to gain from it?

"Are you sure Charles, Janice Greenwood's grandfather on her mother's side was Edward Creighton-Ward? I thought he was supposed to be your grandfather. You told me he had died in an air crash, somewhere if Kent if I remember"

"Actually, I said just outside RAF Andover in Hampshire, not Kent. You are right though,

Edward was my grandfather, but what I told you about his death was just a fabrication. It was an attempt on my part to throw you off the scent, get you to give up and move on.

You see Lee, the family found out what he was doing, killing, murdering for fun. He had become a member of an old order, a cult as you would call it today. So, he was thrown out of the family home, ostracised and so he moved away. This didn't stop what he was doing though, the slaughter continued. He revelled in the blood and suffering, he actually enjoyed it. I guess a modern-day psychologist would call him a psychopath.

Anyway, he was struck from the family records, so far as the family was concerned, he didn't exist. The trouble was of course, he did still exist and so did his terrible crimes. You have to remember the time in which this was going on Lee. Things were different back then, they weren't broadcast, they were dealt with by the family. You wouldn't get away with it nowadays, and quite rightly so.

So long as Edward kept a low profile then the family left him alone. They feared any connection with him, their reputation would have been destroyed. So, lies were fabricated about his death in 1930, he disappeared from any family records, Edward Creighton-Ward ceased to exist.

He vanished for a while, then it came to light he had been married to a property and oil millionairess. They had a daughter, that daughter had got married to one Jonathon Greenwood, they became mother and father of your Janice. So, my grandfather is Edward Creighton-Ward and Janice Greenwood is therefore some relative of mine, I guess you might call her a half-sister!

Edward would have been the leader of this cult by then, and it seems he recruited his son-in-law, Jonathon greenwood into it's folds. It is my understanding that the killings began to increase at that time. The two of them together were the perfect storm, no one was safe. Reports were made to the local police, but the members of this cult were powerful, they simply had the investigation shut down, for ever. You accuse my family of such things Lee, but at least we don't try to coverup murder!"

"This is one hell of a story Charles. I have heard some astonishing tales during my time as a cop, but this one takes the biscuit. If, and it's a big if, what you are telling me is true, then why didn't Janice tell me herself?"

"I fear she has an agender here Lee. We banished her grandfather, left him out in the cold. He had no money, no family and nowhere to call home. She wanted revenge for that, retribution for him, the man she loved as a little girl. I am certain that it's about implicating my family in this case. Bringing shame on our name, encouraging gossip and speculation, perhaps even investigation and prosecution. If she can get people to believe we are responsible for these terrible crimes, then our reputation will be destroyed. To that end, she has done rather well don't you think. After all, you are sitting right there in front of me"

"She has never set out to implicate anyone, this was all my doing"

"Are you sure Lee? Ok, her records stated that Edward Creighton-Ward ordered these rings. Do I assume she didn't mention the truth behind this man and the fact that he was her grandfather?

Did she mention that her mother attempted to bring her father's crimes to light. She went to the police to report what she knew. She disappeared shortly afterwards, she was never found.

Did you know that Janice Greenwood is one of the wealthiest women in these parts? She owns properties and businesses all over the northwest of England. Or has she just relied on the image of an elderly spinster living in a large Victorian house in Southport?

Did she say that she's been married four times. Odd that two of her husband's disappeared without a trace whilst out sailing. A third died when the brakes on his Daimler Benz failed in a motor race. I have never known a woman with such bad luck when it came to husbands.

I think Janice Greenwood has been feeding you just enough information to keep you interested. She has been guiding you with false records and evidence. I am also certain that the break-in and the stolen records was a pre-arranged job.

Most disturbing of all is one report that I received a year or two ago. Do you want to know what that report was Lee?

"Go on, surprise me"

"That your Janice Greenwood is now a very important member of this secret cult. She has inherited her father and grandfather's position of standing within the group. After all, why should it only be men who undertake such terrible crimes? Now this information comes from a reliable source but not one that can be substantiated. However, if it's true, you are dealing with the devil incarnate Lee, and you might be the next one dead in the sand"

"Charles please forgive me, but this all sounds somewhat far-fetched"

"It does Lee, I have to admit. Things like this often are though, that's why they go unnoticed, they can't possibly be true, can they? The question you need to ask yourself is, what is the truth and who is telling it?

If its Janice Greenwood, then you are sitting in front of a mass murderer. If I am telling the truth, then you have been duped and the life of your PA lies in the hands of your current employer.

Look, let's go and search this house, every room, all the cellars and stores. We can then go over to the estate buildings, the barns and the riding school, my mother's dance studio on the first floor. Ring your friends in the police, they don't need any kind of warrant. They can send as many officers as they see fit, they are free to look wherever they choose"

"And what about your golf club, who's to say you aren't holding Jan there?"

"Gold club Lee, my golf club?"

"Yes, the Southport and Lancashire club. I have been there, it's huge, you could hide a thousand people inside"

"That club doesn't belong to me or my family Lee. She obviously hasn't told you, Janice Greenwood owns that place too. Her grandfather Edward set it up with the money he inherited when his wife died. As it happens, I know the men's captain, give him a ring, he will confirm it. Alternatively ring the planning office at the local council, I am sure they will say the same"

An overwhelming feeling of dread grew in my mind. I felt uncontrollable panic boiling inside, I had to take a breath. Had I been wrong all along, was Jan now in the hands of Janice Greenwood? What if James Creighton-Ward had been lying and still was? It seemed too strange to be true, too far-fetched. The thing was, I couldn't help but contemplate it, after all, it had an air of logic.

Why would Charles make the story up? All he needed to do was deny the whole thing and throw me out into the night. I had no real proof of anything, he must have known that, so why bother even talking to me. Most importantly of all, if he was telling the truth, Janice Greenwood had Jan and that changed everything. Not so long ago I thought I knew where she was, now I had no real idea.

I tried to gain control of the turbulence in my mind, grip the black whirlwind. Who did I believe, what did I believe? The terrifying reality was, Jan was out there somewhere and there was nothing I could do about it. I had to make my mind up, take a path and stick to it. I needed to choose, James Creighton-Ward or Janice Greenwood, but who was telling the truth?

"Listen Lee, I am sure you can take this conversation away and replay it in your mind. You can debate with yourself the truth of what I have told you. However, if Janice Greenwood has your PA, you need to find her, and find her fast"

"Well thanks for stating the obvious, but where the hell do I start?"

"Ok, we as a family have kept close tabs on Edward and his descendants, ever since it came to light about his marriage and his return to society. My family pay a firm of lawyers to regularly establish Janice Greenwood's business activities, property dealings, etc etc. We have comprehensive records of exactly what she has been doing and to a certain extent, what she is planning.

It's a form of protection, just in case she tries to slander us, drag us into some sort of situation in an attempt to destroy our good name. We really fear what she could do. She has money and an amount of influence, we need to be prepared for any move she might make. Our family prefers to operate out of sight, in the shadows, never in the public view. I am sure you can appreciate this Lee, not that we involve ourselves in anything illegal to be sure. It's just, well, the people and deals we involve ourselves in are best kept out of sight. Our business partners and customers prefer anonymity, they enjoy privacy and confidentiality"

"Ok, so you are up to some dodgy deals, so what has this got to do with rescuing Jan?"

"I can contact our lawyers, see what she had been up to recently, maybe she has acquired a new property somewhere. Perhaps she has been seen in the company of others entering a particular address. We have suspected her involvement in this cult for many years, let's see what the lawyers have to say about that. It's possible that they have some information that could prove useful"

"So why haven't they said anything before now?"

"That's not what we have tasked them to do Lee. They watch her financial dealings. Is she trying to poach our business contacts, buy stocks and shares that could damage our finances. This is all about business, most of that happens behind closed doors. It occurs on computers, through stock exchanges, during conference calls around the world. That's why we need to be watchful with what she does. Things can happen so quickly in business, once they begin, it can be too late to stop them"

"Right, then make the phone call, let's see what they know"

A Dark Place.

Jan sat naked and trembling on the hard wooden bed. She had been told that tonight the ceremony would begin. She had been cleansed inside and out, rubbed with sweet smelling oils and told to wait. The fear burning in her mind made it difficult for her to breath. The pressure inside would surely cause her head to explode. This was the end of her life and there was nothing she could do about it.

She gasped from time to time, swallowed down the bile, tried to be brave. This situation was totally incomprehensible, it was surely a nightmare, but she knew she would never wake up.

The woman who had been attending her would soon be back. She had said she would bring handcuffs and a blindfold. The woman had explained what would follow. A ceremony, humiliation, pain and sacrifice. She would be given to the devil, a gift to elicit his good favour.

She would be laid on an oak table, her hands and feet secured. Then the ceremony would begin, a special ceremony for a new Principal. This would be the first such ceremony for many years and there was keen anticipation within the membership. Blood would be drawn from every part of her body and given to the devil for his delectation. Parts of her body would be removed, offered to the devil's acolytes to help sustain them in their work.

Through all of this she would remain conscious, the principal doctor would see to that. After many hours of suffering her throat would be slowly cut open. She would be able to feel what remained of her warm blood run down her naked body. She might begin to choke as it surged into her throat. These would be the last terrifying moments of her life, as the congregation gathered around to watch her die.

She heaved and coughed, the room began to spin about her. The last thing she remembers was hitting the cold stone floor.

DC Stephen Burton's Toyota Rav 4.

The Rav 4 made steady if somewhat slow progress towards the Creighton-Ward estate. The passengers held on with white knuckles as DC Burton drove through the increasingly deepening snow. One mistake and they would all end up in the nearest ditch.

The windscreen wipers coped admirably with the blizzard outside. This is more than can be said about the malfunctioning heating system of the old car. DI Smith and DS Shacklady hardly noticed the cold though, the fear of imminent death kept them very warm indeed.

"How much longer Steve?"

"About twenty minutes Shaz, shouldn't be any more than that"

"Well let's get there in one piece Stephen. I don't want to freeze to death in this car, laying upside down in a drainage ditch"

"Don't worry boss, we will be fine"

Before DI Deborah Smith had time to respond, her phone began to ring. Pushing her gloved hand into her pocket she retrieved the rather scratched and battered iPhone 7 and pressed 'answer'

"DI Smith"

"Deborah, it's Lee. You are not going to believe what's happened and where I am"

"Let me guess Lee. You are in the manor house and James Creighton-Ward is holding you at knife point"

"No, no Deborah, we might have a clue as to the whereabouts of Jan. I haven't got time to explain but we think she is in an old hotel in Freshfield"

"Sorry Lee, what the hell makes you think that? The last time we spoke you told me she was in the basement of the golf club, not to mention the stables at the manor house. Next thing you will be telling me she is being held in the local police station"

"Deborah, you have to believe me, that's where we think she is. As I said, I haven't got time to explain, you need to get some uniforms over there and quick"

"You might not have time to explain, but I do. Take a look outside Lee, it's a bloody blizzard out here. Secondly, I can't just drum up a whole army of local police just because you 'think' something. Lastly, who the hell is 'we'?"

"Sorry Deborah, I am at the manor house with James. He has managed to convince me of a few things, or at least put some doubt into my mind. If he is telling the truth, we might be able to free Jan. If he's talking bollocks, it's a quick look around, then you can arrest him for wasting police time. Either way, it's worth a try"

"Fucking hell Lee, you will cost me my job one day. Ever thought of becoming an ice-cream salesman, at least that way you wouldn't bother me ever again! There is no way we are getting hold of any local plod at this time of night, and in this bloody weather. The only thing I can suggest is we go there. That is me, DS Shacklady and DC Burton. What's the address, we will have a quick look and that's all, understand?"

"Great, thanks very much Deborah, I owe you. James and I will set off in his Range Rover, we will see you there. The address is 4 Longstaff Villas, Freshfields. It's a line of half a dozen old abandoned Victorian houses. Huge four or five story places, right on the edge of the sand dunes. They are mostly derelict, they were left when the ground started to shift, and their foundations crumbled"

"No, no Lee, you will stay away, do you hear me?"

It was too late, the line had already gone dead. DI Smith slammed the phone down on the dash in frustration.

"That dam Lee Hunter. Please remind me to make some charges up against him so I can bang him up for the next twenty years in the local jail. We need to get to Freshfield, some half ass idea that his PA is being held in an old house. I can't believe I am even saying that"

"Then why are we bothering boss?"

"Because Stephen, every time Lee 'I know it all' bloody Hunter says something like that, he's always right. I can't just ignore it, we at least have to have a look"

DC Burton turned the car around and headed out towards Freshfield, with DS Shacklady navigating via Google maps.

James's new £130,000 Range Rover HSE Executive roared out of the main gate and off towards their target. It's latest four-wheel drive system made light work of the prevailing conditions. He knew these roads like the back of his hand, and it showed.

"What makes your lawyers think she might be being held at the old villa?"

"It's somewhere she has been seen on numerous occasions. Our lawyers have a team of investigators. They follow her from time to time, nothing overly detailed, just general checks. She arrives at this property normally late in the evening, as do several other people. They have never been inclined to ascertain why she goes there, it's not in the remit we gave them"

"How long before we get there?"

"About fifteen minutes, don't worry it won't take long"

We battled on through the snow without another word. Fear was now the main emotion in our minds, would we be too late, was she even there? I began to question the sense in what I was doing for a living. If we were too late, Jan would be the second person close to me to die. In all the time I had spent in the police force, I had never lost anyone like this. Perhaps I was overlooking the obvious truth, getting other people involved in my work was simply too bloody dangerous.

DC Stephen Burton's Toyota Rav 4 slid across the road and not for the first time. Despite his very best efforts, it was becoming evident that the weather was winning the battle. They skidded again and for the final time, spinning like an out-of-control whirlwind as it careered across the landscape. DC Burton tried his best to correct the slide and bring the errant vehicle back under control. Despite his efforts, the Toyota finally slid off the now invisible highway and into a ditch.

The whole world came to a shuddering stop. A sickening screech of metal rang out into the night as the vehicle twisted and bent under the impact. It pitched forward, rolled over and over as the energy of the crash dissipated. The three occupants were thrown around in the rolling car without any possibility of control. Finally, the twisting and turning stopped and a silence descended.

The Final Act.

Her time had come.

She had been handcuffed, blindfolded and was being led to goodness knows where. The fear was overwhelming, the shame at being naked in the presence of others made her feel so very vulnerable. She had hoped the fear would subside once the final act had begun but that was not the case. She wanted to cry out, but her throat was dry, she wanted to run but strong hands gripped her.

Someone whispered in her ear, a male voice, one not familiar to her. His low hissing tones made her feel sick with terror, the words made her freeze inside.

"Just ride the pain dear, try not to resist. Many have and it doesn't work, just accept it and wait until it all ends. Eventually the agony will go away, the torment will cease, just remember that as they cut into your flesh"

The cold feel of ice.

Eventually the tumult ended, and peace returned. There was some noise, perhaps that of a wheel still turning, a slow creaking noise somewhere close by. She could feel the cold touch of ice on her face, her clothes were wet, her arm and leg numb. DI Deborah Smith tried to push against whatever was holding her still but to no avail, she was trapped. There was a smell of diesel in the background, and the sensation of cold snow falling on her face.

DS Shacklady opened her eyes, she was gazing at the dark night sky, black and foreboding. There was no light, no stars or moon just icy snow falling on her, making her eyes sting as she gazed into the abyss. There was an overwhelming pain, her head felt broken, split open like a rotten apple. Then shock hit her like an express train, she tried to move but the tidal wave of pounding pain stopped her. The night flashed red and white, and her consciousness drifted away into the storm.

DC Burton pushed himself out of the vehicle and rolled over and over into the inky depths. He stopped with a jolt, his face buried in the ice, he gasped for breath but to no avail. Instinctively he pushed out his hands in front of himself. They plunged into a cold semi liquid, instantly freezing his exposed flesh.

Ten minutes to go.

"How long now James, we need to get there, I have a feeling about this, we might already be too late"

"Listen Lee, if we go any faster, we will end up smashed and upside down in one of the local rivers. I understand that you are concerned but better get there in one piece than not at all hey"

I just couldn't shake the feeling that we had already run out of time. Jan was a truly innocent bystander in all of this and now she was probably dead. Why the hell had it all happened on a night like this. That bloody snow just wouldn't stop, the windscreen wipers were just about coping, if it got any worse, we wouldn't get there at all.

What would happen if this wasn't the address, had we jumped off on a mere whim? Self-doubt wracked my mind, should I have listened to James, why would he tell me the truth anyway? Was this just a smoke screen preventing me from finding out where she really was? Yes, I had been taken for a fool, Janice greenwood was the innocent party in all of this. What the hell was I thinking about, the leader of some satanic cult, I must have been out of my mind. James had taken me for a fool, and I had gladly accepted the role.

On the other hand, what had he got to gain from weaving this lie, he could have just thrown me off the estate. We were speeding across the countryside in a blinding blizzard and for what? He must be telling the truth, why else go to this amount of trouble?

Her time had come.

Strong arms held her still. There was silence, somewhere a smell of incense, burning candles and polished wood.

"We must wait here until the master calls for us. It might be a moment or two, it depends where they are in the ceremony. Once we go in, you will be tied to a table at it will all begin. Don't speak, don't try to run, and don't call out, do you understand?"

She couldn't answer, her mind was overwhelmed with the things that were to come. They had been clever, sadistic, and cunning in telling her what was going to happen. This had been going on for several days, building up the fear, the expectation of terror and pain. They could have said nothing but what would be the point. Telling her everything would increase their pleasure, knowing that the horror was intensifying inside her.

The cold feel of ice.

"Deborah, can you hear me, Sharron, where are you?"

"Stephen, I am trapped in the vehicle, something is pinning my ankle. I don't think there is any damage, but I can't seem to pull it loose. How far away from the address are we?"

"Can't be more than a few hundred yards boss, bloody ice and snow. Can you see Shaz, she was sitting right next to you?"

"I can't see anything, hang on. Sharron, where the hell are you?"

There was nothing, no response, no sound at all. DI Smith reached out as far as she could. Several familiar objects came to hand, a seat, some carpet, part of the plastic from inside of the door. There was no sign of DS Shacklady though, she seemed lost in the darkness.

"Sharron, where the hell are you?"

Again, the silence washed back in, like the approaching tide covering the sand.

"Listen Boss, this is bad. I think the side of the old car has been torn open. I am sitting in a deep snow drift, my head is bleeding, and I can't seem to stand. Every time I try the pain in my back just fucks me up. I need to get under cover before the cold starts to kill me, or I bleed to death"

"Well, I can't move Stephen, and Sharron is obviously unconscious. Try to get back to the car, you need to help me pull my leg out. If we all can't find some shelter soon, the lot of us will be goners"

Ten minutes to go.

"This is it Lee, we are on the old lane that leads to the abandoned houses. The problem is, I can't see where the road ends and the ditch begins. The Range Rover is good in the snow, but it has limits"

"What do you suggest?"

"We need to get out and walk. There is a torch in the glove box, the villas can't be that faraway"

I grabbed the torch from the glove box and pulled the catch to open the passenger door. The force of the wind was colossal, I had to use my legs to force the heavy door wide enough for me to get out.

Before I even set one foot outside the cold assailed me, tearing into my flesh like a rabid dog. The freezing snow drove into my eyes, the sub-zero air assaulted my lungs causing me to cough and gasp.

I fell out of the vehicle and straight into a snow drift. The bitter cold ran through me as did fear. What if this storm was too much for me to endure? Perhaps I would freeze to death long before finding the villa where Jan was being held. I tried to stand, at first the snow caused me to slip and fall back. I tried again, this time using the Range Rover to steady myself.

I switched the torch on, it's white beam cutting into the knight. I swung it right and left. James appeared in front of me, he didn't speak, he just beckoned me on into the teeth of the storm. I followed as he seemed certain as to the direction of the villa's, perhaps he had been this way before.

It wasn't long before I caught site of some lights, somewhere off in the night. They flickered on and off, like some distant star. Perhaps I just imagined them, maybe the cold was beginning its inexorable grip on my life. I stumbled, as did James, my clothes were soaking wet, my feet numb in my sodden shoes.

I could feel the cold clammy hands of death wrapping themselves around me. I felt tired, sleepy, I wanted to lay down and rest. Just a few moments of sleep, it would make me stronger. I wondered if James felt the same, alarm bells started to ring in my mind. Don't give in, don't succumb to your yearnings, stay awake, Jan needs you.

Her time had come.

The door opened in front of her. She couldn't see past her blindfold but the air inside the room was warm. There was chatter, perhaps some laughter in the background. Her legs gave way underneath, she stumbled to her knees, but strong arms pulled her back.

"Stand up dear, you are here now. Just a few more steps and you will be at the altar. There will be a couple of speeches, some words and chants you won't understand, then the ceremony will begin.

Don't forget what I told you, just relax. You will be laid down on the alter, your hands and feet will be secured. The blindfold will be removed then the proceedings will start. You can't stop what is about to begin or stop the agony you will endure, so just accept your fate"

She collapsed once more, her breathing began to fail, stars whirled around in the blackness in front of her. The terror raging in her mind was unbearable, the thought of what was to come unimaginable. She cried out but the noise was pitiful, choked by dread and dehydration.

The strong arms carried her forward once more, ten or perhaps fifteen steps. It was just about to begin and there was nothing she could do about it. A voice rang out somewhere behind her, it was loud, powerful and controlling. Its deep tones resonated through her, struck fear into every atom of her being.

"Members of our illustrious order, we are gathered here tonight to welcome our new master. Through the centuries we have assembled to celebrate the inauguration of our leader here on earth, and tonight we do so again. The ceremony of inauguration will be new to many members, as it has been many years since it was last enacted.

We will sacrifice this pathetic woman in celebration of the inauguration event. Also, as a mark of respect to the one true god, honouring the true and one divinity. We will feed her body and soul to those who would do his work, the true believers and followers. She is our sacrifice to him so that his power forever rains over this earth. One day he will rise and take control and we will be his true servants, doing his bidding until the end of time itself.

Here, at the inauguration of our new master of our order, her blood flow and her flesh will be consumed as she still lives. This will seal the reign of our new master and help quench the desires of the one true god, and mark our respect to him"

Chants rang out around the room, "the one and true god, the one and true god".

She was pulled backwards, forced down on a cold stone table. Her legs and arms pulled apart and tied tightly at each corner. The straps bit deeply into her flesh, a silence descended over the place, not a sound could be heard.

The cold feel of ice.

DS Sharron Shacklady awoke with a start, she gasped a deep lungful of cold frigid air. The pain in her head was overwhelming, pounding as if someone was hitting her with a hammer. She hurriedly tried to remember the events leading to this situation. There was a car, DI Smith, DC Burton, the snow, cold, a storm, then darkness. Why was she laying in the snow?

Then the events started to re assemble themselves like a thousand-piece jigsaw. They had skidded, rolled over and over. She was thrown out of the vehicle, into the dark night. They had crashed, but where were the others? She had to sit up, find them, help them.

Pushing her hands into the deep snow, Sharron dragged herself upright. It was difficult, as she pushed downwards into the snow her hands and arms disappeared into the freezing depths. Eventually, she managed to get onto her knees and then stumble upright. It wasn't easy, her head swirled with pain, the freezing wind buffeted her left and right.

In the distance she could see someone, perhaps two figures struggling against the storm. She cried out, waved her arms and almost immediately, the beam of a torch light struck her in the face. The two figures came closer, their faces occasionally lit by the light of the torch.

"Sharron, what the hell's happened, what are you doing here"

"Lee, we crashed, the car slid off the road. I have no idea what happened next, I just woke up"

The three looked about them. The torch helped but the falling snow obscured the light.

"Listen, James you stay here, help Sharron and try and find that car. Deborah and Steve must be trapped inside. You need to get them to safety somehow, even if it's back to the Range Rover. They will be warm and reasonably safe until we can get help. I am going to find that villa and stop whatever is going on"

"Lee, you won't be able to do that by yourself, there might be dozens of people in there. They aren't simply going to stop because you said so.

Sharron, can you make it back up this road? My car is open, follow our tracks back to where we started. Here, use my phone, the light will help you find your way, the fob to start the engine is in the glove box. Get the engine running, warm yourself up. Lee and I are going to find your colleagues and then try and find Jan Talbot. Do you think you can manage that?"

"Yes, I will be ok, go and find Debs and Steve, they might be trapped. I will wait in your car, find them Lee, don't let them die out here"

I stood there for a moment, James was right of course. We needed to find the missing cops, then move into the villa. Maybe they might be fit enough to help, and we simply couldn't leave them out here to freeze to death. Sharron moved off into the inky blackness. If she followed the road, she would be safe in James's vehicle in minutes.

"Right Lee let's get looking. They can't be far from here, Sharron must have been thrown clear as the car rolled.

Her time had come.

The blindfold was taken away, bright lights burnt her eyes, she tried to blink away the pain. There was someone standing above her, she craned her neck to see. That person was clothed in purple robes with a golden hood, which covered their whole head. There were two small eye holes and an embroidered opening for the mouth. They stood above her head with a large curved knife. It shone like polished silver in the bright lights.

They spoke words she did not recognise, waved the knife around in alarming movements. Eventually, the knife was raised above her head before being placed between her naked breasts.

"This edge of Satan will soon cut deeply into her flesh. The red blood will flow, we will drink that life and thank him for his patronage. I will use its keen edge to remove her flesh and whilst she still lives, we will eat that flesh and pray to him.

Soon after, I will open her belly and remove that which would offend him. It will be burnt on our fire, she will see it burn and we will pray that he is pleased.

I will begin the cutting, her arms will be opened, then her thighs. Prepare my brothers, prepare to catch the bounty in your hands. That red life will be warm, we will drink and indulge ourselves.

Once her body ceases to live, we will remove its skin and use it in the installation of our new master. That new master awaits in the anti-chamber and will be admitted once the exultation to the one true god finishes"

She could sense the gathering around her, people dressed in robes were all about. Some in white, others in red and blue. They chanted together a rhythmical hum of unknown words.

They came closer and closer, she could feel the power, the knife was raised, soon she would feel the pain. Its cold edge touched her right arm, it ran up and down without assaulting her flesh. They were going to draw this out, she was going to suffer for a very long time.

"Let the cutting begin"

She felt the knifes edge enter her, an intense burning sensation ran down her arm. It stopped abruptly but Jan Talbot could feel the blood beginning to flow. She shuddered with unimaginable panic and horror, this was it, her life was going to end.

The cold feel of ice.

They pulled at the twisted bulkhead and DI Deborah Smith managed to free her trapped ankle. DC Stephen Burton joined them, he was fine apart from a few sore ribs.

"Right let's go, Jan is in one of these villas, we need to find her fast"

"Lee, it's the middle one. When the snow eases a little, I can see the lights, it's definitely the middle one"

"Right James. It can't be more than twenty yards away, let's go"

The four started towards the villa. Lee Hunter led the way with his torch. It was no more than a few seconds later that they reached the main door.

"Right, there is no time for subtlety here, I am going to kick that door in, and we go inside. Look about, pick up any kind of weapon you can get your hands on, this isn't going to be pretty"

I kicked at the old front door. It simply bounced me back into the night but after another three attempts, it split and opened like Aladdin's cave. I led the way, I had the torch for a weapon, Deborah kicked over an old table and broke off three legs, giving one to Stephen and discarding another. I took a moment to look about me. There stood DI Deborah Smith, limping but ready for the fight, DS Stephen Burton, bleeding from a head wound but keen and alert. Then there was James Creighton-Ward, was he telling me the truth, was this just a plan to entrap me, I would soon find out.

Despite the location and outward appearance of the villa, the inside was very will maintained. This appearance fortified my hope that we were in the right place.

"Right, my guess is the basement. They would be too vulnerable above ground, anyone might see them"

There was a black panelled door to the side of the central staircase. Without any further thought we opened it and rushed inside. There was a long corridor with small rooms leading off left and right. Modern lights lit the way, white LED illumination was certainly not prototypical Victorian!

Along the whitewashed corridor and then finally a righthand turn. To my horror, someone was standing outside a huge double oak door. The man looked over at the four of us with a look of total disbelief and shock on his face. I didn't hesitate, I attacked him without delay, smashing the Maglite torch over his head. I turned to look at my companions, they seemed eager for the fight. A large brass key secured the lock, I turned it slowly.

"Right, I think we can assume whatever is on the other side of this door is not going to be pleasant. We need to go in there and assert our authority, either physically or by persuasion and probably both. They certainly won't be expecting us, so surprise is on our side. Get into them, don't hold back, hopefully shock and fear will stop them in their tracks"

"Lee, open the bloody door, my ankle is killing me, we need to finish this"

I opened the doors with as much force as I could muster. They swung back revealing a large well-lit room. In the middle was a gathering of perhaps fifteen people, all dressed in robes. They were congregated around something, it was difficult to see exactly what from where I was standing.

DI Smith stepped forward. She spoke with an authority developed over many years in the force. I hoped it would do the trick, I didn't fancy fighting against such odds.

"I am Detective Inspector Deborah Smith. You are all under arrest, stop what you are doing and sit down. My officers will be here in a few seconds to process your details"

For a moment or two it worked, then panic set in. These people had been caught doing something, probably murder and they didn't want to hang around.

They rushed for the door, I was immediately knocked off my feet, Deborah hit one or two as they passed, Stephen dragged another to the ground. I got up, hit a man in green robes with the trusty Maglite torch, he stumbled and then fell to the ground. I could see James wrestling with a man, dragging his hood off before hitting him square on the jaw. It was complete chaos, people in coloured robes, the sound of crunching bones and yelps of pain. It felt like a wild west saloon, punches being thrown, people all about me.

The rush seemed to be over in a second. I looked about me, three people were lying motionless on the floor, no doubt at least one poleaxed by DI Smith. DC Stephen Burton had another in an arm lock. James Creighton-Ward had a third around the neck.

"Well guys, that's five. I am sure you folks down the station will get at least one of them to talk as part of a plea bargain. After all, better betray your mates than go to jail hey"

Then there was a cry, I looked to my right, there was a large white stone plinth, and tied to it was.........Jan, we had found Jan.

I rushed over, she was shaking uncontrollably, her right arm oozed blood but she was alive. I picked up a curved knife off the floor and cut the leather straps holding her. DI Smith took off her coat and wrapped it about her naked body.

"Jan, I thought you were dead, I am so sorry, you are safe now, nothing more is going to hurt you"

She looked up at me. She was in shock, her eyes flitted from left to right, there was no real recognition of who I was, but she was safe. The whole adventure had been one of miss opportunities and wrong decisions, but at least we had Jan back and I was thankful for that.

Epilogue.

We had tried to stop anyone else leaving, but with just the four of us it was a pointless exercise. The robed bodies simply disappeared into the night. It must have been a hell of a shock as we busted into the ceremony. I guess many of the participants were important people with a lot to hide. My guess is, they won't be participating in any more ceremonies any time soon.

Janice Greenwood was nowhere to be found, she was not at her home, at her friend's house, or any known acquaintances. I wondered if she was at the ceremony, if she had been, then we will never know. Perhaps James was right, and she was the leader of the cult, maybe she was, perhaps. She will surface again I am sure, a woman of her standing and wealth can't remain hidden for ever. Maybe we will lock horns again in the future.

Many questions regarding the cult remained unanswered. This thing ran deep, and people didn't want to talk. The five DI Smith had in custody were too terrified to even give their names. Two tried to commit suicide in the cells and one went on hunger strike. Like the assassin who tried to kill me, death seemed preferable than telling the truth about the cult.

There have been some arrests, including Tom Toc and his mate from the graveyard. It's going to take a long time to achieve anything with the investigation, but DI Smith is determined to succeed. My belief is it will surface again. The organisation has been in existence for many years, perhaps even centuries. It has money, power and influence, things like that don't just fade away!

The Southport and Lancashire golf club was closed and thoroughly searched. Guess what, another ten bodies were found on the ninth, not the ninth hole, but the practice hole called 'the ninth'. It had been a burial ground for many years. There were four more couples, all facing each other and wearing Janice Greenwood's father's rings. Additionally, there were two individual graves, one has been confirmed as the young Italian back packer Vittorio Bruno, who went missing whilst on his way to a camping site near to Formby point.

What of my PA Jan Talbot? Well, she is progressing nicely, the wound to her arm was not so bad, and the doctors soon had that on the mend. The physical injuries were easy to treat though. The psychological ones are much more problematical. It will be a long time before she is her old self again. I still feel responsible for what happened to her. I seem to have this effect on people. Maybe working by myself is a better idea or becoming an ice-cream salesman as DI Smith suggested.

Speaking of DI Smith, she was awarded a medal for her actions, as was DS Shacklady and DC Burton, well done to the three of you.

James Creighton-Ward has gone back to his business dealings, whatever the hell they are. I guess I won't ever be invited to the manor house, but without him, Jan would be dead, and the case would remain unsolved.

Tony Bianchi has been a rock, without him, I would certainly be dead. You would never guess he is a murdering psychopath. Anyway, we went out the other night, not sure what time we got back. He does like his whiskey, his newest favourite is a 25-year-old Dalmore, cost over a thousand pounds a bottle! Not certain my liver can put up with his nights by the fire much longer.

So, where do I go from here? I will keep the business going, stay at the new offices, I do like the space. I won't be taking on any cases involving mysterious sects, or devil worshipers that's for sure. I am going to concentrate of divorcees, tax evaders and people defrauding the Department of Work and Pensions. Very boring but very safe, I like safe. Oh yes, smelly Ken. He is back with Mike at the rehab centre in

Ormskirk. Not sure for how long, but he promised me he would give it a try, let's see!

So, I am going to visit my daughters in London for a week or so, looking forward to that. I really need the break, away from here, away from near death experiences, then back to work. Let's see what drops into the inbox, something nice and simple, I hope!

"Well good morning everyone and welcome to the breakfast show, this is your host Russ Broadbent, taking you all the way from 7am to 10am on this crisp morning, glad to see the snow has finally melted away.

This morning we are having an 'open mike' phone in. So, whatever you want to talk about, just give us a call and let's hear what you have to say. First on the line is James, what's on your mind James?"

"Hi Russ, thanks for having me on the show. I would just like to say that I am looking forward to the wedding this Saturday. We will be meeting at the big house, the rings are ready, the couple are properly prepared, and the ceremony will be fantastic. I am sure everyone who's going will be looking forward to seeing her at the ceremony. Anyway, must dash and thanks again, bye bye"

"Well thanks James, he seemed in a rush. A bit of a cryptic message perhaps, who knows?

Anyone else going to a wedding this weekend, if so, give me a call"